THE
HARBOUR
MASTER

DANIEL PEMBREY

NO EXIT PRESS

First published in 2016 by No Exit Press,
an imprint of Oldcastle Books Ltd,
PO Box 394,
Harpenden, Herts,
AL5 1XJ
noexit.co.uk

A CIP catalogue record for this book is available from the British Library.
This is a work of fiction. Names, characters, places, and incidents either
are the product of the author's imagination or are used fictitiously,
and any resemblance to actual persons, living or dead, businesses,
companies, events or locales is entirely coincidental.

ISBN
978-1-84344-877-8 (print)
978-1-84344-878-5 (epub)
978-1-84344-879-2 (kindle)
978-1-84344-880-8 (pdf)

2 4 6 8 10 9 7 5 3 1

Typeset in 11.5pt Garamond MT
by Avocet Typeset, Somerton, Somerset TA11 6RT
Printed in Denmark by Nørhaven, Viborg

For more about Crime Fiction go to www.crimetime.co.uk / @crimetimeuk

CONTENTS

Part I:

The Harbour Master

1

THE DISCOVERY

THERE'S A SPOT DOWN by the harbour, with bicycle seats mounted on bollards like fishing perches, where you can't help but feel alert and vigilant. Even, or especially, at six in the morning. But maybe I'm biased. My forebears were fishermen and port workers, longshoremen and mariners.

In the March morning light, the water looked glassy; the flat mist was cool and clammy around my eyes. It called to mind generations of ancestors setting out at dawn and sailing off into the North Sea, unsure of what destiny lay before them.

We Dutch remain at heart a seafaring people: a small but proud collective who once traded with the furthest reaches of the globe – as attested to by the pale, stone maritime museum across the harbour, and the eighteenth-century vessel moored there, her masts blurring into the fog. These monuments to the 'golden age' appeared faint and ghostly, like some dim recess of my memory.

I let my finished cigarette drop to the ground; it fizzled out in a puddle as I exhaled the last puff of smoke. I thought about how it might be a fine time to quit, approaching early retirement as I was.

There was no one around except a lone dog walker and a vagrant talking to himself, louder than easy contemplation allowed. It's hard to find silence in this city: the movement of vehicles on the ring road, the rumble and creak of trains entering and leaving Centraal station, a faint foghorn out in the sea channel. After thirty years as a cop on this beat, I can confirm that peace only comes from within.

I eyed my watch: still plenty of time before I was due to meet my wife. We tried to meet for breakfast on a regular basis now that Nadia had left for university and the nest had become empty again. Perhaps it was good for me – a routine for retirement? Though I was planning on telling Petra about the trip I'd discussed with Johan, my old army friend and fellow BMW motorbike owner.

My gaze remained on the dog walker, who had taken an alert stance similar to my own, his hands buried in the pockets of his charcoal-grey raincoat. So much of police work comes down to making quick and accurate character assessments. Maybe I needed to get a dog, I thought – a retired police one, perhaps, so we could be co-retirees together – when suddenly the man's hands flew up out of his pockets and waved above his head. 'Hey,' he yelled. His dog's bark was like a gunshot across the harbour. 'Hey!'

I was off my perch and running towards them. Before I'd even got there, I caught sight of a fleshy greyness breaking the water surface. My sinking stomach and the buzzing in my ears confirmed what my brain already knew: it was a body, with a floating corona of hair.

I reached for my phone.

*

'I've got it, Henk,' Bergveld said, resting his hand on my shoulder. The hand was more controlling than consoling.

Sebastiaan Bergveld was barely more than half my age. His sandy hair was short on the back and sides but floppy on top; he wore a designer raincoat, and shiny black shoes wholly unsuited to the harbourside. He was one of Jan Six's boys – on the up, politically.

But this wasn't the time to dwell on the ascent of Jan Six ('Six-

Shooter', as he was known) to the top of the Amsterdam police force, or Bergveld's rise through the ranks at the IJ Tunnel 3 station where he and I worked.

The reality was simple: Bergveld had tactical command of the situation now.

I'd arranged for a hoist to lift the corpse out of the water. Its engine was revving to power the hydraulics, sending a cloud of smoke between Bergveld and me. The body was raised, cradled in a black mesh harness, water dripping off it. It was like a funeral in reverse – a marine exhumation, you might say. The man with the dog had stayed, his head now bowed respectfully. The dog, a cocker spaniel, whimpered softly. Bergveld asked them to move along, explaining that this was a police matter.

I had my phone out, in order to film the removal of the body. The woman's thighs and arms had swollen to Frankenstein-like proportions, her dark trousers and top so stretched that they'd ripped at the seams. Her fingers were like little sausages; I couldn't help but look away. As I did so, I caught sight of a crowd gathering on Prins Hendrikkade. Mopeds buzzed to a halt, idling; cyclists stopped abruptly, pointing. Words were being shouted; I didn't catch what. Something prompted me to point the phone in their direction.

'Can I borrow that?' Bergveld gestured at my mobile, surprising me. 'There's something wrong with mine.' He was looking at the onlookers, too. 'Where's Larsson? This is turning into a circus.'

Kurt Larsson was the medical examiner, a Swede known for his indestructible joviality on the job.

Bergveld was fumbling with my phone.

'Here,' I said, reaching for it. 'Larsson's in my address book…'

But Bergveld had already found the number.

The hoist lowered the corpse gently onto the dull paving stones, the harness remaining beneath her bloated form. Her skin had taken on a pearlescent-grey tone in the light that was breaking through the mist. She appeared to be young. Once out of the water, her hair was fairer.

Her eyes were closed. Hypothermia would have put her to sleep within minutes of entering the water – unless she had been already unconscious, or dead, upon entry. There was a third scenario: the shock of entering the freezing water had caused cardiac arrest. The visible parts of her flesh – face, hands, ankles, feet, and the mid-section of her thigh where the seam of her capri pants had split – appeared unmarked.

No shoes and no coat, on what had been a cold night. The shoes could have come off in the water. Theoretically the coat too, if she'd struggled and it had impeded her movement. The harbour wall was high and slick here: hard to get out without help.

I looked at her swollen feet. I couldn't see any abrasions on the toes from where she might have tried to scramble out, though I was too far away to be sure; Bergveld clearly didn't want me closer. There was a swirling black mark on her ankle, perhaps a stray strand of seaweed or some other flotsam.

Had she fallen off a pleasure boat? No, it wasn't the season for those. A student who'd tumbled in, drunk? I thought of my daughter Nadia at the University of Amsterdam nearby. Had the girl been walking this way alone? Anyone accompanying her would surely have helped her out…

'*Hoi oi*!' a sunny voice greeted us. I turned to find Larsson, carrying an Adidas holdall and wearing knee pads over his jeans. Sometimes I wondered whether he cried into his vodka at the end of each day, to compensate for his happiness at work.

Bergveld greeted him curtly, then took a phone call. On his own phone. Funny, it seemed to be working fine now. What had been the point of using mine? Some kind of power play? A mind game?

Larsson had his SLR camera out and began photographing the scene: the water, the harbour wall and the body.

Next he pulled on a pair of thin rubber gloves, knelt down, and examined the woman more carefully. I wanted to remove the flotsam from her ankle, perhaps out of respect, I don't know. I stopped myself long before Larsson needed to warn me about tampering with evidence; the smell had begun to waft along the dock... a salty, putrid odour, like rotting seaweed. Larsson, however, appeared perfectly at ease.

He reached for a pair of scissors and began, very carefully, to cut open the woman's trouser pockets, looking for identification. A short, single shake of the head in Bergveld's direction indicated that there wasn't any.

There was no time or justification for erecting a medical tent here at the scene, so Larsson unwrapped a black vinyl body bag from his holdall. The hoist operator, a wiry man dressed in stained blue overalls, stooped down to help him position the bag under and around the body, but Bergveld intervened, pausing his phone conversation to do the helping himself.

Once Bergveld resumed his call, I quietly asked Larsson: 'What's your best guess at the time of death?'

He looked at her closed eyes and straggly blonde hair. 'Thirty-some hours gone,' he said.

That put it at about midnight of the day before.

There were still a few onlookers on Prins Hendrikkade: two cyclists, a moped rider. The harbour wall led only out to the hulking, copper-clad Science Centre, built over the mouth of the IJ Tunnel to North Amsterdam. Of course, the science museum would have been closed at that hour.

Or would it have been?

I didn't want to get my phone back out to film or photograph the body again; Bergveld was still talking on his phone, but he was keeping an eye on us.

'What tests will you run?' I asked Larsson.

'The usual: tox, dental.' He smiled toothily.

Toxicology tests might throw up something. Dental checks

assumed records existed to match the woman's teeth. If she was from out of town, this could become a resource-consuming task: coordination with other police forces, Interpol even. It would become political, in other words.

'If this is foul play, what are the chances that it goes straight into the unsolved file?'

'Under the new regime?' Larsson glanced in Bergveld's direction. 'High, I'd say. Someone may step forward, saying they're missing a family member. Otherwise…'

I prompted him to continue.

'There are a lot of things competing for police resources just now,' he finished.

I looked at the mystery girl one last time as Larsson zipped up the body bag.

Bergveld was back, his call finished. 'Shouldn't you be somewhere else, van der Pol?' he asked me.

'I should,' I replied.

I was late for my wife.

2

DE DRUIF

I WALKED ACROSS PRINS Hendrikkade, texting Petra to suggest that we meet at De Druif, a locals' bar hidden around the back of the police station. Even though I wasn't handling the case, a longer breakfast at our usual café felt inappropriate now. Not that I included any of that reasoning in my message.

OK, came the terse response.

Then I called Liesbeth Janssen, the third woman in my life – my police partner.

'A body in the harbour?' she said. 'Who?'

'We don't know yet. No ID.'

'Wow.'

'Could you do a quick missing persons check? Female, probably in her twenties, Caucasian, height between one sixty-five and one seventy. Fair haired.'

'By "quick", you mean fast and thorough?'

'Start with the university, would you? Also – could you see if there were any events on at the science museum the night before last?'

'You think she was there?'

'I don't know, but it can't hurt to check. Even if she wasn't, there may still have been witnesses. What else is around there?'

'The Sea Palace – that floating Chinese restaurant in Oosterdok, near the train station?'

'Yes, we should make enquiries there as well.'

'Um… isn't this Bergveld's case?'

'It is. But let's do our part.' A sense of annoyance flared up, unbidden.

I was about to hang up when Liesbeth said, 'By the way, I have news.'

'Oh?'

'I got engaged.'

I paused. 'Well done.' Lucky Marc. Her intended was a trial lawyer. One of the good guys, I had to concede. 'Karaoke tonight then?' I said.

'I think we must!'

It was how things were celebrated at IJ Tunnel 3. Liesbeth's news could only bring cheer to the squad room. With the possible exception of Bergveld, who had quite a serious crush on her. Most of the men there did, innocently enough. Not me – she was young enough to be my daughter.

I'd briefly hoped that Nadia might have been interested in the police force, too, but no. Nadia wasn't a battler like Liesbeth, and that worried me sometimes – this liberal arts, 'go with the flow' approach to life… the world isn't so hospitable to that anymore. It wasn't just about careers and getting on professionally, it also had to do with basic safety. I'd seen enough muggings and violent assaults around Amsterdam to know that attackers had an innate gauge of a victim's vulnerability; they could see it in the way she held herself, walked even – how purposefully. There was something so primitive and predatory about it all.

My thoughts remained on the girl in the harbour as I entered De Druif. A heavily made-up woman wearing white cowboy boots was perched at the bar itself. Petra had found a table in the little seating space up a short flight of steps. The whole place was no bigger than a modest-sized living room.

'We haven't been here in a while,' Petra said tartly. 'Are you OK?'

'Yes. What would you like to drink?'

There was no food here.

'My usual,' she said.

I went to the bar.

'Henk.' Gert nodded his angular, shaved head.

'Gert,' I said quietly. 'Get me a jenever, would you? And a milky cappuccino for Mrs van der Pol.'

He raised an eyebrow and retrieved a clay bottle from beneath the bar. 'Bad start to the day?'

'You could say.'

Petra was facing away from me but I wasn't trying to hide the alcohol. Whenever we sat in a restaurant, I had to face the room, which meant she was required to do the opposite. Ask any cop in the world: they're never comfortable with a door at their back, unless they're with their partner. Police partner, that is.

Gert filled a little bulbous glass to the rim with the strong spirit. Then he turned his attention to the coffee machine.

I stared at the clear liquid, heaved a sigh and then downed it, feeling it burn through me, making me more alive again.

'Make that two cappuccinos – the other not so milky.'

'Okey-dokey,' Gert said.

I returned to Petra.

'So... what's up?' she asked.

'Found a body in the harbour this morning.'

'Dead?'

I was about to make a joke, squad-room black humour, but stopped myself. 'Yes.'

'That's awful,' Petra said, screwing up her face. 'Who?'

'We don't know yet. She wasn't carrying any identification. A "Jane Doe", as my American counterparts might say.'

'Can't they use fingerprinting or something?'

'She's a victim, not a suspect,' I said. I did wonder whether Larsson might try lifting prints in addition to gathering DNA... although the girl's sausage-like fingers might not even give up that much. I felt a chill pass through me.

Petra was silent, taking it all in.

I looked askance at the little drawbridge onto Entrepotdok, vaguely aware of the hiss of the milk foamer. The skies, once promising, had darkened.

'Here, I just had time to get you a roll from the market.' Petra fished out a paper bag containing the fresh-baked bread. 'I thought the harbour master might be getting hungry.'

She liked to tease me about my early morning meditations down by the water, but I enjoyed the jibe. It's important not to take life too seriously. On the other hand...

'Who will handle the case?' she enquired.

'The girl? Who do you think?'

We paused as Gert set down the coffees, one slopping into its saucer. Sebastiaan Bergveld didn't drink here; it wasn't nearly trendy or expensive enough for his tastes. Still, it was unwise to talk shop so close to the station.

I tore off a piece of the roll and put it in my mouth, noticing an older guy joining the cowgirl at the bar. He was surveying the place too, and our eyes briefly met. But he didn't have the air of a cop about him. Too unkempt. A tattoo on his neck had lost its shape with the folds of skin that had formed there.

The bread was too floury and stuck to the roof of my mouth; I washed it down with a slurp of my cappuccino, which was scalding hot, burning my mouth and making it worse.

'You're especially quiet,' Petra remarked.

'Yes. I'm worried about our daughter. She seems so distant all of a sudden.'

My wife frowned. 'She's right here in the city. What are you talking about?'

'But do we know what she gets up to half the time? *Any* of the time?' I corrected myself.

'Henk, she's a student. What do you expect? What did *you* get up to as a student? I imagine it's rather the same. She's discovering herself... leave her alone!' Her mouth made a humouring moue.

'Maybe that's what I'm afraid of,' I said into my coffee,

blowing on it to cool it down. But something else was nagging – something I couldn't yet put my finger on.

'You and I have the same challenges,' Petra said.

'How so?'

'We're both being invited to let go of what we're holding on to.'

I set the cup down and ran my hand over my stubble, evaluating her statement.

It was true. Petra was a journalist for *Het Parool*, the Amsterdam daily newspaper, and a features writer of thirty years' standing. But features were becoming ever shorter and ever shallower 'human interest' pieces now, with the relentless online onslaught of free news and trivia. We'd talked about it enough times, just as we'd talked about Jan Six and Sebastiaan Bergveld from my own, parallel world of frustration. Though the conclusions we'd reached had never been voiced so starkly as this morning.

'And it hurts,' she added.

'Any suggestions about what to do?'

'Yes, we should go away. Not...' she added quickly '... on a sailing trip.'

I took a cautious sip of coffee. 'You really couldn't imagine spending any time on a boat?'

'Henk, we *live* on a houseboat.'

'Where then?' I was thinking about the biking trip with Johan.

'What about spending some time in Delft with my cousin? I'm sure Cecilia could use a little help with that conservatory she's trying to get built...'

'Hmm.' I eyed my watch. 'I should get to work.'

'Will you give it some thought?'

'I will.' I got up, then stooped again to kiss her on the forehead. 'Thanks for the roll.'

As I left, the unkempt man beside the cowgirl got up too, our eyes meeting once more. And that's when I worked out what had been nagging at me. The tattoo on his neck – it reminded me of the black mark on Jane Doe's ankle. Not seaweed. *A tattoo.*

3

LITTLE HUNGARY

I STOOD OUTSIDE THE police station – a little fortress of brick with high, bracketed security cameras – checking the photos on my phone. Or rather, attempting to. I was sure that I'd taken photos of the body, but they didn't appear to have been saved. I was losing my edge.

'*Hoi!*' a couple of colleagues called, passing me. I stepped out of their way and, after some deliberation, called Larsson.

'I just uploaded those photos,' he said.

'That was fast.'

'Not really. Bergveld asked for them.'

I paused. 'You have one of her ankle? There was a mark there. Struck me afterwards that it might have been a tattoo, distorted by the bloating?'

'You're right. I'm running a test on the ink.'

'Could you also email me a photo?'

'Should I though?' he said, half joking. 'Will it get me in trouble?'

'You should. It won't.'

He laughed. 'To your work email, OK?'

'Of course.' I thought about asking him not to mention this conversation, but decided against it. 'Thanks Kurt.' I ended the call.

I was about to enter the building, but paused to check my email on my phone first. Larsson's email had already appeared with the photo attached. I turned around and walked away from the station.

*

Johan answered first time.

'Henk! How are we looking for the trip? You spoken to your missus about it?'

The bike trip.

'What about Denmark?' he went on. 'Copenhagen? Ferry over to Rødby?'

It sounded like a helpfully brief itinerary. Everything would fit nicely in the BMW's metal panniers. 'There's an idea,' I said. 'But I wanted to ask you about something else. A tattoo, actually.'

'You finally decided to get one?' he asked approvingly.

For years now, Johan had been trying to persuade me to get a regimental tattoo – just like one of the various tattoos he had on his arms. Most of the men in our regiment had one. But I'd always resisted those types of tribal affiliations. Holland was already becoming too insular, too protective – too uncertain of its relations with minorities, in particular. Though maybe I'm biased. I'd grown up outside the country.

'You still there?' Johan said.

'Sure. Listen, you know about tattoos… I'm working on a case right now where I'm trying to identify one. If I send you a photo, could you take a look?'

'What kind of case?' he asked.

'A girl was found dead in the harbour this morning.'

'Oh.'

If you don't say anything, you don't hear anything, I reasoned. 'We're trying to identify the body, only I'm struggling already with it.'

'That prick Bergveld trying to run you off the case again?'

'No comment.'

He sighed. 'You want to meet for coffee, talk it over?'

'I want to work the case, Johan. Thanks for the offer though.'

'Send it over.'

'Don't share it, it's an official autopsy photo.'

'You don't need to say that.'

'Unfortunately, in this political climate, I really do. Hold on.'

I paused the call and forwarded the photo to him, double-checking that the email address in the 'To' line was Johan's.

'You should have it now.' I returned to the call.

There was a short pause. 'I do. I'm looking at it on my Mac.'

I bowed my head as I saw Joost van Erven, the station captain, approaching. He discovered a sudden interest in his own phone as he passed me.

'Now,' came Johan's voice again, 'do you want the good news or the bad news?'

'Both, in that order.'

'The good news is that I think I can make out what this is, or was – an insignia. Eastern European, it looks like.'

'What's the bad news?'

'It's probably Hungarian. Vicious bastards. You know that.'

I did.

Had she been branded?

*

The Red Light District, there beside the harbour and the train station, is a curiosity: a flesh market operated by foreigners, for foreigners. Very few Dutchmen ever go there, and even fewer Dutch women work there. Yet the oldest part of the city holds a curious claim on my soul. My forebears would almost certainly have stopped there on their long-awaited return to land, before going on to a bar like De Druif – or getting another tattoo.

I'd left the police station with Liesbeth. It's always striking how quickly the normality of Nieuwmarkt – a wide, brick plaza that has a market on most days – gives way to the narrow lanes and canals of the RLD proper: the cooking smells of cheap restaurants, the glitter of tacky tourist shops, and of course the neon-lit windows promising dark delights.

The sky was now an iron lid. Heavy raindrops began to fall.

Liesbeth updated me on her enquiries as we walked: 'I called the university and the science museum, as you asked. Zero for two, I'm afraid. No missing persons report, and no event at the museum the night before last. I also called the missing persons info line, and the Sea Palace – the restaurant out in Oosterdok… they weren't too helpful.'

'It's a busy restaurant,' I conceded. Sometimes Petra and I went there at the weekend for dim sum.

'Yes,' Liesbeth agreed. 'And that's about all I can do for you, without clearing it with Sebastiaan.'

I nodded. I hadn't told Liesbeth about the dead girl's tattoo; I didn't want to implicate her in my investigations, which were fast becoming semi-official. As far as Liesbeth knew, we were here in the RLD for routine checks – to ensure that the women were working out of free will, which was legal… 'free will' being the operative words. A female police officer's presence was standard procedure.

'Let's walk down Molensteeg,' I suggested. 'Keep your eyes on the doorways.'

And the men loitering in the shadows there, I implied.

Molensteeg is a narrow lane known as 'Little Hungary'. Aptly so, as Hungary was, almost exclusively, the homeland of the girls in fluorescent bikinis trying to draw my attention. We were in plain clothes, Liesbeth wearing a navy-blue wax jacket. I was in my moss-green bomber jacket, vinyl and less waterproof, but at least padded; beneath, in a pancake holster, was my service weapon.

The RLD could be a trial, I won't deny. Sex was still good with Petra, but not wild and abandoned like at the beginning, when our need for each other was like a constant hunger.

Things evolve. I locked eyes with Irena, a Hungarian woman of indeterminate age in a tiny, silly police uniform complete with shiny black cap, and heeled boots that prevented me seeing her ankles. She gave me a hesitant, knowing smile. We kept walking.

'See anything?' Liesbeth asked.

'No. You?'

She shook her head. There were CCTV cameras in most parts of the RLD, causing the pimps to make themselves scarce. But all these girls wouldn't have come here from so far away without handlers. We passed one in a tiny orange bra and underpants, expression beseeching; she tapped the glass aggressively. There, distinct on her ankle, was the swirling insignia – a bit like a yin and yang sign.

We emerged out into the airy square by the Oude Kerk, a huge brick church that spoke to my Calvinist soul.

'Look,' Liesbeth said.

Further down the canal, a white four-poster bed was floating, tethered to an old merchant's house. The thin, blue-white veil around the bed appeared ethereal in the dim light. It was as if we'd suddenly left the RLD and found ourselves in Venice.

'Idea for your honeymoon?' I ventured.

Liesbeth smiled. 'Marc's organising that. And he won't tell me anything.'

There was something rehearsed about her response. Perhaps because she'd had to deal with the suspicion that she might be improperly sharing information with her prosecutor fiancé.

'Probably for the best,' I remarked. I thought about treating Liesbeth to coffee and cake, but there wasn't time. 'Let's double back along Molensteeg. I want to talk to one of the women there.'

Irena was still in her window, wearing her UV-bathed police uniform. We stopped at her door. She opened it warily and turned on the harsh overhead light, instantly ageing her. The cabin was tiny, too small for the three of us. The instruments of her trade lay around: a pair of handcuffs, none too sturdy; a skin-coloured sex toy, not so large as to make the customers feel inadequate; rolled, clean towels for the unclean bed; a little washbasin, and a bin beneath – good-sized – for used condoms.

I was supposed to keep my gaze at eye level – except when there was good reason not to. A dark-green mark peeked out beneath the hem of her black hot pants.

'It is old bruise,' she said.

I nodded. Pimps used violence far less often these days. Too easy to spot, and bad for business. Psychological methods were preferred, namely blackmail. There was a stigma about prostitution in the women's home countries, and it only took one camera-phone photo…

'You remember my colleague Liesbeth?' I said in English.

'Hello again.' Liesbeth smiled warmly.

'I hope it's OK for us to drop by, to see how you're doing,' I continued.

'I'm OK,' she said. Her eyes flitted between mine and Liesbeth's, her lashes clumped with mascara. You might imagine that the women would be more comfortable talking to female police officers, but this wasn't the case. Shame among other women? Or competitiveness? Something more basic, I'd come to conclude. They kept hoping for a person who'd protect them. A guy with a gun was a good start, in their world.

'Business still good?' I persevered. Sex workers could clear a couple of grand a day here in the RLD.

'Sure,' she said. The sides of her mouth crinkled into a smile, but so briefly that she may as well not have bothered.

'And you're still sending money home to Budapest?'

I'd never received a good answer as to how she was converting euros back into the crumbling Hungarian forint.

She waved a hand over her face, sweeping a stray section of her fringe over one ear. Always with half a mind to seduce… though she was trembling.

'Sure,' she said again.

Of course the trembling could have been drugs, another method of control – but I was getting the feeling she was holding back out of fear.

Time to turn up the heat, then. 'Could we see some of the money? To satisfy ourselves that you're receiving it.'

'It's gone. I took it to the bank this morning.' She was looking beyond me now, out into the lane.

'Dressed like this?'

'Could I speak with you alone?' she said to me.

I turned to Liesbeth. Secretly, I'd been hoping for this development.

'I'll get us some coffee,' Liesbeth said, the little bell by the door tinkling as she left.

I sat on the red, PVC-upholstered stool in the window – the one she normally occupied – and crossed my arms. 'Go ahead then, Irena.'

But she was looking past me again, at something – or someone – outside. I thought it might be Liesbeth, but I didn't want to turn and lend weight to the object of her gaze.

'You must leave me alone now,' she said.

That was odd. A moment ago she'd wanted to speak to me. 'I'm a policeman, Irena. Even I don't get to choose to do that.'

'You are putting me in danger.'

I thought about showing her the photo of the tattoo, but decided against it. 'There was a body, a young girl, found in the harbour this morning,' I said instead.

The blood visibly drained from her face.

'Would you, or any of the other girls here, happen to have heard anything about –'

'Please go.' Her voice rose. 'Go!'

Not part of the plan.

I backed away, hands up in a gesture of surrender. Her entire slight frame was shaking in the tiny blue shirt.

'You know how to reach me,' I said.

I exited the cabin onto the street, my eyes adjusting to the duller light. Liesbeth was waiting.

We walked a few steps towards Nieuwmarkt and the police

station. 'Everything OK?' we both asked, almost in unison.

'No,' we said together.

'You go first,' I told her.

'A man showed up. He was trying to see into the cabin, while staying out of the range of the cameras.'

I looked up at one: a spherical, 360-degree camera strung between the buildings above the lane like a street lamp.

'Did you ID him?' I said.

'Partially, but his back was to me. He left pretty quickly. He was on the phone.'

'And you didn't think to follow?'

Liesbeth paused. 'I thought we were just doing routine checks here today? Is there something you're not telling me?'

'Irena was afraid,' I said, sidestepping her question. 'More than afraid.'

4

SLAVIC

LIESBETH AND I STOOD in the cramped CCTV-monitoring room at IJ Tunnel 3, Stefan de Windt at the controls of the grey bank of dated monitors. Stefan was a young, fair-haired cop with a tendency to wear his gun in a shoulder holster at all times around the station. He needed to get out more. Unfortunately for Stefan, he'd become rather too good at making sense of the hundreds of camera feeds dotted about the station's precinct, which – following the first of several planned reorganisations – covered the RLD.

We'd been going over the feeds from the cameras on Molensteeg, with Liesbeth trying to identify the man who'd sent Irena into a state of terror.

'Could be him,' she said.

On the monitor, a figure jumped between frames down the narrow lane. Stefan froze the recording that offered the best view.

'No,' she said. 'His jacket was darker, I'm sure.'

The frustration in the small room grew. It should have been a day of celebration for Liesbeth. To both of my younger colleagues, this sudden quest to track down a pimp probably appeared quixotic. Crimes in the RLD were rarely assigned a high priority. No Dutch householders were implicated; no precious voters in the inner or outer suburbs were affected...

But I was convinced of the incident's significance. Any pimp or handler would have known about the cameras in Molensteeg: the stakes and urgency must have been high for him to risk appearing on one.

Stefan sat back, sighing. 'I'm going to need you to get Joost to prioritise this.' The station captain was another of Jan Six's boys (like Bergveld). 'There's too much else in my inbox.'

I wondered if that included a dead body in the harbour. 'Just a couple more minutes,' I said. I patted him on the shoulder, and he leaned forward with another sigh.

We went back over the time frame once more, from another camera angle. Again Liesbeth came into view, beside the door of a Chinese restaurant. 'Wait!' she said suddenly. 'What about him?'

A well-built guy had appeared in the doorway opposite Irena's window.

Stefan played with the controls, getting us a grainy, partial view of the man's face.

'That's him,' Liesbeth said.

'You sure?'

She nodded firmly.

Stefan did something to send the image of the man's profile to his laptop. Here was the reason he wasn't allowed to get out more: he soon had a program open and was fixing red dots on the man's features. It was like something they might use in an animation studio rather than an outdated CCTV-monitoring room. The identification was soon made.

'Looks to be one Jan Tőzsér,' Stefan said, pausing to read another window that had popped up alongside the image. 'Hungarian national found living in the Netherlands illegally in 2007… a couple of cautions for minor offences, including possession of methamphetamines…'

'Anything more?' I asked, leaning in.

Stefan was silent for a second. 'An arresting officer comments that he goes by the street name "Slavic". Widely feared.'

They usually were.

Stefan looked at me, seeking direction.

But something else was nagging: I'd seen this Slavic before. Where?

*

'Henk, could I see you for a moment?'

Joost had put his bald head and scrawny neck around the door.

'Sure.'

He led me out of the monitoring room down the corridor. In his hand was a paper file. Joost was one of the few to have his own office. But instead of taking me there, he showed me into an empty conference room, the kind used for conducting briefings on operations. The motion-sensor lights flickered on and he closed the door behind us.

'Take a seat.'

Why?

'I just wanted to check in with you,' he said, answering my unspoken question.

'Check in? Should I have someone present?'

I smiled to let him know I was joking.

Half joking.

He smiled back. 'At ease, Captain Henk.'

He liked to conflate my old army rank with first-name terms.

'Bas mentioned that you weren't looking too well this morning.'

Bas.

I thought back to the morning's events with Sebastiaan Bergveld. 'Shouldn't you be somewhere else, van der Pol?' Bergveld had asked at the harbour.

'The case you called in,' Joost reminded me.

'Yes, I know.'

I was now on high alert. Joost was an intensely political creature with a knack for remembering details of events and conversations.

'A dead body is always a shock,' I said.

He nodded. 'Especially the younger ones. This one would be around the same age as your daughter, I think?'

I cleared my throat, about to say something but changing my mind.

'How is she doing, by the way?'

'My daughter?'

'Yes.'

'Well, thanks. Enjoying university.'

'You must be looking forward to seeing more of her when you retire?'

I recalled something else from that morning – my wife's words. *She's discovering herself... leave her alone!*

'Yes,' I replied.

'Or will you be getting away? Taking a cruise with the wife?'

I sat forward on my chair. 'Is something wrong?'

'It really depends on how you look at it.' He paused, nodding very slightly, as though affirming a decision he'd just arrived at.

But no decisions were spontaneously arrived at by Joost.

'You can go early, Henk. If you want to. Full pay through your last six months, pension unaffected...'

'Why?'

'Why not?' He gave a defusing smile. 'Come on, Henk. What are you working on these days?'

'Controls in the RLD...' I nodded towards the monitoring room. 'Just made an ID.'

He gave me a wry look.

Small fry, it said.

It was suddenly important to me that he continued to believe that.

'You've been a good cop, Henk. My advice? Have people here remember you that way.'

I looked him straight in the eye. 'Why wouldn't they?'

'I can't put you on a bigger case,' he said. 'I need to give the younger ones a chance to come through, to prove themselves. Plus I hate transitions – when you *do* leave…'

'Well, it's like you say… not long to go now.' I got up to leave.

He nodded. 'That'll be all then.'

I left the conference room. As I looked back through the slatted blinds screening the glass wall, I saw him reach for his phone.

*

Stefan and I stood beside the Oude Kerk and the little bridge there that turns into Molensteeg. The canal water was solemn and dark. 'Thanks for getting me out of the station,' he said.

'Thank Liesbeth,' I said. 'Or rather, thank her engagement, and her prearranged karaoke night.'

I noticed that the white floating bed in the canal had vanished.

Reaching for my pack of Marlboro Reds, I offered Stefan a smoke.

He refused politely.

It was dusk. Changeover hour in the Red Light District. Couples and tourists departing to be replaced by stag parties and night crawlers. I watched a guy in a tan leather coat and dark baseball cap do his second loop of the canal, sizing up the women in the windows. They could become lost in this process for hours, like on the Internet. Just another modern-day corruption of the primordial hunt.

'You think he'll show up?' Stefan asked.

'He has to at some point, it's his territory after all. He's pissed on it.'

The evening hour was changeover time for the women, too. Oude Kerk was the closest cars could get to the narrow Molensteeg; it was a known pick-up and drop-off point. But it was quiet. Maybe the spot had become too known – the drivers, bodyguards and 'boyfriends' moving further out?

I looked up at the buildings. The drizzle sparkled in the light beams that illuminated the big church behind us. Aside from the Oude Kerk, all the buildings were canal-side merchants' houses with steps up to the front doors and high dormers with hooks for winching merchandise. All built from and for trade. None more than six storeys tall. My gaze swept the lower storeys and returned to the narrow lane directly ahead.

I flicked my spent cigarette into the dark canal. At some point, I needed to get along to Liesbeth's karaoke night myself. Just for a short appearance. Especially short if certain people were there. Joost probably wouldn't leave his station post. Bergveld, on the other hand...

'Look,' Stefan said in a low voice.

A brief movement in the shadows around the dark mouth of Molensteeg. 'That's him, no?' Stefan was saying. 'On foot...'

I didn't doubt Stefan's powers of recognition. We started walking, but the man was moving quickly. I hastened my step as we crossed the bridge, the blood starting to pump in my thighs. We were only just keeping up, dodging passers-by who were looking left and right into the neon-lit windows. Deep reds and purples reflected off the man's slick jacket and his haunches as he moved, animal-like, up the narrow street. Stefan tripped over me at one point – as though I needed a reminder that he was a rookie street cop. But I had to take my chance while I had it.

We crossed another canal, the bridge there crowded, the Old Sailor bar on the corner loaded to the gunwales. A bright block of green on the TV screen inside announced a football game. When British clubs played here, the bar was a known flashpoint, often at the Ajax fans' instigation. Tribal affiliations again.

'Where is he?' I said, looking up and down both sides of the canal.

'Ahead!' Stefan stretched out his arm, pointing to the second, narrower section of Molensteeg. We broke into a jog.

'What will we do when we catch him?' asked Stefan, panting.

It was extraordinary how quickly the man had dissolved into the shadows. '*If* we catch him, we search him.'

Under money-laundering legislation, anyone with more than a thousand euros on their person could be brought in for questioning.

'I'll go ahead, Stefan. Stay behind, don't let him double back.'

I ran soft-footed up alongside him, adrenalin pumping. He'd stopped beside a disused bank of cabins, a black door among them. He unlocked it. As he turned to look around before entering, I suddenly had an awful realisation. We were opposite Irena's cabin. Her curtains were closed, but it would only take the split second as a customer left her cabin for them to open.

I couldn't have her implicated this way.

Slavic's eyes, like rivers of darkness, found mine. I shivered. His cheeks were gaunt, his cropped hair nail-file grey. He had rope-like cords of muscle in his neck where it twisted to look at me. Searching for a tattoo, I didn't see one. I almost let him be, but some part of me couldn't allow that.

I pushed him through the door.

Stefan followed us in.

'Police!' I pulled out my warrant card. 'Turn on the lights.'

The small space was lit by the screen of a desktop computer. There was a sour, unwashed smell about the place – the tang of petrol and mechanical parts.

'Turn on the lights!' I repeated.

He reached sullenly for a desk lamp behind him, its light putting him into silhouette. 'Close the door,' I told Stefan, whose mounting unease was clear. I knew he was wondering why we hadn't questioned the man in the street.

'You can't come in here,' Slavic was saying in broken English. 'You need warrant.'

'We can with probable cause,' I said, omitting that it was for a judge to decide. I forced that thought aside. 'My strong sense being that you're more of a payment-in-cash kind of guy than an American Express man, Slavic. Now empty your pockets.'

When you've done a career's worth of police work, you get

a feeling about some people – that somewhere, deep down, there's a piece missing, mentally. They can be normal-looking and presentable (Slavic being both), even worldly or charming. But you know never to trust that things around them will be OK.

'You make a mistake,' he said.

'Really? Because it looks to me like you're the one who's cornered.'

I made a show of looking around his makeshift den. Cash-drop bags in the shadows, a stowed moped, the computer whirring and clicking away. Right here in the middle of the RLD, almost within gaze of the cameras that had ID'd him earlier – how did he think he could get away with this?

I let my jacket fall open to reveal my holstered weapon. 'Empty your pockets.'

I waved Stefan alongside me. I needed to be able to see my partner, communicate with him non-verbally.

Slavic didn't move. I held his inscrutable stare. Did he think we were rogue cops on the take? Did he have something else on his person that he didn't want me to find?

Stefan had his service weapon on display, mimicking me. I could tell he was nervous, and I started to feel a sick sensation.

But I couldn't back down now.

There was a flash of movement as Slavic finally went for his inside pocket. But the movement was Stefan, unholstering his Walther P5.

Slavic sprang forward, forcing Stefan's arm up; there was an orange flash and a bang so loud that my ears rang. Instinct took over as I used Slavic's movement and momentum to force him to the ground with a thump and a gurgled *ungghhh*... I pressed my knee into the small of his back. Quickly I found my cuffs and forced one of his wrists into them, then yanked the other back before he had a chance to recover, snapping on the second cuff and locking it.

I was aware of ceiling matter drifting down like snowflakes, and the singed smell of cordite.

The street outside was quieter all of a sudden.

'You OK?' I asked Stefan. He was nodding, shaking.

'You want to call it in?'

He was still nodding, but not doing anything.

Slavic remained face down. I thought to check his pockets but he remained adequately restrained, so I reached for my phone.

'Dispatch?' I said.

'Go ahead.'

'This is Officer 6-19. I need a car on Zeedijk, corner with Molensteeg – now. Bringing a suspect in...'

I hauled Slavic to his feet. His eyes were expressionless.

We frogmarched him out onto Molensteeg. A small crowd had gathered outside. I noticed that Irena's curtains remained closed. Perhaps because she'd gone home: shift changeover, of course. I cursed myself for not having thought of that earlier.

Later, I'd wonder what might have happened if Liesbeth had been with me instead of Stefan, and whether the whole day might have gone in another direction without Joost's little chat and the way it had left me feeling...

But those were excuses.

And excuses wouldn't help the woman hoisted out of the harbour. She didn't need excuses, she needed justice.

5

KARAOKE

WE SAT IN A bare interview room at IJ Tunnel 3, Slavic with his arms folded and his chair pushed back.

Just the two of us, me leaning in with my elbows on the steel table between us.

I'd let Stefan get back to his day job – but not before asking him to dig further into Slavic's police record.

There was still time to turn this situation around – to get some kind of result. But for that I needed Slavic to feel intimidated. Not physically. That's not the way cop interviews work these days.

We prefer psychological methods.

'We'll get started in a minute,' I said, taking off my watch and placing it on the table.

I needed him to believe that I'd got something on him – a minor offence at least. My objective was to turn him into a snitch. He might be feared on the streets, but a street-level pimp is low on the criminal food chain. I wanted him to help me find whoever was responsible for the body in the harbour. More than anything, I needed him to stay away from a lawyer.

The door opened and Wester, the custody sergeant, handed me a sheet of paper. I thanked him as he left.

Slavic watched intently, his brow knitted.

'You prefer Jan or Slavic?' I asked.

It was like offering him white or black in a chess game, an imaginary board between us. My hope was that I knew how to use the more powerful pieces. Then again, these Hungarians could be good at chess.

'Let's go with Slavic,' I said.

His face was blank. The knee of his right leg bounced.

'I'm holding a list of items found on your person,' I continued, making a show of looking down the sheet. 'Item four: three thousand, six hundred and sixty euros. Made up of seventy-two fifty-euro notes and three twenty-euro notes.' I put the sheet down. It had done its job. 'That's a lot of fifties to be carrying, Slavic. Care to explain where they came from?'

He shrugged his shoulders, but his knee began bouncing more quickly.

'If you've got more than a thousand euros on your person we can open a money-laundering case on you.' I leant in further. 'Look into your phone records. Your tax affairs, your employment and residency status: lots of different ways in which life can become very troublesome for you...'

'You hear of Schengen?' he said.

So he knew of the EU's Schengen Agreement, which had been extended to Hungary at the end of 2007, meaning he was no longer in danger of deportation – unlike earlier that same year, when he'd been living here illegally.

'But what about the source of this cash, Slavic?' I persisted, raising my voice. 'How long do you think it will take for us to prove that it's coming from coerced prostitution?'

'You think you get girl to testify?' he said.

His knee was still. It was hard to tell from his broken English whether 'girl' meant plural or singular. Whether he was talking about girls on the Molensteeg, or specifically Irena. I suddenly wondered whether Irena had gone home for good – whether that might have been her last shift.

His expression turned quizzical as Stefan entered. Stefan sat beside me, handing me a cup of coffee and setting his own down. He didn't offer Slavic one.

My coffee was black. This was the pre-agreed sign that Stefan hadn't been able to dig up anything more on Slavic, specifically concerning the earlier methamphetamine case. Our guest was staring at Stefan, smiling slyly now.

I pulled his attention back to me. 'Slavic, when we prosecute a theft case we don't need the stolen goods in order to testify. And when we prosecute a drugs case, we don't need the drugs. Are you seeing a pattern here? We don't need *girl* to testify.'

'So charge me.'

We stared each other down. There was something in the depths of his eyes, a dark knowing.

'That's not how it works, my friend. First we open a case. And we investigate. Get to know you very well, crawl over every aspect of your life –'

'You should not enter my property,' he interrupted.

Would he know that a lawyer could invalidate any evidence collected through a search without a judge-authorised warrant?

'The evidence on this occasion – the money – was gathered here by a custody sergeant, Slavic. Right here at the IJ Tunnel 3 police station, at the front desk.'

But something wasn't right. It was something I'd seen in his den, or maybe in his confident posture; of course, there'd been the gunshot too…

'So investigate.' He shrugged. He was looking at Stefan, whose discomfort I could sense. 'Show what happen,' Slavic said.

'Sure. We can throw in refusal to cooperate with the police, assaulting a police officer…'

The tables were turning though. A gunshot incident report would pose awkward questions. What had been our operational plan? Why had Stefan been there and not Liesbeth, my regular partner (especially in the RLD)?

I replayed the scene in my head. Stefan drawing his weapon on Slavic… Slavic responding, forcing the gun back upright. There was no jury to convince here in Holland, but even the harshest judge would see instincts of self-defence in Slavic's move as opposed to him attacking a police officer unprovoked.

I thought too about the ballistic evidence: the 9 mm parabellum that would be lodged somewhere in the rafters of Slavic's den. They were standard-issue bullets for police and street criminals alike, meaning it could have come from anyone's gun, but there was also the witness testimony to consider. A good-sized crowd had gathered on Molensteeg after that bang.

Check, Slavic might as well have said.

Again, the memory of his den sent a shiver through me; there was something I'd noticed that I couldn't yet put my finger on…

Slavic was smiling that sly smile again.

'Maybe I see lawyer now,' he said.

*

'What the fuck, Henk?' Joost exploded, once the door to his office was closed.

Stefan was with me. We'd left Slavic in the interview room, in the capable hands of Vincent van Haaften – an extra-sharp defence lawyer, sharp-suited too. Clearly there was money behind our guest – considerably more than the 3,660 euros that Wester had emptied from his pockets.

'Well?' Joost pressed, walking behind his desk to underscore his authority.

'As I briefed you earlier, I was just doing controls in the RLD… making an ID.'

'You didn't tell me you were going to break into someone's property and fire off a round into the guy's ceiling!'

Vincent van Haaften had spoken with Joost, then.

'I followed Slavic into his place. It felt risky to confront him on the stree –'

'Don't' – Joost held up a palm – 'prejudge the verdict of the incident team I'm required to appoint.'

He had his head bowed in thought.

Behind Joost were shelves of awards – and photos of him

receiving awards. Some at the police academy, but also one with a rosy-faced Jan Six. Six-Shooter was standing between Joost and a politician that I recognised as Rem Lottman, a big figure in every sense – a 'kingmaker' within the city's fragile coalition government.

'Who fired the gun?' Joost looked up with alert eyes.

I glanced at Stefan. Pale-faced, he was shaking once more. His eyes met mine, beseeching.

How old was Stefan? Twenty-eight? Thirty? A whole career ahead of him, with a clean sheet so far in station operations. An adverse incident report could set his career back years... permanently, even.

One thing about my own status and relations with Joost: I had very little to lose now.

'It was me,' I said quietly.

Joost canted his bald head. 'And if we were to run a GSR check on you, it would confirm that?'

I knew they weren't going to test me for gunshot residue; Joost already had the result he wanted.

'Sure.'

'OK, Stefan,' Joost said, 'you can go.'

For a moment, Stefan stood still, too confused to move. Then he bolted.

'We'll need to check your gun,' Joost informed me.

'I'll get it.' Fortunately, I'd left it locked up in the squad room. I made a mental note to fire it someplace, fast. But where?

'It's not looking good for you, Captain Henk.'

The pity appeared genuine.

'What the hell were you thinking, trying to get back in on the harbour case?'

His words almost passed unnoticed. But how would he have known about that connection? Had van Haaften told him? But I hadn't mentioned the tattoo to Slavic, van Haaften's client... Or even to Stefan.

Kurt Larsson?

'That'll be all,' Joost said, dismissing me.

Had it been a guess, or a very subtle warning on his part? An uncharacteristic error even?

His back was already turned.

*

I needed answers, but more than that I needed a drink.

My watch showed nine o'clock as I made it to Liesbeth's engagement celebrations. It was a short walk to the karaoke bar, a place where cops knew they wouldn't be hassled. And Joost wouldn't be there; I'd at least managed to leave him buried beneath fresh paperwork.

But as I entered, I saw none other than Bergveld at the mike, singing along to the 80s track 'Jessie's Girl'. He looked out, steely-eyed, from under his floppy fringe, the glint of a disco ball dancing across him, turning him into some past video idol.

The place was full. Through the bobbing heads I could make out Liesbeth, looking radiant – along with several others from the squad room. I wanted to offer them a drink, but there were too many people in between. I forced my way to the bar and asked for the strongest beer they had. The music and laughter were loud, causing the barman to lean in, cupping his ear. The Dubbel Bok he poured had travelled all of a kilometre from the local IJ Brewery.

There's something about that Rick Springfield song Bergveld was singing – the obsessive quest for someone else's woman – which always unsettled me. Or maybe I just ached for the 1980s again. In any event, Bergveld was trying too hard with it, like he really *was* the star, yet the words were someone else's. There was something symbolic in that, someplace.

I took the head off the flavoursome beer and sighed.

'Henk,' a voice said to the side of me.

Marc Vissering, Liesbeth's fiancé, was the prototypically tall Dutchman with pale eyes. He clasped my hand warmly.

'Loosening the vocal cords?' he asked with a boyish grin.

'Marc, can I offer you my congratulations?' I hugged him and thumped him on the back. 'She's a lucky woman, and you're a luckier man. What are you drinking?'

'What did you say?'

I guided him further along the bar, away from the speakers.

'Drink?' I repeated my offer.

'No!' he said. 'We've got a tab going. Let me add that beer to it.'

'That's OK, it's paid for... So, how does it feel?'

'Hold on,' he said, getting his order in, shouting it over the bar. That done, he turned back to me. 'Actually it feels pretty amazing. This is now a double celebration.'

I raised my Dubbel Bok in acknowledgement. 'How so?'

'We got a major conviction today.'

'Oh? Which case?'

The barman leant over to clarify one of the drinks ordered. 'Without ice,' Marc confirmed, before facing me again. 'Organised vehicle theft. The suburbs will be sleeping quieter tonight.'

'Ah, car alarms.' They'd even arrived in my neighbourhood. No one acted on the bloody things, especially when the owners were away – which was often enough, apparently.

'High-end stuff: Mercs, BMWs...'

I'd heard chat about this around the squad room. Operation Boost, was it? It had to be. It was one of those cases that you weren't supposed to know of, but always found out about.

'Not BMW *bikes*, I trust,' I gave him a sidelong look.

'Not valuable enough, I'm afraid,' he laughed.

I smiled. 'So who were the bad guys?'

'Eastern European syndicate. Taking the vehicles up to Rostock then shipping them across the Baltic. Lot of demand for baubles out East these days. Tens of millions of euros' worth, in fact.'

Suddenly he had my full attention.

His drinks appeared on a tray.

'How did you get the testimony?'

'You should know,' Marc said, picking up the tray. 'It was one of your guys – Sebastiaan' – he nodded ahead – 'who directed the infiltration operation.'

I turned to look at Bergveld. The track had ended and Liesbeth was now at the mike for 'Ademnood', a staple of weddings and karaoke nights. A chorus of female voices joined in around the room.

Bergveld was walking straight towards us. I didn't doubt that he'd received a text from Joost by now.

But then there was a stir around the doorway as someone strode in. Jan Six, instantly recognisable: he was wearing a flowing black overcoat, and was red-faced as usual. Six-Shooter had rustic features – a squashed nose and rough skin – and he smiled a lot, giving off an air of geniality, but his political moves to get to the top of the Amsterdam police force spoke for themselves.

What was he doing here? It must have been a spontaneous drive-by, otherwise Joost would surely have been here to greet his boss. Had he come to wish a highly regarded young prosecutor well with his engagement? Or rather to claim paternity for a successful police operation: success breeds many fathers, after all…

Operation Boost had clearly been a big deal.

Bergveld and Six converged not two metres from me, clapping each other on the shoulder. Marc drifted over to them; his body language invited me in, too, but that was checked by Bergveld's turned shoulder as he steered the group away, towards the swaying crowd of happy squad-room staff.

Coming the other way was Wester. 'How many times must we be tortured by this song?' He shook his head, pressing his palms into the wooden bar. 'For God's sake, Henk, get up there and sing something.'

I looked over at Liesbeth and her happiness; all I could do was smile and hold my hands up in surrender.

'By the way,' he said, 'I'm sorry your guy was cut loose today. Handing all that money back… It felt like I was giving him the green light to go on doing whatever he's doing.' He glanced at me, perhaps hoping I might enlighten him.

Not wanting us to be overheard discussing Slavic, I changed the subject. 'So what *would* you have me sing?'

'André Hazes?' he suggested, not missing a beat.

Though now deceased, the Dutch singer was still wildly popular.

'I wouldn't know which song to choose,' I said.

Only, I would… *For me, no garlands on the wall.*

6

THE NIGHT WATCH

HAVING FOUND MY MOMENT to say goodbye to Marc and Liesbeth, I slipped out of the karaoke bar and headed home along Entrepotdok. The mist had come back in, blotting out the former warehouse buildings lining this historic waterway.

The smell of whale oil, resin and other goods once kept in storage here was gone. Even when we moved here back in the 1980s, the dockside buildings had mostly been abandoned. The area then underwent the classic cycle of urban renovation and gentrification: the social housing originally intended for these units was supplanted by an influx of architects, 'creative' types and start-up kids, their designer furniture arriving by van instead of by boat. Things evolve.

We were glad to be living on the water. At least, I was; Petra would probably speak for herself on that point.

I stepped across the gangplank onto the houseboat and opened the door, hit by a welcome blast of hot air from below.

'*Hoi*!' I called.

I could hear the TV.

'*Hoi oi*!' came the response.

I took off my coat and gun holster and negotiated my way down the narrow wooden steps. Mrs van der Pol was in her house slippers, watching a rerun of some talent show competition I vaguely recognised, working her way through a jar of English liquorice. I stooped to kiss her on the forehead, and joined her for a moment. A Chinese singer appeared onstage. A judge named Willem yelled, 'What number are you going to sing for us? Number thirty-nine with rice?"

'Is this all that's on?'

She shrugged.

'Do you want a drink?' I went through to the kitchen.

'Tea,' she called back. 'Rooibos, please.'

I put the jenever bottle back, reasoning that tea might help me sleep. I switched on the kettle and pulled out a couple of mugs, feeling the boat creak. Sometimes vessels passed by, causing groans in our hull with their wake.

'Nadia phoned,' my wife called out.

'Oh?' I stepped back into the living room. It was gone eleven, I saw, as I checked my watch: too late to call her back. 'Everything OK?'

'Yes,' she said, looking up from the TV. 'I think.'

'You don't sound certain.'

There was a flash of green at eye level.

Our boat – which I'd restored over many years – featured a varnished wooden ceiling in the living area that popped up a little above deck level. I'd fitted portholes to allow in light. Only, it was dark out.

Another flash of green.

'What's that?' I said.

'What?' My wife strained to hear me over the noise of the TV.

I grabbed the remote to turn it off – then hit the switch of the standing lamp with my foot, plunging us into darkness.

'Hey!' Petra said.

'Shh.'

'Don't shush me, Henk.'

The creaking again. Definitely a creak, not a groan from boat wake.

'Listen.'

She was silent.

Creak.

'There!'

'I'm not hearing anything,' she huffed. 'In particular, I'm not hearing my TV show!'

In my peripheral vision I caught a sneaker with a fluorescent strip.

'Someone's aboard.'

I went to get my gun.

A creak, louder this time, along with a muffled voice. There were two of them.

Over the thirty years we'd lived on the boat, we'd experienced our fair share of students, tourists and vagabonds finding their way across the gangplank – but these intruders felt different. Stealthy… acting with intent… I checked the magazine and action of my P5 in the pale glow of the boiler's pilot light.

'Henk?' Petra said, sounding uncertain.

A white torch beam sliced through the dark, glinting off the brass chandlery of the galley and kitchen, then moving back, searching – and coming to rest on the side of Petra's face, which she turned away, gasping.

I paced quickly to the stern. There was a hatch, originally intended to take goods onboard. I eased it fully open into the night air, waiting for the hydraulic arm to catch, then silently hoisted myself up into a standing position, braced and ready.

But the two men were already retreating down the gangplank. In the mist, all I could see was that fucking green flash.

I aimed my gun at the water – between the boat and the shore – and punched out a round with a flash and a loud crack. The 9mm shell casing landed on deck with a clinking sound. I heard a foreign curse; the men were taking off, the gangplank bowing like a springboard, the green stripes scything through the misty darkness.

My heart was thumping.

A moped droned, rising in pitch yet softening as it gathered pace down Entrepotdok.

I realised a car alarm was sounding, set off by the gunshot.

Mrs van der Pol wouldn't thank me for reinforcing the 'cop neighbour' stereotype among the knick-knack designers now populating the neighbourhood (assuming they even knew who I was), but I'd at least managed to fire off a round from my service weapon before handing it in to Joost.

*

I didn't sleep a wink that night. I tried napping in the hammock slung amidships, but resorted to standing in my usual spot in the cabin, where I could look out of the windows. It afforded a clear view across the ink-dark water. I spent so much time here that I'd even fixed up a little shelf for the cups of coffee or evening jenevers that I liked to drink while I stood, watching.

Eventually, the mauve morning light crept over the dockside skyline and into the boat. I doubted our visitors would be returning now. Putting on the coffee, I woke Petra, who hadn't slept well either and was probably about to throw something at me – not herself, alas. I slipped on my bomber jacket, checking I had my phone, and crossed the gangplank.

It usually felt good to be awake at this hour, while others were still in bed, but this day was different, in ways I couldn't yet fathom. I got a Marlboro on the go and headed for the harbour as usual.

Once, the neighbourhood cafés and diners would have been for dockhands and barge pilots, but now they didn't open much before ten – broadly the time the start-up kids rolled into work. Pretty much the only place to get a coffee this early was the Ibis hotel opposite the police station. There, Sonja served me a cappuccino and a fresh roll. As she set them down, I noticed the headline of the day's *Het Parool*:

YOUR CARS ARE SAFE WITH SIX
New police commander makes major inroads into organised vehicle theft
– by Marianne Brouwer

I read the article quickly, intently…

> *The long-running undercover operation allowed Amsterdam police to successfully dismantle a major criminal network supplying hundreds of high-end vehicles to cash-rich buyers across the Baltic states, Hungary and Ukraine.*
>
> *'The suburbs will be sleeping safer tonight,' said Alderman Rem Lottman, from Amsterdam's coalition council. 'Although we must continue to work on all fronts to ensure the kind of social security and stability we need…*

I finished the article, tore out the page and folded it into my inside pocket, thinking over what I'd just read.

'Undercover operation' didn't usually mean cops changing identities to infiltrate criminal milieus. Too risky – and too resource-intensive. Rather, it was often a euphemism for cultivating snitches.

'You OK, Henk?'

'Sure,' I replied, leaving a five-euro note for the €3.80 I knew it cost. 'Thanks, Sonja.'

Making a mental note to ask Petra about this Marianne Brouwer, who was a colleague of hers after all, I quickened my step down to the harbour.

Everything looked like it usually did.

Except everything felt different. I bypassed my usual perch and walked over to the spot where the girl's body had been hauled out the previous day.

There was no evidence of what had occurred, no residue left on the pavement.

I looked across to the old ship with its masts and rigging, the science museum, the floating restaurant… my gaze swept around to the main street, Prins Hendrikkade. I recalled taking some footage on my phone. My fingers fumbled with the touch screen; I couldn't find it.

I looked around again. There was something else…

But what?

I decided to call Larsson, the medical examiner. He'd taken photos. But it was too early, he didn't pick up.

So I walked over to the station. Wester wasn't in yet; the night-time desk sergeant was new, we didn't know one another.

I unstrapped my holster and handed it to him. 'Ballistics need to run some tests on this, per the station captain. Could you send it over to them?'

Joost wouldn't be in yet. I wanted it on record that I'd handed the gun in at the earliest opportunity that day.

The desk sergeant raised an eyebrow as if to say: *Can't you do it yourself?* But I prevailed.

Then I stepped back outside and tried Larsson once more. He picked up this time.

'*Hoi?*'

'It's Henk.'

There was a pause.

'Henk…'

'I had one more request about the harbour case. The body.'

'I'm sorry, I…' He sounded jovial enough, but I heard something else in his voice. 'It's been made clear to me that you're not on the case, Henk. I'm sorry. If it was up to me…'

'No, that's OK. Catch you round, Kurt.'

'So long.'

I checked my phone for any calls or texts.

Then I left a voicemail for Stefan.

*

My daughter didn't answer my call, and she didn't return it immediately either. I was struck by that saying: how children need you, until they don't need you.

I decided to go and see her. She worked certain mornings and lunchtimes in a café beside the university called the Kriterion, which was also an art-house cinema. One of her courses was film studies and the job gave her free access to the films shown there, as well as providing some income. Or so she'd told me, the last time we'd met.

The Kriterion had a decidedly retro, studenty feel. A vacuum cleaner was whirring away as I walked in. The films advertised on the posters and flyers looked like arty, fake porn but perhaps that was unfair. I hadn't seen any. Petra and I preferred the real thing.

'Nadia,' I called.

She was wiping down the bar top and looked up, a little confused, but finally managed a smile. 'Dad… hi. What are you doing here?'

'I was passing.' As I got closer, I couldn't help notice… 'Your hair's redder –'

'Dad,' she said, coming out from behind the bar, away from her colleague. Her face had gone the same colour as her hair. She gave me a quick, self-conscious hug.

'And is that a nose stud?'

'*And?*' she said, crossing her arms.

'Is there anything else?'

'Christ, Dad! Would it matter if there was?'

I checked the frustration I felt at the growing distance between us.

'That depends. I heard you called last night. I just wanted to stop by and see if everything's OK.'

We stood for a moment, her fidgeting slightly.

'Could you put those excellent bar skills of yours to work and fix me up a coffee?'

'We're not open yet.' She rolled her eyes good-naturedly enough. 'OK, then.'

'That's my girl.' The chair scraped as I sat down at a table. I nodded at her gaunt-cheeked young colleague. He looked like he hadn't eaten in some time. Or was the goth look coming back?

Nadia said something to him, then returned.

'Your boyfriend?' I nodded towards him. Then I looked harder. 'Is it wise for him to be out in daylight?'

'Dad, please. You're being ridiculous now. What's up?'

'That's what I wanted to ask you. You don't normally call home on weeknights. We're lucky if we hear from you at the weekend –'

'*You're* the ones going away,' she said.

'Are we?'

'Mum said you were probably heading to Delft for a while, to stay with Cecilia.' She screwed up her face. 'Aren't you?'

Mrs van der Pol's plans were gathering momentum.

'We'll see,' I said. 'We're thinking about it… That, or a trip some place else. Depends also on my retirement, and hers.'

'When is that, now?'

Had it already happened?

'We're working it out.'

'Christ,' she said, exasperated. 'I wish you guys would just make a decision.'

Slightly stunned, I had to acknowledge the trait in me that I was increasingly objecting to in her. 'You seem on edge,' I managed.

'I just don't like –'

She paused as her colleague set down my coffee. It had a heap of milky foam and what looked like nutmeg sprinkled over the top; I thanked him for his creation.

'It's just taking a little longer than we'd hoped to work out our plans,' I said as decisively as I could. 'But we'll do so soon enough.' I sipped the mochachino, or whatever it was.

She couldn't stop herself from laughing.

'What?'

'Foam on your nose. You really *do* look ridiculous now.'

She pulled the long sleeve of her cardigan over her hand and used it to wipe the foam away.

'So everything's OK?' I asked.

'With me? Yes.' She thought. 'Well, I did get this strange phone call yesterday. You know sometimes, when something just doesn't feel right?'

She had my fullest attention.

'At first the caller said nothing. I was about to hang up, then he said: "Give my regards to officer six nineteen."'

The temperature seemed to drop.

'I thought at first he'd got the wrong number and was after the Student Housing Office, but something in the way he said it' – her voice was coming to me as if from underwater – 'was strange enough that I thought to write it down...'

My blood was turning to ice.

Even Nadia didn't know my officer number.

I could recall exactly where and when I'd last given it out: *This is Officer 6-19. I need a car on Zeedijk, corner with Molensteeg ...*

7

MILITIA MEN

I CALLED PETRA AS I walked.

'Hello?'

'Henk –'

'You still at the boat?'

'No, I had to come in to the office early.'

'I need to see you,' I said. 'Now.'

'Why? I can't.'

'Why not?'

'Because things are afoot here at the paper. What's come over you?'

I stopped midway across the drawbridge onto Entrepotdok. If Petra was at *Het Parool*'s office, then at least she was safe in the middle of an open-plan newsroom. Which reminded me of something...

'Do you know a reporter called Marianne Brouwer?'

'Er... why do you ask?'

'She broke a story this morning about vehicle theft. Involved some of our guys.'

'No, she's a freelancer. But it's funny you mention her.'

'Why?'

'The paper's moving.'

'Office?'

'No, in political direction. And this Brouwer woman is connected to it somehow.'

'Moving politically how?'

'Look Henk, this really isn't the time. I'm sorry we missed our breakfast. Let's talk tonight, OK?'

I went over Marianne Brouwer's article in my head, and remembered the mention of the alderman. 'Is Rem Lottman relevant to this political move?'

There was a pause. I could hear the newsroom's babble and the ringing phones. 'Henk, this just isn't the time.'

'Fair enough, but I've been thinking about Delft. Maybe we should go sooner rather than later. Take Nadia with us.'

'*Nadia?* In the middle of a university term?' She made it sound like I'd gone mad. 'This is definitely a conversation for later, Henk. I'll see you tonight.'

If I couldn't put Nadia and Petra out of harm's way without upending their lives, I had to remove the harm itself. But how? It would be impossible in an official police capacity now.

I walked home, stopping to check my motorbike. It looked fine – nothing awry. I patted the saddle tentatively.

Boarding the boat, I went down to the galley and pulled the article out from my pocket.

'The suburbs will be sleeping safer tonight,' said Alderman Rem Lottman, from Amsterdam's coalition council...

My phone buzzed. Stefan.

'*Hoi.*'

'Henk,' he said. 'I can't tell you how grateful I am for what you did yesterday.'

'Don't thank me, just send me the information I requested earlier.'

'What you asked for in your voicemail?'

'Yes.'

'I can't. The harbour case is locked. Larsson won't share anything without Bergveld or Joost's written authorisation.'

'OK, something else then. Could you send me Slavic's mugshot?'

'Er... sure. To your work account?'

'No, print it off and meet me on the corner of IJ and Prins Hendrikkade instead. *Do not* send it from your work email account.'

'OK,' he said, bemused.

I locked up the boat and looked around quickly, then strode over to where we were meeting. I lit a cigarette; by the time I'd finished it, Stefan had arrived with the printout.

'Are you going to be all right?' he asked. 'With Joost, I mean?'

'I don't know. But if not, it's not your fault. I was the senior officer in command – I shouldn't have put us in that spot.'

'Shit,' he said. 'I hope they don't need me to write a report accusing you. Will they?'

I patted him on the shoulder, reckoning that Joost would only be looking for one report: my own. A report, confession and resignation all in one. 'Get back to work, Stefan. You've got a bright future ahead of you.'

He nodded and left.

I looked at the hi-res image he'd handed me. 'Rivers of darkness' was how I'd thought of Slavic's eyes, and that came through even on paper. There was a mole above his left eye that I hadn't noticed before.

I walked down to the harbour again, returning to the spot where the body had been hoisted ashore.

I held up the photo, trying to find the through-line, the pattern of connections that was at the dim margins of my consciousness, refusing to reveal itself.

I'd stood *here*...

Larsson was *there*...

And Bergveld *there*...

That's when the memory struck me. *There were still a few onlookers on Prins Hendrikkade: two cyclists, a moped rider...*

I reached for my phone, searching again for that brief video footage I'd taken.

The moped in Slavic's den...

I looked at the printout, then back at Prins Hendrikkade...
Slavic had watched it all.

*

Whatever impression people might form about Johan, my motorbike-riding, regimental-tattoo-sporting friend from the army, it's probably nothing like the real thing. He's one of the coolest, most laid-back guys in the world... until he's in a fight, and then you definitely want him on your side. He was the best man at my wedding, as I was at his.

These days he had long, silver-grey hair swept back into a ponytail. But the same clear eyes and tall, stolid facial features. Often to be found smoking an American Spirit roll-up – only not now, in the dark little mariners' chapel off Kattenburgerstraat. It was one place I knew we wouldn't be overheard.

His hand grasped mine firmly. 'Henk,' he said solemnly. I gestured for us to sit in one of the aged rosewood pews and caught him up on everything that had happened since I'd asked about the tattoo design: the trips to the RLD, Slavic, Bergveld, Joost and Jan Six, not forgetting the vehicle-theft case that had been mentioned in the paper.

'So you handed in your P5. They'll want your warrant card next. You no longer have your 225?'

He was talking about my army-issue Sig Sauer P225, but it was a statement rather than a question. Most went 'missing' after active service; not mine.

I was silent.

Johan sighed deeply. The old smell of the resinous rosewood blended with the spicy scent of the votive candles. The chapel was one of my favourite places in all Amsterdam, but not at that moment.

'You need to take this Slavic guy off the board.'

'Off the board? How?'

He left a gap for my imagination to fill. 'I'm seeing two things as next steps. First, I'll lend you my 225.'

I didn't like the direction this was going in. 'I'm going to tell Petra to take Nadia to Delft, get them away from here.'

'And so, what... ? Nadia's going to leave university?'

'If need be, yes. For the time being.'

He shook his head. 'Henk, this man has entered your home – your cave. He's tracked down and threatened your daughter. Don't you see? He's using the same intimidation tactics as with one of his street girls –'

'What are the other options?'

'Pray?'

I looked up at a wooden carving above the altar: a ship's figurehead, the mouth of her face agape, a surprisingly lifelike wooden hand wrapped around her eyes.

'You mentioned two things as next steps,' I said.

'A pair of balls, Henk. One way or another, this man has to go.'

But I couldn't descend to Slavic's Neanderthal level. There had to be another way. Not lawyers or tribunals: they'd have no chance, given the politico-judicial forces now ranged against me.

Who was at the top of the chain? Who did Jan Six ultimately answer to? The power broker of Amsterdam city, who'd helped get all these apparatchiks appointed: Rem Lottman.

8

TRADE-OFFS

'Hi Nadia, just wanted to tell you again how good it was to see you earlier. Please could you call me when you get a moment...'

I walked a quick circuit around the harbour, so I could think. From the science museum, above the tunnel, there was the little footbridge across to the new library, then the floating Sea Palace off to the left; somehow it all made me see life on many different levels.

'Petra, please could you call me back as soon as you get this...'

I stopped by the big Saturn music and electronics store beside the DoubleTree hotel, extinguishing my cigarette. Inside, there was a man with a younger girl in hot pants. They didn't look like father and daughter, nor girlfriend and boyfriend. I flipped through some CDs, watching them for a moment as they left, him guiding her by the small of the back.

I looked down at the jewel case I'd picked up from the rack and groaned. Damn that André Hazes...

'Nadia, please call me, I love you.'

Now I had the store to myself. I put back the CD and bought something else instead.

'Petra, why aren't you checking your phone? Please call me, this is important.'

Then I retraced my steps towards the police station.

*

'Hello?'

'Henk, I just came out of an editorial meeting to six missed calls, mostly from you. *What* is going on?'

'Thank God. You and Nadia are in danger. You need to take her to Delft.'

'Henk, are you mad? What are you talking about?'

'A case gone bad. A street thug, menacing us. He came aboard the boat last night, I'm pretty sure.'

Petra was quiet.

'He also called Nadia.'

'Who did?'

'The guy. Slavic.'

I could tell that she was walking, probably away from the newsroom. 'Who's this guy?'

'Like I told you, a street thug. A pimp. Violent.'

She'd arrived in a place where she could speak freely. 'Listen to me, Henk. I am not fleeing my job. Nor is Nadia quitting university.'

'I'm not asking you to –'

'Listen to me! You need to get your colleagues to sort this out.'

'They're protecting *him*, Petra. I brought him in for questioning yesterday. Joost cut him loose. But there's more… I believe he was at the scene of the harbour incident yesterday –'

'The dead body?'

'Yes, and I accidentally shot some footage of him on my phone. Only, Bergveld borrowed my phone for no reason. And now the footage is gone.'

'Bergveld deleted evidence… at the scene?'

'I'm sure of it. The whole case is locked down. Access to information is airtight.'

'A cover-up?'

Part of Petra couldn't help but hunt the story, I knew. 'The girl in the harbour had a tattoo on her ankle, like she'd been branded.

It turned out to be Hungarian. I'm sure she was a prostitute working in Little Hungary, where I've seen the same tattoo on other girls. This Slavic guy controls most of that street.'

'Why would the police be protecting him? Why cover it up?'

'The only explanation is that they're using him as a snitch for much bigger cases – like Operation Boost.'

'What's that?'

'The vehicle-theft investigation. The story your colleague had the scoop on.'

'Marianne Brouwer's not my colleague. She's a freelancer, like I told you. But this is starting to make some sense.'

'What's making sense?'

'Why they used her, and not a staff reporter like me.'

'Who is she?'

'We'll come back to her. What are you going to do about this street thug?'

'I'm talking to Johan about him. I'll have a plan in place by the end of day. And I need you and Nadia to leave town.'

'Henk, that's not happening. Go back to your colleagues and tell them that if they don't protect your family – *our* family – real reporters will land on the story.'

I was almost at the station.

'They'll see that as a threat. This could spiral out of control.'

'They should see it is a warning. You need to bring things back *under* control.'

'I guess I've got nothing to lose,' I murmured, not mentioning the shooting incident and internal enquiry now underway. 'By the way, one thing to keep in mind: if this is the cover-up that we think it is, it goes way above this police station. It goes up to Jan Six, at least. And I doubt it stops there.'

'Even better,' she said.

'Why?'

'Because of the chief puppeteer. It's time he was taken to task for what he's doing.'

I stopped in the street, outside the station entrance. 'Rem Lottman?'

'Has his name been mentioned elsewhere?'

'Yes, in that article. He gave the quote. Why him and not the mayor, who formally controls the police?'

'Lottman has the ear of the mayor on policing and security, surely you know that? He's the one holding the council coalition of aldermen together. That freelancer, Marianne Brouwer, is practically on his payroll. Word is that he's just been chosen by his party for a big European role.'

'In Brussels?'

'It's not yet clear. Looks like he's moving away from the "Dutch First" law-and-order dossier, though, and more towards social policy.'

'*There's* a switch. And he's trying to take the editorial stance of papers like yours with him?'

'Yes, towards social policies that travel... internationally.'

'A dead trafficked girl in his backyard might not be the best start in Brussels.'

'No question. But it's your lever.'

'Yours too. Switching gears, could you talk to Nadia? Tell her to be extra careful? She'll listen to you.'

'Henk, I'll try. But let's not have any misunderstandings here: one way or another, you need to get this Slavic off the streets.'

'One way or another...'

I hung up as a familiar voice called my name.

*

Liesbeth's face looked uncharacteristically pinched and tight. 'What's going on?' she said.

'How d'you mean?'

'Bergveld wants to see me later today.'

'Perhaps to compliment you on your singing.'

The joke landed flat.

'What happened yesterday?' she asked.

I explained everything that had taken place with Stefan, including the gunshot, adding: 'I only took him because I wanted you to enjoy your engagement party.'

'Christ,' she said, shaking her head. 'Will you be OK – with Joost?'

'Course,' I lied.

'Couldn't you have explained this to me before doing it?'

'I was afraid that your sense of duty would get the better of you and ruin your celebration.'

'Henk, please don't do anything like that again. If casework requires something to happen, tell me!'

'OK, then here's something: the girl we visited in her cabin yesterday, Irena… could you check she's all right?'

'Sure,' she said, confused.

'What time are you meeting with Bergveld?'

'This afternoon.'

'Go now, then. I'm worried about her.'

'OK.' She looked at the station, then down the street, deliberating.

I pointed. 'The RLD's that way.'

*

I avoided the squad room altogether and went in search of Stefan. Thankfully, he was in the monitoring room. We had it to ourselves.

'Glad to see you back at work today,' he said. Dark circles around his eyes betrayed a lack of sleep.

'I'm making every last moment count.'

'That bad?'

'It's not good, Stefan. But let's not dwell. Could you pull some footage from the cameras on Prins Hendrikkade from yesterday morning?'

'If this is the harbour case –'

'It's not. It's Slavic. Check and see if his moped was down there around eight a.m., parked up by the harbour wall, would you? Then track it as far as you can throughout the day. We know that by six p.m., he'd driven it back to his den on Molensteeg...'

'Do we?' Stefan said, leaning towards his controls. 'We saw him arrive back at his den on foot – remember?'

'But it was already parked there when we followed him in.'

'Henk,' Stefan said, turning back to me. 'I'll do what I can, only –'

'I know – there's a lot of other things in your inbox. But try to think about what's *not* in your inbox, Stefan. At the end of the day, you wanted to get out on the streets rather than spend the rest of your days cooped up in here. I made that happen. You drew your weapon when you shouldn't have, causing it to go off accidentally. Remember?'

He turned bright red.

I let him sit with that.

*

'Henk.'

This was it. Joost.

He beckoned me into his office.

'I handed in my gun,' I said, pre-empting him.

'I know. Fired once, yesterday: a nine-millimetre round.'

'That report came in fast.'

He nodded. 'Now I need your warrant card.' He held out his hand.

Shocked, I reached for it. Gave it to him.

'You're still a police officer, but you're suspended from active service pending the enquiry's results.'

'Which will be when?'

He shrugged.

'I get it. That part of the process *isn't* so fast.'

I was now formally being run off towards retirement.

'We're reorganising the team here. Bas is communicating it in one-on-ones, starting this afternoon.'

'I see.'

'You were a good cop, Henk. This saddens me. There aren't many of your type left – who've served in the military, who...'

'Handle each case equally before the law?'

A shake of the head. 'Who can't see the bigger picture. You know that we're not immune from public-spending cuts. That there's always more to do than resources will allow. There's always got to be prioritisation, Henk. There are always' – he waved his hand, seeking the right word – '*realities*.'

'And a branded body in the harbour isn't a reality?'

He was silent.

'Why's the harbour case not being worked?'

'How do you know it's not?' He sighed. 'But do you really think the majority of Dutch voters care about some prostitute gone missing, when their Audis and BMWs – which they've worked and saved hard for amid the worst financial crisis in living memory – are being snatched from under their noses? I don't remember anyone inviting these Eastern European thieves and whores to come and live here!'

He composed himself.

'There are always trade-offs, is what I mean to say. Hell, you *know* the mantra. Six hundred known criminals account for sixty per cent of the crime in this city.'

What a nice, shiny new ring it had, with Jan Six at the helm.

'Slavic helped you get one of those six hundred?'

'Two,' he held up both fingers in a peace sign. 'Two of them. Damn it, Henk, you could have been in on that!'

I took a step towards him, towering over him. 'This Slavic is threatening me, personally' – my voice was low but audible – 'coming into my home, calling my daughter up with my officer number...'

'Then leave him the hell alone!' Joost snapped, stepping back. But there was only so far to step.

He changed tack: 'This is between us now, Henk. I didn't want things to end this way.'

'So maybe they don't need to. Every day is a new day and all that. There's always a chance for a fresh start...'

A final head shake. 'Jan's already been briefed.'

So Jan Six was out of the running for legitimate recourse. Good to have it on record.

Joost thrust out his hand. 'So long, Henk.'

I didn't shake it.

I couldn't. My right hand was in the pocket of my bomber jacket, cradling the mini digital recorder I'd bought at the Saturn store in place of an André Hazes CD.

9

IRENA, SASKIA AND STOPERA

LIESBETH HAD MANAGED TO find Irena, who'd still been breathing – just.

We were in the back of a van, making our way to see her at a shelter operated by GendrAid, a women's rights NGO. Judging by the sound of the planes coming in low overhead, we were somewhere near Schiphol.

The shelter operator, Erik Hoffman, explained that this was now standard procedure for all visitors. The previous year, a Ukrainian journalist had been given a tour of the shelter. It turned out that she'd been working for one of the trafficking gangs, who arrived the following day with Heckler & Koch MP5s to reclaim their 'investment'.

And this was considered less serious than vehicle theft?

I'd pointed out to Erik that, as police, we were entitled to make our own way to the shelter, but he'd requested that we didn't. Many of the rescued women there were suffering from post-traumatic stress disorder, and in their home countries the police were typically seen as corrupt – at least, in matters relating to prostitution and human trafficking. Lacking a warrant card, and for the reasons Erik had given, I felt obliged to agree.

The shelter was a former youth hostel, now surrounded by a high perimeter wall, making it look like a prison. I asked Erik what the women did when they got out.

'We have a number of employers around the city who we've

vetted carefully and who are willing to give them a job. But on average, it takes a year here before they're even ready to think about such a step. We just don't have the capacity or resources to deal with all the cases we're now seeing.'

We entered the building and found ourselves in a reception area, where some of the women were sitting alone. One of them, missing a front tooth, was talking animatedly to herself.

'That's Veronika,' Erik said. 'She likes to tell herself stories about eligible suitors vying for her affections, who she's choosing between.' He paused. 'She can't have children anymore.'

Moving on, we walked down a corridor with brightly coloured drawings and finger paintings on the walls, like in a children's nursery. The former hostel rooms still had bunk beds. They smelled institutional. Cleaning products.

Erik turned back to us. 'Given that one of your guys already interviewed her —'

'Hold on,' I stopped him. 'Someone's already been here, from IJ Tunnel 3?'

'I don't remember which station. Surely you'd know? In any event, it was a client who gave Irena the beating, your guy managed to establish…'

Liesbeth and I looked at each other.

'I wouldn't ask her about the beating again,' Erik finished his caution. 'It risks a relapse.'

We turned down another corridor of single-occupancy rooms, finally reaching Irena's.

'You do the talking,' I whispered to Liesbeth, who had a knack of winning immediate trust with victims. I'd told her everything I knew about the harbour case now; nothing had filtered through to her from Bergveld, apparently.

She nodded.

Irena was unrecognisable. Her face was mostly black; one eye was closed altogether from the bruising. A butterfly-stitched gash that started as a split lip ended at her chin.

A nurse sat her up and helped her drink some liquidised food through a straw.

Liesbeth sat on the far side of the bed, so that she could easily see both Irena and me. Irena looked straight ahead, glassily – not even noticing me.

'Hello,' Liesbeth said brightly, taking Irena's hand. 'I can see that the doctors and nurses are looking after you very well. I wanted to start with a simple question. It's just like we're at school again. Can you tell me your name?'

The cracked lips parted. 'Irena.' Her voice was barely audible.

'Good,' Liesbeth said soothingly, patting her hand gently.

'And another name question… Can you tell me the name of the girl who fell into the harbour?'

Irena's good eye went into a thousand-yard stare. 'Saskia.'

'Very good.' Liesbeth looked at me.

Keep going, I gestured.

'And did that naughty man put her in there?'

Liesbeth looked at me again. I nodded. *Say the name.*

'… Tőzsér?'

Irena convulsed with fear. Erik and the nurse stepped forward in unison.

Use his street name, I mouthed at Liesbeth.

'Was it Slavic?'

Irena's eye squashed shut.

'Why did the naughty man do this to her?'

'She escaped,' Irena said, eyes scrunching, clearly wanting this over with.

'From where?'

'Where new girls arrive, by train station.'

'New girls arrive where, Irena?'

'At hotel.'

'Which one?'

Liesbeth looked at me again. There were any number of hotels around Centraal station, but I was starting to see the geography, the little footbridge from the harbour wall where Saskia had fallen in...

'Irena?' Liesbeth prompted.

For some reason, I thought of the hotel opposite the station, a dark behemoth on the very edge of the RLD, with its curiously shut-in feel. It always reminded me of the remote lodge in Stanley Kubrick's *The Shining* in which Jack Nicholson goes mad. I could still recall watching that film on the houseboat, ten-year-old Nadia hiding as the creepy twins appeared, 'redrum' running across the mirror in reverse: *murder...*

Liesbeth was looking to me for direction. I mouthed a question: *Why?*

'Why didn't the naughty man try to recapture Saskia?'

But Irena was trembling.

'Was Saskia pregnant?' Liesbeth prompted.

'I think we'd better stop here,' Erik stepped in.

'Had she contracted an illness?'

If she'd been infected by one client, the next one wouldn't want her; she'd be worthless to Slavic.

'OK, that's enough.'

The nurse stepped forward, helping Irena lie back down. For a second, I wasn't seeing Irena but rather all women, beaten into submission. Surely I could at least keep Nadia and Petra safe?

Perhaps not, with Slavic on the loose.

*

'I'd like to know who from the station visited the shelter ahead of us,' I said to Liesbeth. We were almost back at IJ Tunnel 3, just in time for Liesbeth's one-on-one meeting with Bergveld.

Liesbeth nodded.

A dismal drizzle was falling.

This was the last time we'd be working together as partners. Liesbeth was about to find that out. I thought to tell her myself, but then my phone started buzzing. I juggled it while waving goodbye to her and lighting a Marlboro.

'Henk.'

Stefan…

Had he got anywhere with the footage from yesterday?

'Something's not right,' he said.

'Only one thing?' I walked briskly away from the station.

'First, the camera coverage on Prins Hendrikkade is bad, once it's away from the road junction at the mouth of the tunnel…'

How convenient for Slavic… and Bergveld.

I inhaled deeply on my cigarette.

'But here's the strange thing,' Stefan continued. 'No moped appears at Slavic's den on Molensteeg all day. I checked back to six a.m.'

'Yet the moped was there when we were,' I continued his thought.

'Are you sure it was the same moped?'

Was I?

'I'm pretty certain it was him on Prins Hendrikkade at eight a.m. But it may have been a different moped,' I conceded. 'So… he drops the moped somewhere else, returns on foot shortly before we intercept him…'

'No,' Stefan said. 'He was there earlier, remember? Liesbeth saw him when you went into that sex worker's cabin.'

Irena's cabin. It was true.

I tried to make sense of it. 'So he was there earlier, and he went back out again.'

'Only I don't *see* him going out again.'

'Doesn't add up. You're saying Slavic only returned to his den in the evening, when you and I pursued him to Molensteeg… yet he was already there?'

'So the images show.'

This was turning into a Hungarian wild goose chase.

'Unless there's another way out of his den?' Stefan added. 'A back way?'

I thought about that. 'It's possible,' I acknowledged.

'Especially if he'd identified Liesbeth and me. He may well have retreated to his den, and used a hidden exit...' I weighed up the risk of returning to Molensteeg to check that out.

Another call was incoming: Petra.

'Hold on, Stefan, my wife's on the other line. Please keep looking.'

'What for?'

'I'll get back to you.'

I answered Petra's call.

'Henk?'

'You got the sound file I emailed to you?'

The recording of my conversation with Joost.

'I already visited Lottman,' she replied. 'Or tried to. He wants to see you instead. Right away.'

'At Stopera?'

'Yup.'

Stopera is the seat of city government. There's a music theatre in the same complex; the name 'Stopera' runs together *stadhuis* ('city hall') and opera, an apt label for the melodrama of Amsterdam city politics.

'I'm on my way,' I told Petra. 'You hear from Nadia?'

'Christ, Henk. Is it the street thug or *you* who's harassing her now?'

But I could hear concern beneath her anger.

'I'll take that as a no...'

'I'm on my way over to the university now.'

'Good. Start at the Kriterion.'

'OK!'

*

Stopera is a modern, fortress-like building on a bend in the Amstel river, maybe a kilometre as the crow flies from IJ Tunnel 3. The fortress took decades to plan and build, and the project was mired in controversy from the start. As early as 1915, the city elders had deliberated over a site to house a new city hall and opera house, finally deciding on Waterlooplein square. The Jewish street market that was held there was cleared out by the Nazis during the Second World War.

After the war, plans lurched between commissions, competitions and budget crises. Finally, in 1980, the city council approved a new design by Cees Dam and the Viennese architect Wilhelm Holzbauer. National government approval followed, but so too did fierce resistance from squatters, displaced groups and the Provo protest movement. Riots broke out when construction started in 1982, the year I returned to Holland. The project ran wildly over budget, and it wasn't until 1988 that the new city hall finally opened for business.

I'd been there several times, so knew the layout – and where the aldermen sat. Rem Lottman's office was on the fourth floor.

An impeccably dressed PA closed the thick double doors of Lottman's large office with an unnecessary sense of occasion; I didn't have an appointment, the urgency of the matter apparently requiring no announcement. Clearly, he had something to protect.

Lottman was like a giant beetle: his stomach filling out his dark waistcoat, his hair shiny black, his brow sheened with perspiration. He wore horn-rimmed glasses. Even his thick eyebrows, peeking out over the frames, had a faint lustre.

I walked towards him, feeling the deep carpet give.

His thin pupils bored into me as his plump hand shook mine, weighing me up, evaluating. Then he waved me over to a pair of leather easy chairs beside his desk. The room was lit by an art deco table lamp; beyond the pool of light sat cardboard boxes. *Destination: Brussels?*

'So,' he began. 'Two for the price of one: journalist and cop. You make quite the little power couple.'

I ignored the provocation, taking the recording device out of my pocket and laying it on the glass tabletop. I ran my palms together in the manner of a croupier leaving the blackjack table: *nothing concealed.*

Lottman stared at me, nodding slowly. 'What do you want?' he said.

'To help you. Your police appointees are getting it all wrong. Listen...'

I pressed play. I'd stored a few of the sound bites in the device's memory:

> *'Why's the harbour case not being worked?'*
> *'Do you really think the majority of Dutch voters care about some prostitute gone missing?...*
> *'I don't remember anyone inviting these Eastern European thieves and whores to come and live here... There are always trade-offs...*
> *'Jan's already been briefed.'*

I pressed stop.

Lottman sat still for a second, then shrugged. 'An over-zealous station captain. Most Dutch voters would probably agree with him.'

'They possibly would. But that can't play well on your watch, with the new social-policy dossier I hear you've been handed. People-trafficking is a hot topic in Brussels.'

He was silent.

'You'd better hope this is all Petra and I find out about him – and Jan Six, too.'

He canted his head. 'To play devil's advocate' – he adjusted his bulk in his chair – 'as I occasionally like to... Word has it your wife's not long for *Het Parool*, if that's your intended outlet for this –' he waved his hand at the device, not deigning to finish his sentence.

'But there's always the Internet, Alderman Lottman. Blogs, social media... If you can't beat them, join them.'

He looked at me, entirely impassive. The perfect poker face.

'You'd know better than me,' I continued, 'but I believe there's a phenomenon in media called the sleeper effect? That, over time, people only remember the message, the words… not the source. And words most certainly matter in your realm.'

Thieves and whores…

'You realise this makes you a snitch?'

'I prefer whistle-blower.'

'I'm sure you do. Words matter in your line of work, too.' He paused. 'What do you want?'

'Reinstatement to full police duties.'

Lottman nodded, clearly expecting this. 'What else?'

'There's a street thug named Jan Tőzsér menacing my family. I need him neutralised. Right away.'

He made a show of thinking.

'The police, the prosecution: they all answer to the mayor, not me.'

'Please.' My impatience broke though. 'You have influence at all levels. Everyone knows that. So what if you're moving to a bigger stage? No successful politician neglects their base, and yours is right here in Amsterdam.'

He sat back, interlacing his fingers over his belly.

'Travel's a fascinating thing, isn't it, Henk?' He looked past me at the packing boxes.

'How so?'

'Your father. He was in the merchant navy, I'm told. But there was a problem, as I understand it. A man inexplicably found dead on his watch. And all the fingers pointed to him. Do I have this right?'

There was a dull ringing in my ears, like when I'd first found the body in the harbour…

'No wonder you went into a different service – the army,' Lottman continued. 'But tell me: what was it like, growing up overseas…'

We'd kept moving on whenever questions started to be asked, you see. Questions that never received any answers…

'… feeling banished from your homeland…'

South Africa, Ghana, the Dutch Gold Coast…

'… through no fault of your own. Or *do* you blame yourself, a child growing up that way – an outsider, wherever you go?'

Lottman held up an appeasing hand before I had a chance to answer.

'Let's just be a little careful here,' he said, leaning forward slightly. 'We don't need any more unnecessary hurt caused.'

I picked up the recording device and stood up; my legs felt like lead.

'Perhaps you could let me know your answer,' I managed, before walking out.

10

THE BIKE TRIP

IT WAS RAINING HARD as I left Stopera. I would have turned my collar up but my bomber jacket didn't have one. Just as I was lighting a cigarette, Petra called.

'Henk, I can't find her.'

'Nadia?'

I stopped.

'I went to the Kriterion. They said she left at lunchtime, at the end of her shift.'

'She's still not answering her phone? Even when *you* call?'

'No. And there's something else: I went to the university administration and got her class schedule. She didn't show up to her tutorial this afternoon.'

'She could have just skipped class.' It was my turn to play devil's advocate. 'What about her halls of residence?'

'She's not there. I don't know where else to turn.'

'University security? The campus police?'

'I've been to see them all. They won't do anything till she's been gone twenty-four hours. They asked if she was at a boyfriend's and just hadn't told anyone.'

'Does she *have* a boyfriend?'

'No one serious, I'm pretty sure. She mentioned someone once… I don't know,' she said despairingly.

I attempted to stay calm. 'What about that friend of hers? Famke?'

'I'll try.' Petra was silent for a second. 'What happened with Rem Lottman?'

'He may be able to help. I think he's thinking about it... I don't know, Petra.'

The rain was running beneath my jacket and shirt, trickling down my back. I sought shelter.

'Henk, what do we do?'

'Johan's offered to help. I'm on my way over to see him now.'

If I couldn't put my family out of harm's way, I had to remove the harm itself.

'Henk,' Petra said imploringly.

'What?'

'Be careful.'

'Don't worry. And don't go back to the boat. Check in to the Ibis instead.'

This time, she didn't debate it.

*

I stood astride my BMW on Nieuwmarkt, on the edge of the RLD. It was dark, the rain coming in squalls now, whipping the umbrellas of the few tourists braving the terrible weather.

Fully suited and booted, I kept my hands in the bike's handlebar muffs, partly for warmth, mostly for readiness. Water ran off the visor of my crash helmet in rivulets.

The helmet had a built-in Bluetooth intercom, allowing me to communicate with Johan. It had a video camera as well, though the picture quality was usually too poor for it to be useful, particularly at night.

Johan was a hundred metres away, at the entrance to Molensteeg. Him, not me, in case Slavic recognised my build.

'Copy?'

'Copy.'

The sound via his mike was clear enough. The only interference was the faint sound of the rain.

'How's the repair going?'

'It's looking more and more realistic in this weather,' he said. He was pretending to have broken down, all the while monitoring the street. 'There's still time to go to Rødby,' he joked.

'You think the Baltic Sea would be any better? That's where this weather system's coming in from.'

'OK, Piet. Just keep your eyes on the road, and I will too.'

Piet Paulusma was a famous Dutch weatherman who'd been hit by a car on camera. It was a joke, mocked up for a Kwik-Fit commercial, but it still had an impact when viewed on YouTube.

I watched the cars come and go. Occasionally, a dark saloon pulled up and two or three girls would be helped out. The business of the RLD went on. Little umbrellas folding in on themselves, the girls being hurried along by their 'boyfriends' or 'loverboys' – whatever they called themselves these days.

'Hold on.' Johan's voice came to life again.

'See anything?'

Silence.

'Johan?'

'Nah, it's not him.'

'Did you study that photo at all?' I was only half joking.

'It's strange,' Johan said. 'He has one of those faces that's so hard to fix somehow.'

A police bike trundled past, the yellow livery spectacularly fluorescent against the watery gloom. I couldn't tell who the rider was, but I felt a jolt of unease. In my left pannier was Johan's ex-army Sig Sauer.

'Wait, I think it's him,' Johan said.

'Slavic?'

'Yup, coming up the lane on his moped, weaving between pedestrians…'

I fired the trusty flat-twin engine; it was still warm. 'Is he wearing a crash helmet?'

Silence.

'Johan!'

'No… shit… he's heading the other way, north on Zeedijk. I'm turning round to follow –'

'Towards the train station?'

His mike was still working but he was breathing heavily with the exertion of manoeuvring his bike. I'd moved my motorcycle forward off its stand, ready to follow suit, when a black BMW saloon slowed down in front of me. A familiar figure stepped out of the shadows, reaching for the rear door.

'Johan,' I said. 'D'you copy?'

I could hear the whine of his bike moving at speed. 'Copy.'

'You've got the wrong guy. Slavic's getting into a car right ahead of me.'

'You sure?' His engine was loud. ''Cause I'm pretty sure I've got him. We're already opposite the station, bearing right…' *skkrrrr* '… Oosterdok…' *skrrrr.*

Shit, the intercom only had a range of one kilometre. I tried to shine my headlight at the car, but the rear door was already closed and the windows were tinted. The only movement was from the rain and the car's front windscreen wipers.

Skkrrrr skrrrr '… DoubleTree…' *skrrrr skrrrr.*

'Johan?' I yelled, my breath misting my visor.

I'd lost him.

The jagged-shaped DoubleTree hotel, beside the station: it made sense, but one of us must be wrong. And I was sure Slavic had entered the idling saloon car that faced me like some dark beast – rain dancing wildly in the beams of its headlights.

I reckoned it was sixty or seventy grand's worth of car, even used. That surely put it above Slavic's pay grade. A money courier's ride, perhaps? But I hadn't seen a bag. Maybe Slavic had the cash concealed inside his coat…

There was a short screech as the car took off to my left, across Nieuwmarkt.

'Johan?'

I was speaking into a void. I kicked my bike into gear and

gave chase, slapping my visor down against the rain.

The saloon was moving fast, down towards Waterlooplein. I gunned the engine and was just able to keep up without endangering the wobbling cyclists we overtook. The car bypassed the turning to Stopera and rounded a dogleg curve to Weesperstraat, an urban canyon of modern buildings. The driver was choosing open roads – avoiding the risk of getting boxed in?

My speed was showing seventy... eighty... eighty-five kilometres per hour – the rain turned to little dancing dots on my visor as I tried to close the gap between me and the tail lights. I tucked in behind the water splashing up in the car's wake, afraid of aquaplaning. I was also trying to read the licence plate in my headlight beam, but it was heavily mud-spattered – how convenient.

The red tail lights flared, flying towards me as the car braked to turn right towards Stadhouderskade. The bike's telelever suspension barely prevented the front end from diving as I squeezed the brake hard, veering to follow.

We shot past the Amstel Hotel and over the river there. My speed was at eighty... ninety... one hundred... I dropped back – I couldn't risk being pulled over carrying the gun. Traffic lights spangled green as we continued past the Dutch central bank. I thought of Rem Lottman, Brussels-bound, and how little my meeting with him seemed to have achieved in this unfolding nightmare.

We were racing alongside the Singelgracht canal, getting ever more central. The monolithic brick Heineken brewery, another vivid reminder: this time Freddy Heineken and his infamous kidnapping, one of my first assignments. I'd been a junior member of the rescue team, no older than Stefan was now.

Around the side of the Rijksmuseum we swung, past the diamond houses at the foot of Paulus Potterstraat, gaining speed once more. Suddenly the car's tail lights reddened again as it turned right into the rear of the Conservatorium Hotel.

I slowed but didn't follow it in, instead riding around to the front and parking further along Van Baerlestraat. I pulled my crash helmet off; I was cold, but sweating too. Something about this whole situation – make that *everything* – wasn't right.

The odometer showed that we'd done four kilometres in as many minutes. But we couldn't have travelled further from the sleaziness of the RLD. The Conservatorium was Amsterdam's ritziest, most fashionable hotel. A new glass structure had been added at the rear, creating a giant, open atrium. I started to jog around the building, reluctant to leave the Sig Sauer in the bike's pannier but with no time to lose. I pulled out my mobile to call Johan as I went. There were missed calls from Petra.

As I approached the rear entrance, phone to my ear, the BMW saloon pulled out onto Paulus Potterstraat and turned back towards the Rijksmuseum. It was travelling more slowly but there was no time to return to my bike and give chase now. I cursed the evening's events.

'Henk?'

'Johan, where are you?'

'Still by the DoubleTree. What happened?'

'I tracked him to the Conservatorium, I think. But I've lost him. Shit.'

'Henk, I'm pretty sure he's here, at the DoubleTree. I could've sworn I saw him enter the lobby not five minutes ago. His moped's outside. I've got camera footage from my crash helmet.'

'Of him?'

'Er… of the moped.'

'That just can't be, Johan.'

But I'd begun to doubt myself. The moped rider on Prins Hendrikkade – had I been wrong about him? The tattoo on the body in the first place… Was I so obsessed with Slavic that I'd created the very problems for me and my family I was now desperately trying to solve?

'Did you ID the car?' Johan was asking.

'Licence plate was too dirty.'

'Convenient.'

'That's what I thought.'

'What nationality?'

'NL, I think.'

'I'm going to hang out here at the DoubleTree… talk to reception.'

'As you wish.' I was walking past the glinting Porsches and Bentleys parked behind the Conservatorium. 'Let's talk again in the next ten minutes. No more than ten.'

The doorman wore an expensive black coat with a blood-red scarf. He was large, courteous and mistrustful; I was in my biker gear, dripping wet.

'There was a car here a few moments ago,' I said. 'A black BMW saloon. Did you happen to see who it dropped off?'

His eyes narrowed. 'And you might be…?'

'A police officer.'

He looked me up and down. 'May I see your warrant card?'

My warrant card – now with Joost.

'It's probably better that I speak to the reception staff.' I walked straight past him before he had a chance to argue.

Welcome warm air, like entering a hothouse. Inside was Amsterdam's beau monde – chic men and women lounging in expensive chairs, surrounded by artful knick-knacks and champagne on ice.

This was some watering hole.

I strode over to the reception desk, aware of dripping onto the pale stone floor. Coming the other way was none other than Jan Six – with an unnaturally beautiful young woman, cheekbones like blades, and a female member of the hotel staff.

Had he seen me?

I dodged over to the stone steps that led up to a gallery of boutique shops. There was a viewing spot at the top of the stairs, looking back out over the entire atrium. I stood back slightly, staying in the shadows. Six's companion made an equal impression from the rear, her white satin dress revealing almost as much as if she hadn't been wearing one. Lots of skin on display… Six's mistress? She looked too young though – young enough to be his daughter. An expensive escort, maybe? Was Slavic into high-end prostitution? Or was I fitting the facts to my own, increasingly fractured story?

Was I projecting my fears onto the 'other' – this outsider… this Slavic?

No, there was Irena's testimony and the BMW that I'd just followed from Little Hungary.

But what exactly was I observing here? Just another important figure, Jan Six, showing off a beautiful woman on his arm? The big beast in his natural habitat?

He hadn't turned around. The hotel staff member was guiding them towards a lift at the base of a little glass tower, a separate structure within the atrium building. Six and his female friend parted ways with a companionable kiss. I watched through the layers of smoked glass as the lift ascended to the second floor and he entered a meeting room with three other figures; from where I was standing it was impossible to tell their gender even, let alone whether one of them was Slavic.

My phone started ringing.

I turned to walk through the gallery of boutiques and answered just as it became a missed call.

Johan.

There was a text too, from Petra: *At the Ibis, please come soon as you can. Please.*

I was hurrying back out to my bike when I got hold of Johan.

'Could you go to the Ibis hotel right away? Petra's there, I'm worried about her.'

'Where are you going?'

'I'm heading there too, but you're closer.'

'OK. I talked to reception here at the DoubleTree – they say a man *possibly* fitting Slavic's description checked in with five young women, claiming they were all in town for a talent contest –'

'Never mind that, just get to the Ibis. I need to call Petra. I'll see you there. Please hurry.'

11

REM'S WORLD

FROM PETRA'S ROOM AT the Ibis, you could just see IJ Tunnel 3 further along the opposite side of the busy street.

Johan stepped outside; I nodded my thanks to him.

Petra's eyes were puffy from crying. I hugged her but she broke away from me.

'Henk, I can't do this.'

I sat down on the edge of the bed, ready to talk. I was still in my biker gear. The room felt hot and stuffy.

'Pushed out of our own home. Unable to find our daughter,' she said.

'It's just for a night or two, then we'll go back to the boat. Nadia's safe, I'm sure of it. Just incommunicado, for whatever reason –'

'Henk. No.' She looked around the room. 'I can't function here. I don't have any of my things!' There was a wild look in her eyes; I'd seen it before in the homeless, the dispossessed – that lack of a secure place…

I stood up and gently placed my hands on her shoulders. 'I'll go back to the boat and get your things. What are you missing?'

She waved her arms meaninglessly and began sobbing.

I tried to hug her again but she pushed my hands away, more fiercely this time.

'What will you do about Nadia?'

'I'm dealing with any potential threat. That way she's safe, wherever she is.'

'I don't even know what that means!' she cried.

I just needed time to think. 'Is there anything to drink here?' I couldn't see a minibar.

'No! It's all on the boat.'

'I'll go there, then, get whatever we need.'

She shook her head. 'My daughter –'

I left the room.

Johan was outside, pointedly out of earshot. 'Where to?' he asked solemnly.

'Could you stay here a little longer?'

'Er... sure. But where are you going?'

'The boat.'

'D'you need help?'

'No, please stay with Petra.'

I took the lift down, contemplating my next move. In the time it took to cross the lobby, I was resolved. I strode past my parked bike, crossed the busy street and entered the station.

*

Bergveld was in the squad room working late, and so was Liesbeth. They looked cozy together – police partners now?

'I need a word.'

'Are you talking to me?' Bergveld looked up, incredulous.

'Who the fuck else?'

Liesbeth was staring hard at her computer, avoiding eye contact.

Bergveld stood up, and as he did so I charged at him, shoving him through the door behind him into a conference room. He clattered over a chair onto the floor as the lights flickered on, his fringe flopping over his reddening face. '*Yesus*,' he managed, winded. 'Liesbeth, call Wester!'

But there was no force to his voice. I had him by the throat. 'I've been a cop for thirty years, Bergveld. My daughter's missing, my wife's in a hotel room – you owe me and my family protection. You *owe* me that!'

His face was bright red, and sweating. I let him go and he collapsed back onto the floor, gasping. For a second he just lay there breathing, his chest rising and falling. Then he picked himself up, eyeing me with steely contempt.

'D'you ever wonder if there might be other considerations, van der Pol?' he asked hoarsely. 'Ever allow for the possibility that *you* might be missing something here? You're like a fucking bull in a china shop!'

He pulled himself up to a chair, composing himself. The mask, the face I'd seen at karaoke, was back on. I remained standing.

'We told you to leave that guy alone.' He looked at me and then out into the squad room, calling: 'Liesbeth, fetch Stefan.' This time his voice carried, and Liesbeth acted.

'Slavic's lawyer is Vincent van Haaften, I'm sure you're aware. It's looking like you might be getting to know Vincent a whole lot better if they pursue their case.'

'What case, you little shit?'

'Harassment by a suspended officer. There's a chain of command here, Henk.'

'As the Nazis once said.'

He shook his head.

'Where's Joost?' I suddenly asked. Was he with Jan Six?

'Offsite.'

With Slavic?

Stefan appeared in the doorway, looking sheepish.

'Tell him,' Bergveld commanded.

'Sebastiaan asked me to –'

'Tell him!'

'I pulled more footage from the Molensteeg,' Stefan stammered, not making eye contact with me. 'And also from the vicinity... and it appears that... you and another, unidentified male were conducting surveillance on Jan Tőzsér... I'm sorry...'

'That'll be legally discoverable,' Bergveld promised, 'if van Haaften and Tőzsér decide to file suit.' He was standing now.

'Someone here talked to Irena,' I said. 'She confirmed that Slavic killed Saskia.'

Bergveld screwed up his face. 'Who the fuck's Irena? Who's Saskia?'

'The woman in the harbour.'

'I don't have a clue what you're talking about –'

'Of course you don't. So why's the harbour case sealed?'

'And I've no spare resources to protect paranoid former officers from themselves,' Bergveld continued. 'Take your family away for a while, Henk. Do us all a favour,' he said in a low voice. 'Take a break, or –'

'Or what?'

'Accept the consequences.'

'Is that a threat?'

'It's a warning. It's a fair and final warning.'

'It's certainly the final warning I'll accept from *you*,' I said, staring him down before turning away. Stefan had left.

Liesbeth wasn't in the squad room either.

I walked straight out into the night, heading to the boat, when a black stretch Mercedes pulled up. The rain had eased up some. For a moment nothing happened – there was just the faint idle of the engine and the billow of the exhaust, like those New York street vents you see in movies. Then the rear passenger door opened as if under its own power, and out stepped Joost.

He didn't meet my gaze, but rather walked straight past me into the station.

'Get in, Henk,' the remaining passenger said, a hand beckoning.

*

Alderman Rem Lottman amply filled the capacious black interior. The car was icily air-conditioned; it smelled faintly of cigar and expensive cologne, or maybe perfume – an aromatic fridge. The armrest featured a traditional phone handset. In front of it was a recess containing expensive-looking glassware.

The back of the seat in front of him had a built-in TV, which was flickering silently.

'Drink?' Lottman offered. 'Whisky?'

I nodded.

He lifted a decanter, pouring generously first into one and then a second cut-glass tumbler.

'Cheers,' he said, raising his glinting tumbler.

I raised mine too, not stopping till it reached my mouth. I drained half of it, the immensely welcome fire spreading through me.

'You impressed me earlier,' Lottman said. 'Not everyone could do that, come to see me like that. Takes balls.'

It made me think of something – a trip to the zoo, with my dad. Where would that have been... Cape Town perhaps? We're standing in front of the lion enclosure and a fully grown male, rangy-looking, is pawing at the cage, trying to get out, trying to get at *us*. I'm absolutely terrified. My dad puts his rough hand on my shoulder, says: 'Never show you're afraid, son. That's when they really come for you...'

'Congratulate my wife,' I told Lottman. 'She contacted you first.'

'But it was *you* who married your wife, Henk. So congratulations are still in order.' He tilted his glass again in acknowledgement. 'There are no coincidences,' he went on. 'The people we meet in life, we meet for a reason: people who have a lesson to teach us, or some lesson to receive from us. But most often, people who just reflect us – show us some aspect of ourselves...' He pushed his glasses up the bridge of his nose with a fat forefinger. 'You grasp the realities, Henk. Yes, I'm going to Brussels, and no, I can't neglect my base here in Amsterdam. Weren't those your words?'

'Well remembered. Or recorded?'

'Mmm,' he said, mid-swallow. 'Which reminds me. Servaas, would you do the honours?'

The burly driver got out and walked around the back of the car, opening my door.

I climbed out and Servaas patted me down, hesitating only over the large fob for my motorbike keys. Eventually satisfied, he let me back inside the car.

'Sorry about that,' Lottman said, 'but I'm sure you understand. Things have been getting out of hand around here.' He waved a hand towards the police station. 'Quite a mess to clear up.'

'Good thing you have Joost,' I said. 'And Jan Six above him.'

He shook his head. 'Too many chiefs, not enough Indians.'

We sat drinking in silence as I digested this remark. I was wondering about Sebastiaan Bergveld, his status on the chief–Indian scale, and exactly what mess Lottman was referring to, when he turned to me.

'You could be inside the tent.'

'Huh?' I met his eye. 'Why me?'

'I see something of myself in you.' A pause. 'I, too, struggled greatly till I found a cause, and a mentor.' He pushed his glasses further up his nose. 'We all need that figure in our lives.'

Did we?

Did Nadia?

'I can teach you.'

'Alderman Lottman –'

'Please, call me Rem.'

'I'm a fifty-four-year-old father. Do you not think it's a little late in the game for a community elder to be stepping forward and offering me guidance?'

'It's never too late to learn, Henk. Don't let anyone tell you otherwise. It's all up here' – he tapped his temple – 'in the mind. Doubtless it shocked you today when I brought up your father. I'm sorry. Everything to do with your father is in the past, I know. That was then, this is now. The questions we face are: How can we be useful? How can we serve? Knowing that there are always trade-offs, compromises…'

He shifted his bulk towards me.

'And if you can take that…' He cupped his plump hands together, like he was clasping some imaginary vessel. 'If you can channel that…' The exact word seemed to evade him. 'You could be very useful to me,' he concluded.

Or had *he* evaded the word?

Guilt? *Shame*?

More than anything… *anger.*

'What exactly are you offering me?' I said.

'Delete that recording of our station captain, and any intent to use it with your wife.'

'And?'

'You'll be reinstated to full active service.'

'What about my family? Their safety?'

'What's your answer, Henk?'

I leaned in. 'Are you holding my daughter hostage too now?'

'No! Henk –'

But I was already out of the car.

'Henk!'

12

INTO THE TUNNEL

I RODE MY BIKE back to the boat. As I approached, I felt a sinking sensation: there was a light on where there shouldn't have been. I slowed down and hit the bike's kill switch, the engine dying obediently.

The BMW rolled to a stop thirty metres from home.

I eased the Sig Sauer out of the pannier, unsheathing it from its oilcloth.

Someone was definitely aboard.

I ran along the waterside and crept up, crouching behind a couple of parked bikes. It was drizzling softly but steadily. I could see a moped parked further down Entrepotdok. The light I'd seen on the boat was dancing; it was a torch, a little handheld one that the intruder had clamped between his teeth. Slavic was trying to unpick the lock of the cabin, but he was failing. The lock had five tumblers instead of four; I'd fitted it myself.

I eased my crash helmet off and set it down, then checked Johan's gun, re-familiarising myself with the old army weapon. I wanted to put a bullet in Slavic's upper leg or pelvis right there and incapacitate him for good, but I was still running that last conversation with Bergveld through my mind: could a clever lawyer like van Haaften spin it a different way? Client comes to reason with persecuting ex-cop; vigilante ex-cop uses excessive force on him, or some such... As of now, Slavic was simply fumbling around on deck.

There was a shape-shifting quality to the man. I felt my heart beating hard at the thought of squeezing the trigger. Every now and then, the light of his torch reflected off the glass of the cabin windows and back onto his face. Once again, I felt the sense of my mind playing tricks on me: was I seeing Slavic, or someone else in his guise?

Somehow I knew I'd got things wrong. This lowlife's crude attempts to break into my boat just didn't jibe with seventy-thousand-euro cars and trips to the Conservatorium Hotel, where lurked the likes of Jan Six. What were the 'other considerations' Bergveld had mentioned, the 'trade-offs' and 'compromises' Joost and Rem Lottman had referenced?

A tinkle of glass – he'd given up on the lock and broken the window of the door.

'Police! Don't move!' I yelled. I stood up, my gun in a two-handed grip, sighting at his centre-mass as I edged forward.

He dropped the torch. One arm, in silhouette, raised a translucent shape, like a litre-bottle of water.

'Don't move!' My heart was thumping in my chest. 'Put your hands where I can see them!' I was contradicting myself.

His other hand raised a little block with a wire dangling from it: the most improvised explosive device I'd ever seen, but doubtless a deadly, effective one. Clearly he'd hoped to break in and hide the device somewhere aboard. Had he reckoned on it igniting while Petra and I were asleep? I'd modernised the boat as much as possible, but it was still over fifty per cent wood and tar. Slavic had devised our crematorium.

The temptation to put a round into him was almost overwhelming. I looked over my shoulder, up at the expensive apartments in the old brick packing houses. Would his death spasms trigger the device?

I edged closer, to see better. My eyes were adjusting to the dark. He'd brought the bottle beneath his chin. Its cap must have been off, because I caught the wavering fumes of the accelerant – petrol? white spirits? – before I saw his eyes, those rivers of darkness, shining back at me. He'd managed to draw me in close enough that the fireball would engulf us both if the device went off.

I stopped, lowering the gun slightly, as he moved crab-like down the gangplank. He backed away towards his moped. I had to give chase – but that meant getting on my bike, which was thirty metres away. I ran, hearing a drone as he accelerated away.

The engine fired first time. I opened the throttle and roared down Entrepotdok after him, the belly of the BMW rearing alarmingly as I negotiated the speed humps. I'd forgotten my crash helmet beside the boat; my eyes watered with the velocity. Down to the end of Entrepotdok we flew, swerving to the little drawbridge, when all of a sudden a hatchback was reversing out in front of me. I slammed my foot down on the rear brake and slid around to a halt, tyres squealing.

'Move!' I yelled over the burbling of the bike. With no crash helmet, my voice was unimpeded.

The driver held his hands up from the wheel in a 'what the fuck?' gesture.

'Fucking move!'

Slavic was getting away.

A woman sat in the passenger seat with a crying baby.

Slavic was turning west onto Prins Hendrikkade.

I used my horn to no avail. Then I let out the clutch, nosing around the back of the car. There was faint resistance, and a shattering sound as I ripped the hatchback's rear bumper off; now the driver was moving, getting out of his car as I rode away across the drawbridge. But I could feel that something was wrong with the bike's powertrain. The engine was running fine but the bike was lurching unevenly, the delivery of power to the rear wheel erratic. Something must have been wrenched out of alignment.

Shit.

Slavic was turning right into the IJ Tunnel. My bike gave a burst of speed and I made the turn, too. Why was he heading to North Amsterdam? The bike lurched violently again; I knew it was now or never.

I yanked the throttle fully open. All that prevented the front wheel from flying into a fatal wheelie was gravity as I swept downhill into the mile-long underwater tunnel. But when my front wheel rejoined the tarmac I saw his brake light flying towards me as he slowed for the traffic. I slammed into him; his moped and body skittered separately between traffic, crossing the central reservation.

My own bike flew out from under me. I could feel the gritty tarmac.

Cars were stopping behind me. I struggled upright in their glare, tasting something tangy, metallic: my own blood.

I pawed my wet, naked head.

The central reservation was made up of traffic cones at the mouth to the tunnel. Slavic and his bike had slid straight through them.

He, too, was stumbling to his feet, into the path of an oncoming red city bus. It blared to a halt, hydraulics hissing, everything amplified awfully by the tunnel's acoustics.

My gun was in my jacket pocket but drivers were out of their cars; one was pointing a camera phone at us.

I staggered over to Slavic, who was retrieving something from the open luggage compartment of his moped, the seat ripped clean off.

He held up the bottle of liquid. In his other hand was a Zippo, the little flame menacing.

His face wavered again in the dancing light.

Perhaps he wasn't thinking straight after the crash, because liquid was dribbling down his other hand; the smell of it reached me just as everything bloomed and blossomed orange, and the next thing I knew I was on my arse again amid floating cinders.

He was running, burning, away from the tunnel. I stumbled after him. Flames licked at his legs and arms. Further up, the wall became short enough to tumble over to the harbourside. He staggered to the water's edge. I could smell his burning flesh.

He slipped in noiselessly.

I made my way unsteadily over to him. He was thrashing in the water, turning it white. My phone trilled.

A text from Petra. I struggled to read it, my fingers bloody.

Nadia had called… she was at her boyfriend's house on the coast… Pieter was Nadia's boyfriend, the guy from the Kriterion… the goth?… Nadia was OK…

But Nadia could never be OK while Slavic was alive. I looked up from my phone at him. He would always be there, in the shadows, waiting, lurking…

'Shh,' I managed, raising a finger to my cracked lips.

He was moving – just.

My voice sounded distant to me. That old conundrum: *What's so fragile that when you say its name, you break it?*

His dull eyes barely communicated anything, starkly pale and deep-set in his blackened head. Pieces of his skin were falling off. Soon he was immobile, the hypothermia having claimed him.

'Silence, Slavic. *Silence…*'

It felt like an eternity, but eventually his charred head slipped beneath the icy water, the harbour sucking him under.

*

I walked up towards the Ibis hotel.

Blue lights flickered wildly, Liesbeth appearing among them. 'Are you OK?'

Bergveld joined her, wide-eyed, reaching for his phone.

'I'm leaving town,' I pre-empted him. 'Going away. Don't worry.'

I started walking away again as a call came in.

PRIVATE NUMBER.

'Henk.'

Lottman.

I wondered where his Mercedes, his mobile communications centre, was now. The first TV reporters had arrived on the scene with a satellite truck, but the images of a burning tunnel would already have hit the social networking sites. Rem's networks, too.

'They were a package deal, Henk.'

My phone was wet with trickling blood. Liesbeth was following me, mouth agape.

'What do you mean, *they*?'

'A package deal just like you and your wife, when you contacted me. They were brothers.'

'Brothers,' I repeated dumbly, feeling a plunging sensation inside.

A male paramedic had caught up with me, at Liesbeth's insistence. She was standing next to him, eyeing my head. I waved them both away.

'Jan and Zsolt Tőzsér,' Lottman said into my ear.

'*Twins?*' I was incredulous. You couldn't make that up. But it was now clear where all the confusion had sprung from...

'Actually not. They were almost identical, but if you looked closely, you would have seen distinct differences. One had a mole above his left eye.'

'Slavic with the mole?'

'Come by my office first thing tomorrow,' Lottman said. 'We can discuss it then.'

*

This time his office didn't look so big. There were more cardboard packing boxes, indents in the deep carpet where furniture had stood.

'Slavic had the mole, yes,' Lottman confirmed. 'Or rather, Jan. It was Zsolt who you followed to the Conservatorium Hotel. Who was also parked on Prins Hendrikkade, on his moped, surveying the aftermath of his younger brother's handiwork...'

I'd never got close enough to the older one to see the difference. 'Who is Zsolt?'

'The older brother, living in North Amsterdam.'

'But what does he do?'

Lottman sighed, like a storyteller feigning reluctance.

'The Tőzsér brothers came here to Holland during the financial crisis. Zsolt as the brains, Jan the brawn. Various schemes involving fraud, extortion and intimidation, bribery, blackmail –'

'Blackmailing how?'

'Prostitution was Jan's speciality. Photos, videos that they threatened to send to wives, colleagues. A lot of bankers were being laid off, there was a lot of fear.'

'What a gift to society.'

'Welcome inside the tent.' Lottman pushed his glasses up his nose. 'Jan – or Slavic as you know him – was a problem from the start. His methods were too crude, he ran too many risks.'

'He was caught.'

'Yes. Only, while Jan was nothing but a headache to us, his older brother Zsolt turned into the most productive informant that the Amsterdam police force has ever known.'

'Operation Boost?'

'Not just vehicle theft. All kinds of high-value goods: stolen art, diamonds. High-end prostitution, too. Paedophilia, drugs and guns through Rotterdam –'

There was a tap at the door and his assistant appeared, looking like a twig in comparison to Lottman.

He stood suspended, mid-sentence.

'Your next appointment –'

'Two more minutes.'

She withdrew, the sound of the closing door barely perceptible.

Lottman went on: 'Your Jan thought he had carte blanche to do things.'

'Like dumping bodies in the harbour.'

'I'm still awaiting Joost's report on that, but I think we can anticipate the results.'

Had Joost been the one to visit Irena at the shelter?

'As you wish,' I said. 'But one question... how did you satisfy yourselves that Zsolt and Slavic weren't playing both sides, all the way along?'

'By creating our own force within a force, specialising in handling these types.'

Jan Six. Joost. Bergveld...

'IJ Tunnel 3 was a guinea pig,' Lottman went on. 'But it all needs to be rethought now. Time to clean house. Brussels beckons, old Henk.'

I nodded.

'And here's where it becomes difficult for you – if I'm understanding events down there at the harbour last night correctly. The Tőzsér brothers were intensely loyal to one another – that was their strength, and their undoing. It was what caused a lot of our problems in handling them.'

'Go on...'

'You know very well where I'm going. It wouldn't do well for you if Zsolt got wind of how his brother died.'

I tried to say something, but no words came out.

'So, returning to what we were discussing in my car: do we have a deal, Henk?'

13

DUTCH LIGHT

Six months later

WATERLAND (that's the name of it in Dutch), to the north-east of Amsterdam: location of another body, found submerged in a dyke.

Just beyond the remote hamlet of Ransdorp and its brick church – squat-looking, as though huddled against the elements. Bright clouds scudding across the sky, alternately diaphanous white and silvery-grey.

There's a rinsed quality to the light in Holland. None of the particulates that create those rosy glows in warmer climes. You'll see this austere cleanness in any Dutch master's work.

'This is where it was found,' Stefan indicated.

I nodded. The dyke water was dark and still – brackish, giving off a putrid odour.

I thrust my chin down into my coat, using the lapels as protection from the wind to get a Marlboro going.

'Two nine-millimetre shots. One to the head, one to the chest. Guess they weren't taking any chances.'

'Any ideas about the model?'

'Sounds like it might have been a Sig Sauer.'

'It's a common enough weapon,' I said.

'Army model, isn't it?'

'Yes. Many go missing after active service.'

'Really?' he said. 'I bet yours didn't.'

'No.'

He looked around. 'There's a tool rental place at the north end of Ransdorp. I guess we should speak to them.'

'Why?' I asked.

'In case they saw anything? Look at how flat it is…'

Holland's blessing and curse. All that waterborne navigation moving goods and items around so easily… the dead-level horizon… the barely reclaimed, primordial swamp. This scene wouldn't have looked much different in the Middle Ages.

The low flatness of Holland could make a man mad.

'Worth a try.' I made a point of looking around too. The church tower was the tallest structure for miles.

That and the pylons scarring the horizon.

My phone buzzed. A text from Petra: she was meeting Nadia later that afternoon for coffee. They'd started a news blog together, which was getting traction. Google was already paying them meaningful amounts of money to advertise on it.

Wish my new schedule allowed for it. Give her my love. I thumbed the message into the device, then slipped it back into my inside pocket.

Liesbeth walked over; she'd been going from house to house down the bricked main street of the hamlet.

Both Liesbeth and Stefan were on my team now.

'There's a caravan park over by the water. We should probably ask around there too,' she said. 'What d'you say we get a coffee and a sandwich at the Swan, then I'll head over?'

The Swan was the name of Ransdorp's only bar. How fitting. Serene on top, frantically kicking beneath. 'I need to get back to the station. But you two carry on.'

As I turned towards my unmarked police car, my phone buzzed again.

'Henk.'

'Joost.'

Jan Six's sudden successor.

'The murder of Zsolt Tőzsér leaves a major gap in police capabilities,' he said evenly.

'Indeed.'

'Any preliminary findings?' His steady voice dripped with accusation.

'I'm guessing it was a settling of scores. He would have had some determined foes by now, after all those years as an informant…'

'Really.'

I paused, allowing him to fill the gap that ensued.

'This changes things.'

'No doubt.'

'We're all going to have to do more with less, Henk.'

'Agreed.'

I was ready.

Things evolve.

Part II:

The Maze

14

DAY TRIP

PETRA AND I WERE beside the Old Harbour in Rotterdam when the call came in.

PRIVATE NUMBER.

'You're not going to take it?' she asked.

'No. They can manage without me.'

She raised both eyebrows in surprise. This was the first time we'd been away in months. Leading a team at the IJ Tunnel 3 police station wasn't proving easy.

'Why don't you have some more of that cranberry brownie?' she said.

I grimaced.

We were sitting outside at a Danish café. The Old Harbour is all that is left of old Rotterdam, a city whose marine fringes form Europe's biggest port – 'the Maze', as it's called. All that cargo moving around those labyrinthine docks...

The city itself must have been a fine-looking place once – when my father first knew it, perhaps, before he joined the merchant navy. That is, before the Germans flattened Rotterdam. Then the architects got to work, turning it into a series of geometric shapes and concepts that were dead on arrival. The yellow and white creation hovering above the old harbour buildings was known as the 'flying saucer'... or was that one the 'wilted sunflower'? Either way, the older buildings before us were the only ones left with any life in them. *Nooitgedacht* ('Who'd've thought?') read the name of one of the old wooden boats opposite us in the harbour.

'Do you want anything else?' asked the café's owner, a stout lady with ruddy cheeks. She was ready to clear our plates.

'We could use an ashtray.'

Petra shot me a look. I was down to two cigarettes a day now: one after lunch, the other after dinner. It only made me want them more.

'Sure,' the owner said.

No fuss from her.

Rotterdammers are like that: down-to-earth and humble, certainly in comparison to the materialism and hot air found in Amsterdam these days.

I lit a match and took infinite pleasure in that first draw on my cigarette. The gulls called out above us, the putter of an engine crossed the water.

'What time are we meeting Nadia again?' Petra asked.

'Hmm?'

'Our daughter. What time are we meeting her?' she repeated.

Nadia was here for the Rotterdam International Film Festival.

'Five, I think.'

'Let me call her and check.'

She began pressing the screen of her phone.

I let the sun bathe my face. I was starting to relax, the muscles in my neck de-tensing for the first time in weeks. The light streamed blue-white off the water, splitting prismatically through the table's glassware. Sometimes I flatter myself, imagining that I glimpse the world as a great painter does, seeing the rents in the filter of everyday life that allow the bigger world to come tumbling in. But maybe I just have my head up my arse.

Petra was arguing with Nadia.

'We've come all the way to Rotterdam!'

Pause.

'A whole hour on the train, young lady!'

Pause.

'Well when, then?'

Pause.

'*What time?*'

Petra was shaking her head in exasperation. 'See you then.' She ended the call. For a second, nothing. Then: 'I think she has a new boyfriend.'

'Oh? What happened to Pieter the goth?'

'Who knows? I don't like the sound of this one.'

'What time are we meeting her now, then?'

'It's not clear, but I think eight. She's going to call back.'

'Oh well.' I patted my wife's hand, which was still gripping her phone. My own rang again.

PRIVATE NUMBER.

'Let me just get rid of it,' I said, pressing accept.

'Henk,' my wife and the caller said at the same time.

The voice on the phone was Rem Lottman's, now attaché for the Dutch energy minister in the Council of Europe.

'Where are you?' he asked.

'I'm enjoying old Rotterdam on my day off.'

'Excellent! So much closer to Brussels. Can you come here? There's something I'd like you to help with.'

I was about to refuse and end the call there and then, but I thought of the difficulties I was having at IJ Tunnel 3 with Joost (who was the new Amsterdam police commissioner), and how helpful some support from high up might be. 'When did you have in mind? Late next week would be better if possible –'

'Can you come now? It's rather urgent.'

'You've got to be kidding me.'

My wife looked on intently. The phone went so quiet that I thought I'd lost him.

'Hello?' I prompted.

'Do you see Zsolt Tőzsér's death as a joke now?'

107

The light darkened as if a cloud were passing overhead. I got up and walked away.

'What?' I asked quietly.

The suspicion among certain members of the Amsterdam police force – that I'd been involved in the shooting – just wouldn't go away.

'Don't let this be about you and me,' Lottman said. 'Have it be about Holland, and Europe.'

I tried to make sense of his words but only saw Zsolt Tőzsér's body in a dyke, bullets to the head and the heart. 'How?'

'By coming to Brussels. Now.'

*

We met at a restaurant not far from Brussels Central Station, a Michelin-starred place called Chez Moi. I'd realised that I could get to Brussels and back before Nadia was ready to meet us; I'd left Petra watching a highly acclaimed documentary film about the Ecuadorian cuckoo or something.

The short train ride to Brussels had given me a chance to think about the problems piling up at work again, and what help I might be able to ask for from Lottman. Ever since Zsolt Tőzsér was lost as an informant, IJ Tunnel 3 had been stretched thin in having to deal with rising levels of organised crime. That was the deceptiveness of Amsterdam: people rarely encountered crime (in the city centre at least). But when they did, they encountered it hard. Organised theft, smuggling and gun crime; too many goods moving through the ports, too much to keep track of. And I still only had Stefan and Liesbeth on my team.

'Henk,' Lottman greeted me.

He'd put on even more weight. It wasn't hard to see why, in a place like this. Chez Moi had a discreetly art deco feel, and its warm, buttery tones conveyed an understated opulence. Clearly it catered to the bigwigs. Lottman was in his natural habitat.

The maître d' eyed my bomber jacket as he showed us to

a table in the corner. Lottman was wearing a single-breasted tent of a suit jacket along with a shirt and tie. He nodded his acknowledgements to other important diners. The maître d' asked in Dutch whether the table was suitable and, after a moment's evaluation, Lottman said that it was.

Once we were seated, he dropped his voice.

'It's good to see you, Henk. You're looking well.'

His words caught me off guard. I found it hard to believe the compliment, and I couldn't in all sincerity repay it. He was sweating, so much so that he had to use his white napkin to mop his brow.

The sommelier saved me.

'We'll order a bottle of the usual,' Lottman leaned back to tell him before turning to me again. 'Are you hungry? The veal here is always very good. The fried calf's brain is *exquisite*.'

I could still taste the sourness of the cranberry brownie from earlier and opted for *moules-frites*. When in Rome...

'How's the team-leader role suiting you?' Lottman asked.

'It keeps me off the streets... and on them. How's Bruxelles?' I said, using the French pronunciation.

He snorted. 'I've never known any institution that takes better care of its people. EU employees don't pay tax, not even VAT, in the first year they work here. They have more-than-generous expense accounts, free meals and haircuts, and even their own bus lanes. Whatever the EU doesn't pay for, the lobbyists do. It's perfectly possible to stay here and not spend a single centime. And yet, no one seems happy.'

'Maybe we're born to struggle.'

'Maybe we are. Have you ever been to Ghana?'

'Ghana? In Africa?'

'Yes.'

I paused. 'No.'

My dad had spent time on the Dutch Gold Coast. At least, I think he had; he wasn't around to ask about these things anymore. Maybe that's why I tended to give Lottman, with his paternal presence, the benefit of the doubt.

'Why?' I asked.

'I was just curious. I thought there might have been a family connection, but maybe I am mistaken. Ah –'

The wine arrived – something red, French and no doubt extremely expensive. The sommelier poured a little; Rem swirled it in his big glass, then sniffed, tasted, and pronounced it satisfactory.

A frustrating silence followed as the sommelier decanted the wine, poured two glasses, removed others and generally fussed; finally, once he'd left, Rem continued in a confidential voice.

'There's a man arriving in town, a Mr Lesoto. Ghanaian diplomat. Quite important to our national business here.'

I had to remind myself what Lottman actually *did* in Brussels, apart from drink expensive wine in restaurants such as this one.

'He's been having a rough time of it with the authorities here lately. The Belgians can be pretty uptight when they want to be, you know.'

'Having a rough time how?'

'At the airport, apparently. Suspicion as to what he's carrying in diplomatic pouches. Well, as I'm sure I don't need tell you, that's no one's damn business but the Ghanaians.'

'Agreed,' I said slowly, wondering how I fitted in with any of this. 'Are there any grounds for suspicion?'

'No more so than with any other country's diplomats.'

A curiously evasive phrasing.

'It would be helpful if you could be here when he next arrives in the country,' Lottman continued. 'To ensure that everything's handled appropriately. Just to be certain that his rights are observed.'

'Why?'

'Because he's a friend of our country. And friends look after friends.' He leaned in. 'Do you know what I mean, Henk?'

'Why on earth me? It's not like I don't have enough to do back in Amsterdam. And it's not my jurisdiction.'

'Why? Because I trust you. I'll smooth things over with your boss. You'll be in a better position when you go back.'

That much rang true. I could see the opportunity to interrupt the uncooperative pattern I'd fallen into with Joost.

'Mr Lesoto is planning to make a trip to Amsterdam, via Belgium, I'm told,' Rem went on. 'You can act as a sort of chaperone. I know Belgium's not your jurisdiction, but…'

'Why don't you just speak to Belgian customs? They'll surely listen to you – or any member of government here.'

He gave no answer.

Which *was* an answer: he didn't want any direct involvement with the matter. That gave me pause for thought. But if I were seconded to Rem Lottman for a week or so, the resource and staffing issues at the station would surely gain visibility and urgency. Or so I told myself.

'Let me get this straight. You want me to meet a Ghanaian diplomat on arrival here and make sure he has no problems. Then… what?'

'Spend a little time with him. Like I said, he wants to visit Amsterdam, apparently. You might even have fun.'

He smiled. I think it was the first time I'd seen him do so.

'Why doesn't he just fly into Schiphol?'

'Please, I don't know. Try asking him when he arrives first thing on Monday. Ah, the veal!'

111

15

THE GHANAIAN STAR

MONDAY MORNING CAME AROUND fast, as it tends to. I was standing in the arrivals area of Antwerp Airport – a small, single-terminal affair – full of questions. With me was Sammy, a driver from the Ghanaian embassy in The Hague and a man of few words. He held a sign: *MR LESOTO*. It bore a discreet, primary-coloured Ghanaian flag.

We were early. The flight was showing as on time.

'Where are we going when he arrives?' I asked.

'Who knows?' Sammy shrugged his slim shoulders. There was a bulge in his jacket, as if he were carrying a gun.

Unlikely.

I checked my phone.

'Do you want a coffee?' I needed to call in to the police station, get an update from Stefan.

Sammy shook his head. Diplomatic silence. That left me with all the more time to ponder.

Why Antwerp? It seemed a curious way to get from Ghana to Amsterdam. The flight was arriving from London – a connecting flight from Accra, surely.

I walked into the terminal's dated-looking restaurant and ordered an Americano. The coffee came scalding hot. As I blew on its surface I wondered why a diplomat wouldn't bypass the normal arrivals procedure. Or was that the point – had Lesoto been denied a diplomatic method of entry? It felt premature to track down an opposite number on the Antwerp police force, Rem Lottman not having suggested that I do so.

There was no sign of any arriving passengers.

I called Stefan.

'*Hoi*,' I said.

'Boss.'

'Good weekend?'

'Could have been better.'

'The Ajax game?' I asked.

'Indeed. A travesty. How about you?'

'Much the same. Listen, I've been called away to Belgium.'

'Oh?'

'Not for too long.' I thought about adding more, then decided against it. 'I'll be calling in regularly enough.'

Stefan was developing into a fine police officer, but it didn't take much to throw him off balance. I could sense him trying to process the information.

'Has there been any movement in the Holendrecht case?' I asked. There had been a shooting in Southeast Amsterdam... drugs were involved.

He sighed. 'I thought we had a taxi driver who'd give testimony, but no. Withdrew his witness statement. Can't believe that bastard Hals.'

Frank Hals, the person suspected of running the drugs operation and a man widely considered untouchable, lived in a sizeable residence in our precinct. Hence our peripheral involvement in the case, which really belonged to the drugs unit of the National Police Agency.

So it went at IJ Tunnel 3. We were increasingly being pulled between the pickpocketing and other petty cases that couldn't really justify resources, and the far bigger ones that weren't ours to begin with. And all the while we were being assigned aggressive productivity targets. This was how our new commissioner wanted it. I'd be talking that over with Rem

Lottman before long. Certainly before this Ghanaian odyssey was through.

'Stay involved,' I advised, 'but don't get too sucked in. Anything else?'

'Liesbeth just went off to the Royal... a disturbance in one of the rooms there.'

Hmm.

'Not the kind of place you associate with domestics,' I said. The Royal, on the Amstel river, was one of Amsterdam's most exclusive hotels.

'No, it's not,' Stefan agreed.

Passengers were dribbling through in ones and twos. Mostly ones.

'I need to go,' I said. Sammy had stepped forward with his sign.

'You hear about the death over in Willemspark?' Stefan asked.

'No.' Another posh place – but not our precinct.

'Diplomat found dead in his house there.'

That made me sit up and take note. 'Which diplomat? How'd he die?'

'Norwegian. Sounds like a break-in gone wrong.'

'Try to find out more about that, would you?'

'But it's Bergveld's case.'

Fuck. Of course. Sebastiaan Bergveld, my erstwhile nemesis, had been moved over to the cushier beat of Willemspark.

'Whatever you can find out,' I told him. 'I really must go.'

'Here!' a voice boomed, a perspiring face bobbing above the others. He was smiling at Sammy's sign. Mr Lesoto had landed.

*

He was a huge, square-shouldered man. Sharp-suited. He took my hand with a bone-crushing grip.

The whites of his eyes contrasted vividly with his dark skin. They had a yellowish tint.

Lesoto only had a roller bag. Two uniformed immigration

guards were looking on, a sniffer dog sat obediently by their side.

'Henk van der Pol,' I said in English. Though Ghana had once been a Dutch colony, English was now its lingua franca. 'I'm with the Dutch police,' I added. 'Rem Lottman asked me to drop by and make sure things are OK.'

'Ah, Mis-ta Lottman!' His eyes lit up. 'So long as Mista Lottman is involved, *everything* is OK.' He gathered Sammy alongside. 'Come… Let us leave this most *unwelcoming* place.'

I glanced at the guards again. They stared straight back at me. Law enforcement types tend to ID one another fast.

Sammy led us through the concourse.

'How was your trip?' I asked Lesoto.

'The flight was *quite* nice.'

'You connected through London?'

'Yes.'

Cooler, moist air hit us as we left the terminal building.

'You're just here on business?'

'Business *and* pleasure. There must always be both in life. Yes!' he added approvingly. Sammy had led us to a deep-maroon, four-door Bentley. Diplomatic plates. He opened the kerb-side door for Lesoto.

I jogged around in the drizzle to the other side. The door handle wasn't obvious, but I managed to open it. Inside was another world. Rem Lottman's stretch Mercedes was like a taxi minivan in comparison. The Bentley smelled of rich leather and had a profound silence. A paper box of tissues behind the rear headrests looked incongruously cheap.

Lesoto blinked a couple of times and breathed deeply. His eyes were heavy-lidded – jet lag no doubt. I heard the vague *thunk* of the boot, and it was only when the terminal building glided past that I realised we were moving, so smooth was the engine. Rainwater turned to beads on the windows.

'Where are we going?' I enquired.

'To Amsterdam. But first, I must pick up a gift.'

Sammy didn't react; apparently he knew the plan.

'How do you know Rem Lottman?'

'He is a *good* friend,' Lesoto said with soft insistence.

I held on to the rail above the door with my left hand. We were snaking through the grey Antwerp suburbs, moving quickly. We flew by a dishevelled woman, pushing a shopping trolley beside the road. Homeless, surely.

'Are your people happy?' Lesoto asked me.

'Which people?'

'The people,' he gestured outside the window at the world.

'I don't know,' I said. 'You'd have to ask them.'

'Do you not all speak the same language?'

'Some of us do.'

His eyelids drooped.

Those were all the words we spoke till we arrived, ten minutes later, in the centre of Antwerp. I was beginning to think that this was all a big waste of time, and was planning to report as much to Lottman, when we turned down Pelikaanstraat into the diamond district.

The windows of the shops sparkled. Behatted Hasidic Jews conferred among themselves; crowds of tourists flowed around them like shoals of fish. The place had a desultory, theme-park feel to it. We came to a stop outside an office.

I knew a bit about diamonds. Or rather my father had.

Lesoto leaned forward heavily and said something in his own language to Sammy, who nodded in confirmation. In the wet gloom I could make out the office's nameplate: *Cape Diamonds*.

Sammy got out. The roller bag stayed in the boot. Sammy opened an umbrella and then Lesoto's door, and off they strode to the building's entrance, the smaller man reaching to hold the umbrella above Lesoto. What a couple they made.

After speaking a few words into the intercom, Lesoto was admitted. Sammy returned to the car and got in. As he did so, a gust blew open his jacket and I glimpsed a tan leather shoulder holster carrying a slim semi-automatic.

He'd kept the engine idling. That didn't mean anything in terms of how quickly Lesoto might conclude his business; rather, it was simply to keep the interior cool.

What was Lesoto's business?

Diamonds are dug up in Africa, Australia and Bolivia, and find buyers in Moscow, Geneva and Shanghai. Yet, somehow, over four-fifths of the world's uncut stones make their way through Antwerp's diamond district. And not just the financial arrangements for them, but the stones themselves. Even Amsterdam's role in the diamond trade has all but disappeared – just a few polishers buffing stones for tourists. How had Antwerp held on?

By a mixture of lower taxes and tight regulation, I reasoned, thinking about those two immigration guards at the airport.

'How long will he be?' I asked Sammy.

Sammy shrugged.

He was good at that.

I consoled myself with the thought that international regulation made it almost impossible to profit from illicit diamonds now – even those brought in by diplomatic pouch. Under the Kimberley Process, opportunities to sell on stones are incredibly limited if the stones' non-conflict provenance cannot be certified.

I gripped the hand rail, remembering a diamond heist at the airport here, a year or so ago. A gang had held up a Swiss-bound plane on the runway, relieving it of fifty million dollars' worth of gems. You couldn't help but take an interest in these things in the squad room. With equal parts curiosity and envy, my mind had gone to how the detectives would have interviewed the insiders. (It had clearly been an inside job, given the speed and precision of the robbery.) Which inconsistencies in their stories would have come to light? Which tics and tells? The diamond insurers sitting behind these facades on Pelikaanstraat were assiduous in pressing the police to investigate, generous in making resources available… But the gang had only been caught when they'd tried to sell the stones on, having resorted to using the Internet. The police had raided a chalet in France, near the border with Switzerland. There they found the stones' certificates and, not long afterwards, the gang itself.

The door of Cape Diamonds swung open and Lesoto appeared.

Sammy opened the car door for him. Lesoto was chuckling – like he couldn't believe his luck.

'Where now?' I asked.

'*Am*-ster-dam!' he said. 'We can drop you there, if this is helpful.'

I nodded; it would be.

'Let me show you something.' Out of a small felt pouch he produced a piece of pure brilliance, the like of which I'd never seen before. I took the hard stone from him and turned it between my fingers. It was the size of an acorn, perhaps twenty carats; it had to be worth many millions of euros. To my eyes, it looked flawless. Shards of light wheeled across the roof and seat backs of the Bentley. But it was the skill with which it had been cut and polished… The more I stared at it, the more the diamond turned everything else to dark around it, save for Lesoto's eyes. Soon it was as if we were looking at it down a deep mine shaft.

'It's the Ghanaian Star,' Lesoto whispered.

'And this is a gift?

'Yes.'

'You're going to make someone very happy.'

'Yes. I am.'

16

THE WOMAN AT
THE ROYAL HOTEL

WE SPED ACROSS THE dull low country of Flanders towards Amsterdam, the landscape a mud-brown blur. Lesoto snoozed, his heavy head nodding. Occasionally he'd wake with a start, surprise in his eyes, then relax and drift off again.

I couldn't help but think about the precious stone in his inside pocket. It spoke to something in me. Man's lust for treasure down through the ages, maybe? Or something closer, more familial? Much of what my dad got up to was never made clear.

It struck me that diamonds were a remarkably efficient and discreet way to move financial value around. More so than drugs, gold… anything.

I decided to call Liesbeth at the station. She picked up on the first ring.

'Belgium, eh?' she said, having apparently spoken with Stefan. 'For a few days?'

I needed to be careful that neither Sammy nor the sleeping giant could decrypt my conversation. And I also needed to be a little careful about Liesbeth herself. Though she was a great team member and married to a good guy, her husband was a fast-rising prosecutor who was regularly in contact with my boss, Joost.

'Don't get too comfortable,' I joked, 'I'm back this afternoon. What's this hotel incident?'

'Ah yes, a Ukrainian lady was badly beaten up in one of the suites at the Royal.'

'Who?'

'Still trying to find that out. Haven't located her yet.'

I shifted on the leather seat, trying to make sense of it. 'Then how do you know this?'

'A maid called the police using her own mobile phone. She found the victim in the suite this morning, barely conscious. The maid was Ukrainian, too. But by the time I got there, the victim was long gone.'

'So… who'd booked the suite? What did hotel management have to say about it?'

Sammy's eyes met mine briefly in the rear-view mirror.

'They're checking with their head office about client confidentiality.'

I mulled that over as we sped past the exit to Rotterdam.

Clearly an important guest, then.

'You let them know they had to tell us?'

'I… No. I wanted to talk to you first.'

'Did you speak to the caller in person – the maid?'

'No, I got the call report from the emergency-response phone operators. When I rang the hotel, the manager wanted it all handled by him. My guess is that our maid won't enjoy stellar career prospects there now.'

'Didn't the victim need an ambulance?'

'Apparently not.'

'Hmm.' I didn't like the sound of this. 'Should we both go and speak with them when I get back? What's your feeling?'

She paused. 'If the victim doesn't step forward, and there's no witness to the incident…'

If a tree falls in the forest…

Liesbeth sounded too much like her husband, assessing the chance of success at trial. Prematurely.

'We have a reported crime.' I estimated the journey time from the Rotterdam exit. 'I'll see you at the hotel at thirteen hundred.'

Sammy looked up and met my eyes again in the mirror.

*

We got back to Amsterdam so quickly that I even had time to grab my notebook before heading over to the Royal, so I asked Lesoto and Sammy to drop me near the police station – not remembering, until it was too late, that the police commissioner might be dropping by that day. Getting out of his unmarked vehicle, Joost watched us glide up to the end of the block. His bald head canted quizzically.

I cursed myself for not having asked Sammy to drop me a few streets away.

Still inside the Bentley, I turned to Lesoto and said, 'Call me if you need help.'

All the while Joost was watching... waiting.

Damn.

IJ Tunnel 3 was one of several stations Joost was responsible for, but it was where he'd started out and he took a disproportionate interest in our affairs. Especially since I'd become a team leader.

'I will be sure to tell Mista Lottman that you are a *friend*. A friend of Ghana,' Lesoto said. To make matters worse, he climbed out of the Bentley, intercepted me and gave me a crushing hug. It was like trying to wrap my arms around a house.

Finally I walked over to the station entrance.

'Joost,' I greeted him.

'A word?'

'Sure.'

Joost waited for an explanation.

'It's a personal matter,' I explained, 'not police business.'

'Really.' He eyed the departing Bentley. 'Let's go somewhere where we can talk, shall we?'

He led me, not into the station, but rather to the Ibis hotel opposite.

It gave me a minute to think and plan. Before saying anything to Joost, I needed to report to Lottman, confirming that I'd carried out what he'd asked of me. I was still working out exactly what I wanted in return. It rather depended on how the next few minutes went.

Sonja, my usual waitress at the Ibis, was serving. I waved hello as Joost led me deeper into the restaurant in silence. The lunch trade was sparse and he was able to find us a quiet table with ease, the piped muzak giving us extra cover.

'Not police business,' he repeated. 'A car with diplomatic plates. Just what the hell kind of business is that, exactly?'

'Like I said, it's a personal matter.'

Perhaps Lesoto's hug had given my assertion some credence. Joost considered my words. Maybe he imagined it to be connected with my past?

'Perhaps we can talk about *police* business, then,' he said.

'Sure.' I eyed my phone. I was going to be late for Liesbeth at the Royal after all.

'Where's your update on the Holendrecht case?' The shooting in Southeast Amsterdam.

'I'm sure you know more about that than I do at this point. The National Police Agency are running the case after all, aren't they? There's really not much for us to add.'

'What about here in the precinct? What about Hals?'

Since the shooting of supergrass Zsolt Tőzsér, life had become a whole lot easier for the likes of Frank Hals, the local drug king. Tőzsér had grassed up Hals's competitors and then ceased to be a direct threat himself.

'It's not getting any easier to go knocking on Hals's door.'

Joost's mouth twitched. 'So what exactly *are* you working on, Henk? When you're not sailing around in your friend's Bentley?'

I ignored the barb. 'Managing my team. We're working on a range of cases.'

'Such as?'

'A serious assault on a guest at the Royal Hotel last night.'

Joost's mouth twitched again, like he was about to say something but was holding back. I could tell that my arrival in the diplomatic vehicle had really thrown him, which wasn't easy to accomplish with Joost. Finally he leaned in, his folded arms resting on the table.

'I need your revised targets. To show *all* the work that's going through IJ Tunnel 3, with *exactly* where you are in terms of your goals. We need to consider whether more' – he searched for the words – '*tightly* defined goals might be in order.'

He sat back.

'D'you not think we have enough goals already, for such a small team?'

'The KLPD is doing more and more in precincts such as this one.'

The Korps Landelijke Politiediensten being the National Police Agency – the ones with the real resources to work cases such as Holendrecht.

'Maybe they should have it all,' Joost went on. 'I'm reviewing the station's future.'

Sonja arrived. 'Would you both like to see a menu?'

'I'm fine,' I said, numbed by my boss's threat.

'Something to drink then?'

'We're fine,' Joost snapped, not shifting his gaze from me.

Sonja's eyes widened as she left.

I thought to change the subject. 'What's going on over in Willemspark?'

Joost did a double take. 'Huh?'

'Diplomat found dead over there, I heard.'

'What the hell's that got to do with you? It's not even your beat. That's Bas's case.'

Sebastiaan Bergveld had handled police informants while Joost was running IJ Tunnel 3 – there was a deep loyalty between the two men.

Joost paused, perhaps trying to work out whether the

diplomat who'd died was connected to the one who'd dropped me off.

As I'd hoped.

'Just be careful, Henk. There's still time to open up an enquiry into the shooting of Zsolt Tőzsér.'

So he was laying his cards down.

I watched him get up and walk out of the restaurant, his scrawny form vanishing into the lobby.

I stood up myself, left a five-euro note on the table for Sonja and followed suit – at a safe distance.

*

'Where were you?' Liesbeth asked when I finally entered the squad room. Stefan looked up from his computer and nodded a hello to me.

'Unavoidably detained. Did you go to the Royal?'

'No need,' Liesbeth said. 'The hotel called me.'

'And?'

'They released the name of the beaten woman. Elena Luscovich.'

'Go on.'

'She's an escort.'

'Hmm.' I went over to the little drinks machine, but it was still broken. 'How do you know that? And how did they get her name?'

'She arrived there around midnight. Hotel security required her passport before they'd let her up to the guest's suite.'

There was nothing illegal about 'escorting' in Amsterdam. I wondered if she'd tipped the staff. The higher-end escorts working properties such as the Royal could earn ten thousand euros for an overnight stay. More, even.

'Did they give a description?'

'Yes.'

'You've managed to track her down?'

'Not yet. Still thinking about how to do that.'

'See if she's legal, paying taxes… ?'

'She might have professional insurance.'

'Maybe.' Some escorts insured their physical condition against unforeseen events.

'But first, I was hoping that the maid might help.'

I nodded; Liesbeth was on the right track, as ever. Both the maid and the victim were Ukrainian.

Which reminded me that another beneficiary of the Tőzsér brothers' demise was a middle-ranking Ukrainian hoodlum called Malek, located on the edge of the Red Light District. But it was too early to involve him.

'What about the actual hotel guest?'

'No dice.'

'Huh?'

'Hotel won't give out the name.'

Classic. Anonymity and security always went to the client.

'They say we need a warrant,' Liesbeth went on.

'Then we get a warrant. Make them understand we're not just filling out forms with this one. We want to know what happened in that hotel suite. And we'll want to know if it happens again.'

Liesbeth gave a little salute. 'Yes sir.'

I turned to Stefan. 'What are you working on?'

'I've just finished the Holendrecht report.'

'Good. Now let's take a trip over to Willemspark.'

17

PARK LIFE

WILLEMSPARK LAY TO THE south-west of us, a little outside the canal belt. Flanked by a large, popular park, the houses there are substantial and finely detailed, the streets quiet. Willemspark is home to Amsterdam's wealthiest families and dignitaries. Old money, as opposed to the stuff sloshing around my beat. It's all relative in this city, where prices and rents have become stratospheric. The whole central area is turning into a playground for the rich and privileged.

The dead diplomat, Lars Pelt, was a senior adviser to the Norwegian ambassador and had lived on leafy Koningslaan. We parked a block away from his address.

The afternoon was bright and hazy, the air soft. Tulips stood in the large gardens.

I lit a cigarette. Technically it qualified as after lunch, though I hadn't in fact eaten yet. My stomach rumbled as I thought of Rem Lottman in Brussels, probably on his fourth or fifth course by now. I needed to call him and give my field report regarding Lesoto.

'What are we doing over here?' Stefan was wearing his bemused look.

'I'm not exactly sure yet.' Perhaps I was being led astray by the diplomatic angle, with Lesoto fresh in my mind, but sometimes you have to follow your nose in this game, see where it leads you.

I was heartened to see the capable figure of Wester at the

door of the brick and stone house. The former custody sergeant from IJ Tunnel 3 had been moved – reluctantly – to Sebastiaan Bergveld's beat in Willemspark. 'Resource reallocation', Joost had termed it.

'*Hoi oi*,' he said. 'Didn't expect to see you over in this neck of the woods.'

I shook his hand firmly. 'How are you, Wester?'

'Oh, surviving.'

I knew the feeling. 'Is Bergveld here?'

'No, he's gone off for another meeting with the big cheese.'

'Joost?' He was everywhere all of a sudden.

Wester nodded.

'We were just passing,' I said, trying to see inside the house. 'Dead Norwegian diplomat, eh? Is Larsson the medical examiner on this one?'

'You'd need to talk to Bergveld about all that.'

I stepped aside as a woman appeared from the shadows of the doorway.

'Hullo,' she said in a very proper English accent. Her blue eyes held mine for a second. Then she walked briskly past, out onto the street. She wore an expensive-looking, fitted tweed jacket and skirt.

'Who's *she*?'

'Her name's Lucy something-West. Channing-West, I think it is. I wrote it down someplace...'

'But who is she? What's she doing here?'

'She's an art insurer over from London.'

'Something was stolen?'

'A very valuable painting.'

'That's why Pelt died? He disturbed the burglar?'

'We don't know yet. You'd need to speak with Bergveld about it. Assuming you two are on speaking terms now.'

'Actually, that's why I stopped by. It's time to smoke the pipe of peace. But I'm sure I'll catch him again soon.'

I wanted Wester to characterise my presence here that way, should Bergveld become aware of it and ask.

I watched the young English woman walk along the street. She was looking up and down as though searching for a cab. I suddenly thought to offer her a lift, but a taxi miraculously appeared, a Mercedes from the prominently liveried Amsterdam Executive Cars swerving over to her side of the street.

We were all watching. 'I imagine she often has that effect on drivers,' I said, running my hand over my stubble.

Wester chuckled.

'You know the amazing thing? It's a Verspronck that no one even knew existed. A study for *Girl Dressed in Blue*. Can you believe that?'

'You're kidding me.'

Everyone in Holland knew the *Girl Dressed in Blue*.

I should qualify that: everyone above a certain age. It had once featured on the back of the twenty-five-guilder bank note – my father had given me one, when I was a boy.

'I kid you not,' Wester said. 'But you didn't hear that from me.' He paused. 'There's a question about the provenance, whether it changed hands during the war. Oh look – here comes Bergveld.'

Bergveld was walking towards us in his latest designer jacket, a light-brown suede number that ended mid-thigh. His expression turned from surprise to confusion and then rage. Stefan slunk away towards our car. Bergveld's eyes stayed on me, steeling for a confrontation, his chest puffing up; he was just about to open his mouth when my phone rang.

PRIVATE NUMBER.

'I'm sorry, I need to take this.'

'Henk?' the voice on the phone said.

Lottman.

Bergveld shook his head in exasperation and stormed off towards Wester.

'How did it go this morning with our Ghanaian guest?'

'Plain sailing. Nothing to report. We met him at the airport, went to a diamond house in Antwerp, then drove to Amsterdam.'

'Oh, good.' He sounded relieved.

I was about to mention the stone that Lesoto had shown me when Lottman asked, 'There were no problems?'

'None at the airport.' What problems had he been expecting? 'Lesoto had a couple of gripes about the way he'd been welcomed through immigration, but'– I thought of the two guards eyeing us – 'that was all.'

'Well, that's good then. And how were things left?'

'Er... not in a great way for me, to be honest. Joost happened to be getting out of his car when Lesoto dropped me back at the station in a diplomatic Bentley. I didn't say anything to Joost, only –'

'Don't worry about your boss.'

Easy for Lottman to say, sat there in Brussels.

'Did Lesoto mention where he was going on to?'

'No, but I told him to call me if he needed anything. I think he mentioned that he would be speaking with you. I'm sorry, I was somewhat preoccupied by Joost watching me.'

'Hmm.'

'Look, *about* Joost –'

'You did the right thing,' Lottman cut in. 'Could you let me know if Lesoto does contact you?'

I couldn't bring Joost's name up a fourth time, dammit. 'Sure.'

'Where are you now?'

'Willemspark. The death of a diplomat, Lars Pelt.'

'Ah, what's going on with that?'

Lottman knew about it already?

'I don't know yet, it's not my case. Belongs to Bas Bergveld.'

'Oh, yes.'

'It appears that a valuable painting was stolen.'

'Yes, most unfortunate. I'm late for a meeting. Let's stay in touch.'

With that he hung up, leaving me pondering his last four words. Had my usefulness to him already expired?

Stefan was waiting in the unmarked police car. 'You drive back,' I told him, handing him the keys. 'I want to clear my head. I'll see you at the station.'

'OK, boss.' Stefan nodded and shifted over to the driver's seat.

I walked along Willemsparkweg towards Museumplein, using up my after-dinner cigarette quota. If Lottman wasn't going to help me with Joost, I needed another plan, and fast. *Dammit*. I wish I'd told Lottman where the hell to go when I'd been sat out in the Rotterdam sun with Petra.

I realised my phone was ringing again…

Throwing the end of my cigarette away, I checked the caller ID and answered it.

'Nadia.'

'Dad, sorry it didn't work out at the weekend in Rotterdam.' I could hear outside noise and hubbub on her end of the line.

'Yes, we were sorry too that you couldn't find the time for us.' I checked myself. 'But these things happen.'

Increasingly frequently, I left unsaid.

'So, my passport is set to expire in the next few days, and I didn't get the chance to renew it…'

'Go on.'

'Well, I was hoping to go away this weekend.'

'Where?'

'Dubrovnik.'

'I see.'

'Is there any chance… Do you know anyone who could fast-track a passport renewal?'

I puffed my cheeks and blew out air sharply.

'OK, Nadia, let's just have a chat about it, shall we? Where are you?'

'In town.'

130

'Me too. Let's meet at the café in the Rijksmuseum.' I could see its gold-and-grey towers glinting.

*

The Rijks was mobbed with tourists but I managed to find us a table for two at the café in the new atrium. The entire museum had been renovated over many years, at vast expense, and it had only recently reopened. It resembled an international airport.

Nadia caused a small stir as she walked into the café. She'd certainly grown up of late. Gone was the nose ring and student garb; her hair (once red) was now a rich chestnut brown. She wore a dark jacket, leather handbag and designer jeans – every inch the elegant young Amsterdammer.

I didn't notice it at first. It was only as she set her bag down that the ring on her middle finger glinted at me. Nothing like Lesoto's jewel, certainly less than a carat, but a rose-coloured stone, brilliant-cut, and probably worth a decent percentage of my annual salary. What did it mean to wear it on her middle finger?

'Hi,' she said, giving me a quick hug.

A waitress approached in smart black uniform. 'What would you like?' she asked.

By now I was famished.

'Some tea,' Nadia said. 'No, make that water. Sparkling.'

'Anything to eat?'

'No thanks.'

'And for you?' the waitress said to me.

'Make it a bottle of water, two glasses.'

'Nothing to eat?'

I ordered the Farm Hen Salad, whatever that was.

'So… Dubrovnik?' I asked as soon as we were alone again.

'Yes,' Nadia replied. 'Just a weekend trip.'

'Hmm. Who with?'

'Sergei.'

'Sergei?'

'My friend.'

131

'And what does this friend do?'

She sighed. 'He works in films. Film investment.'

'What kind of films?' I asked. 'What kind of investment?'

Nadia was saved from needing to answer by the arrival of the drinks.

I checked my phone. Two missed calls from Stefan.

Soon the food arrived. I made a start on my late lunch, glancing again at the stone on Nadia's finger. Had my daughter turned into some kind of gangster's moll?

'Look,' she said, 'about the passport renewal – are you able to help with that?'

'If it was some kind of emergency,' I said between mouthfuls, 'possibly. For a weekend away at the seaside?'

'Fine,' she said, reaching for her bag.

'Hold on, Nadia.' I grabbed her hand, encouraging her to stay. 'Just give your mum a call, would you? She was quite cut up, not seeing you at the weekend.'

'Really?'

'Really.'

'I already did, actually, and it sounds like she didn't see so much of *you* either, with your jaunt to Brussels.'

She'd got me there. I picked at a piece of food between my teeth – a piece of nut.

'Do you still have time to work on the website with her?' I asked, referring to the news website they'd started together last year.

'I really need to find my own way with my career now,' she said. 'But, of course, if mum needs help...'

'That's a fine-looking stone on your finger.'

She shrugged. 'Sergei gave it to me.'

'Right. Do you know if it's OK?'

Her eyes narrowed. 'What do you mean, *OK*?'

'Legit.' Finally I managed to free the piece of nut from between my teeth. 'A conflict-free diamond.'

'Jesus, Dad!' She was on her feet again. 'That's hardly a question I can ask now, is it? *Oh, thanks so much for the lovely gift, can I just see the paperwork for it?*'

'I'm just asking.'

'Well... don't!' She rolled her eyes at me, and then strode off.

18

NEW GOALS

'BOSS, THERE'S A PROBLEM,' Stefan said when I returned his call.

What now? I thought. A server cleared my table.

'Joost rejected the Holendrecht report.'

'What?'

'He said we need some kind of result from the case, locally. To meet goals.'

'Just back up there, Stefan. How did Joost even get *hold* of the report? *I* haven't seen it yet!'

'He called and asked me to email it to him –'

'You *emailed* it to him?'

'I copied you in on –'

'I hadn't even reviewed it!'

'I tried to call you.' His voice trailed off. 'Twice.'

'Have the damn table,' I told two tourists who were hovering with a waitress. I stood up.

'What?' Stefan said.

'Not you. What else did Joost say?'

'He asked me to direct him to the part of the report about Frank Hals.'

'And?'

'And... I'm sorry, what's the question?'

'What's the *answer*, Stefan? What does the report say about Hals?'

'Nothing. We never spoke to Hals, did we? I didn't know

what to include, so I didn't include anything.'

'Okay.' I was breathing more easily now. 'What else?'

'Er... Joost said if we don't get a result with Hals, he's shutting the station down.'

Jesus. Joost bypassed me and told Stefan this?

*

I tried to call Lottman, who didn't pick up, but I got hold of his assistant. He was in a 'council session'. Not Amsterdam City Council now; rather, the Council of Europe, as I had to keep reminding myself.

I walked around the museum's big atrium in a slow circle, trying to figure a way out of all this. Perhaps if I could track down Lesoto and engineer some sort of incident, I'd have the pretext to engage Lottman, give him the update he'd requested and force his intervention with Joost. In theory, finding Lesoto shouldn't be too difficult. How many giant African men were rolling around central Amsterdam in a maroon-coloured, diplomatic Bentley?

But I needed a plan for Frank Hals, too, in case Joost did prevail. Joost was a seasoned politician. He wouldn't be issuing threats if he weren't confident of being able to execute them. But from where did his confidence stem?

Maybe he knew that Hals and I had history, and was taking this opportunity to needle me over it.

Frank Hals was truly an Amsterdam institution. He lived on a houseboat of sorts, down in the harbour. Not the kind of houseboat that Petra and I lived on, but a clipper from the days of the spice trade. Strictly speaking it wasn't even a legal residence, but after three decades his right to inhabit it had somehow been grandfathered in by the city. That was Hals: nothing about his life was quite legal, but it couldn't be shown to be *il*legal either.

'Are you coming in, sir?' the man at the security gate to the museum proper asked as I passed by him again.

'Sure. Why not?' I almost flashed my warrant card, but managed to swap it for my museum card in time.

Hals had started off as a free spirit. We'd met at demonstrations in the early 80s, protesting the displacement of people around town as businesses and city government began taking over and developing different locations – for example, Waterlooplein, and the new city hall there. Freshly demobbed from the army, I might have seemed an unlikely candidate for such protests, but somehow they spoke to me, my background overseas and the constant moving around. *Being* moved around, I should say.

Sometimes I wondered what would have happened if Petra hadn't come along when she did.

But just as my life had stabilised and found a fair current, so Hals's life began to drift off course. He'd built up a chain of coffee shops, initially in the Red Light District, and later across the city. The irony was how defensive he'd become over his investments. Over time, his personality had soured like a lemon.

It had been a difficult decision to investigate Hals in connection with the Holendrecht shooting, but investigate him we had to, as he was known to have become vicious in his dealings with those who crossed him.

He'd shown this during his trial a few years ago. It was common knowledge that Hals grew weed in the hull of his ship. It could easily be spotted on heat maps of the eastern part of the harbour; he must have installed hydroponic grow lights below deck. In 2008, he went to court accused of cultivating marijuana for resale. His lawyer, the notoriously sharp Vincent van Haaften, successfully argued that the entire crop had split from a single plant thirty years before – and that this single plant had been acquired for personal use. One of the witnesses at the trial was never seen or heard of again.

I jogged up the stairs to the Gallery of Honour.

Joost's message was clear enough: *With an informant such as*

Zsolt Tőzsér at our disposal, we could have got Hals. Now Tőzsér's dead. So what've you got instead, old Henk?

I glanced down the corridor to the gallery's focal point, the massive *Night Watch*, Rembrandt's iconic band of local militiamen. But it wasn't why I'd come up here. I wanted to see the painting a third of the way down on the right-hand side, almost as popular in its own way here in Holland: Johannes Cornelisz Verspronck's *Girl Dressed in Blue*. And that reminded me of other things about Frank Hals, which I didn't even want to think about. Rumours that he'd developed an unhealthy interest in young girls.

The heads of other visitors parted and there she was: one of the seventeenth century's most enduring mysteries. Who was the girl in blue? No one knew anything about her. Perhaps she'd lived in Haarlem like her portraitist, or perhaps not.

The fascination with the painting is attributed to the way in which the adorable-looking girl is also a little adult lady, there in her Sunday best. I got closer, trying to prevent the other visitors crowding into my sight line.

I beheld her feathery fair hair, rosy cheeks, curiously drooping mouth and glassy, dark eyes. A chill passed through me; now there was a new mystery attributed to her – Lars Pelt's death.

A Norwegian diplomat killed by burglars seeking a priceless artwork.

A Ghanaian giant rolling around town with a huge diamond.

A high-class Ukrainian escort, badly beaten up by a protected guest at the Royal Hotel.

Not to forget the ever-present Frank Hals, just offstage…

What *couldn't* be bought or obtained in this town, by one means or another?

*

Back at the station, I could see Joost in one of the conference rooms – and he was with someone. The blinds were drawn; I couldn't tell who the other person was. 'Who's Joost in with?' I asked Liesbeth.

'I don't know, I just got back here myself.'

'Coffee?' I got up and went over to the drinks machine to see if it would give me a better view. It didn't. I could only see the hem of a brown jacket.

'The machine's not working,' Liesbeth said. 'Don't you want to know where I was?'

'Does anything work around here?' I got back to my desk and sat down heavily in my roller chair. 'Where were you?'

'The Royal Hotel.'

'Good. And?'

'They still won't reveal the name of the guest.'

I sighed.

'They said that their lawyers advised them not to.'

'You told them we'd get a warrant?'

'Yes, only...' She paused. 'A warrant requires probable cause of a crime committed.'

'Er... a beaten woman?' I turned my palms up incredulously.

'But for a crime to have been committed, it has to be proven.'

'Liesbeth, I'm not looking for a philosophical discussion or your prosecutorial advice on this. Get. The. Warrant.'

'But what if the suspect has immunity from prosecution?'

I hesitated. *A diplomat?*

'Why assume that?' I said.

'Why else would the hotel be going to all this trouble?'

'The crime happened on Dutch soil. In our precinct. No one is above the law.'

'But do you really want to spend the resources on this – to have to secure authorisation?'

I sighed again, exasperated, and eyed the conference room. 'Then what *do* you suggest?'

'I think I should focus on tracking down the maid – and through her, the victim.'

'Fine.'

I was mentally preparing a parallel approach when I heard my name called.

*

Sebastiaan Bergveld was with Joost, I was shocked to discover. He was smiling at me, his eyes perfectly calm under his floppy, blond fringe.

It was like a reunion of the station's old guard. Had I been invited along as the entertainment? I nodded at them like none of it fazed me.

'Take a seat Henk,' said Joost. 'I'm just reviewing the station's goals in depth, and yours in particular.' He slid a piece of paper over to me.

Our eyes locked.

'I invited Sebastiaan along as an independent observer.'

I almost laughed.

'As I'm sure you know, Internal Investigations likes such transparency.'

This was fucking unbelievable. 'Internal Investigations?'

Bergveld just kept grinning that grin.

I glanced down at the page and saw a series of numbered points. Frank Hals's name appeared more than once.

'What is this about? The Holendrecht case?'

'It's about many things,' Joost said. 'Primarily it's about a lack of progress here at IJT3 towards goals.'

'Which goals are we talking about? Holendrecht's not even *in* this precinct. The case involves a shooting that was already being investigated by the National Police Agency. Aren't they the natural agency of enquiry now? Didn't you say so yourself, only this lunchtime?'

'I've since had a chance to review the case in full.'

Bergveld's smile broadened.

Joost continued: 'You implied previously that it was linked to a drug deal gone bad and related to a name on the six hundred list – a name known to this precinct. Frank Hals.'

Six hundred known criminals account for sixty per cent of the crime in this city, and that statistic had acquired a nice ring to it under Jan Six, the old commissioner. But now Joost was the commissioner.

'One of your team members went out there trying to obtain witness testimony from a taxi driver.' Joost was referring to Stefan, of course. 'You *made* it your case. So now you need to finish it, Henk.'

He let that thought hang there.

'The KLPD will handle the shooting in Holendrecht,' he went on. 'But *you* need to get a result here in the precinct with Frank Hals.' He tapped the top of the sheet in front of me with his forefinger. 'And you need to acknowledge as much by signing this. In front of us, now. If you want this station to have a future, that is.'

'What am I, a child?'

'Sometimes I wonder,' said Bergveld, barely more than half my age.

Joost made no objection to his comment.

19

MALEK

IT WAS PAST 6 p.m. by the time I got to the old merchant's house opposite the vast Oude Kerk on the western fringes of the Red Light District. The RLD still fell within the station's precinct. *For how much longer?* I wondered. Would Joost really try to close us down?

The sun was low on the horizon: shift changeover for the visitors and workers here. There was something symbolic in that, because the man I was visiting was a very different kind of animal to the Neanderthal street pimps I'd had to deal with in the past. Street pimps such as Jan Tőzsér, Zsolt-the-Informant's younger brother.

I rang the intercom for EWT Services.

'Yes?' said a foreign voice.

'I'm here to see Malek.'

'And you are?'

'Henk.'

'Henk who?'

'Just tell him.'

A pause.

The door buzzed and clicked open.

I climbed the dark wooden stairs and found myself in front of the door to East–West Trading Services.

I rang the bell, and for a few moments nothing happened. Finally, the door opened. The woman who greeted me looked like she'd stepped out of the pages of *Vogue*, so high were her cheekbones. On the sparse, white walls of the reception area were moody photos of other, equally exotic women – all with come-to-bed looks.

She was almost as tall as I was. 'You have appointment?' she asked.

'Nope, I was hoping to catch him for a few moments.'

'Tell me your name,' she said.

'Didn't we just have this conversation? This is me.' I flashed my warrant card.

Like Frank Hals, Malek had benefitted from Zsolt Tőzsér's demise. Only in Malek's case, I'd tried to establish a trade in advance of dealing with Zsolt: an easier life for Malek, in exchange for information. When you clear out weeds, others soon appear, and sometimes you need to tend to them – or so I'd managed to persuade myself.

I'd shared none of this with Joost, my glorious leader.

'Wait here,' the woman said, disappearing through a doorway.

East–West Trading Services was a front for Amsterdam's most high-end 'escort agency'. Malek always maintained that these women had true independence, that the more successful ones made hundreds of thousands of euros a year. That last part may even have been true; it didn't prevent Malek from relieving each of the women of five thousand euros upfront for a photo portfolio, in addition to his ongoing commission.

The woman reappeared. 'He will see you now.'

Malek was tall, with salt-and-pepper cropped hair and stubble. He wore a loose grey top and linen trousers, like an architect or a graphic designer might. But that was where the similarity ended. His dark eyes were unusually alert; his physique was special forces muscular. A star-shaped tattoo on his wrist hinted at a regimental past. We'd never discussed his background properly.

'Drink?' he offered.

I nodded.

At first blush, Malek's office resembled that of a model agency or a fashion company, with its glass trestle table and large portfolios of photos.

This was organised crime: business-like, removed. Always with an eye to plausible deniability.

There were also samples of weed on the desk in bags. That was hardly illegal in Amsterdam, either.

'What's going on?' I asked.

'You tell me,' he said. 'Whisky?'

I nodded. It was always a game of chess with Malek.

On a low table were architects' plans for what looked to be a shop or a bar. Was he branching out?

He handed me a heavy glass tumbler of what smelled like good malt. I took a welcome sip as I decided where to begin. The whisky tasted smoky-sour. I rolled the liquid over my tongue, and resolved to play it straight.

'A Ukrainian woman was found badly beaten up at a hotel near here.'

'Cheers, by the way.' He raised his glass.

Something about his timing with that toast was off.

Way off.

'It happened last night,' I went on. 'Know anything about it?'

'A lot of women come out of Ukraine just now.' He shrugged, staring down into his glass. 'Hard to say.'

'Really? This was at the Royal Hotel. An important client. The woman made an overnight stay. Just thought you might know something.'

His eyes remained downcast, his face immobile.

'Elena Luscovich,' I prompted.

A vein on his temple became prominent. A tell? Then… nothing, his poker face restored.

'So, help me fill in the gaps,' I said. 'Who might the

arrangement have been made through? Which contact or agency? I need to know the client's name.'

'For that kind of client, that type of hotel? Much is word of mouth, not advertised. Recommendations. Everything discreet.'

'Okay, but now it's an official police enquiry.' I made a show of looking around his office again. My eyes settled again on the architects' plans on the low table. 'You might want to get your affairs in order.'

'What do you mean by that?'

I shrugged. I wasn't entirely sure what I'd meant.

'What happened to her?' he asked.

'You didn't hear?' I said sceptically. 'She was beaten into unconsciousness. According to a witness account.'

He took a slurp of whisky. Then he sat down at the glass table, as if he had work to get on with. 'Maybe it did her some good.'

Had I just heard him right? My ears were buzzing.

I couldn't play this snitch game anymore.

I smacked my tumbler down on the glass in front of him.

'I'll see myself out.'

*

As soon as I got out onto the street I called Liesbeth, but she didn't pick up. It was already 6.30 – she would have gone home.

I tried Johan. I wanted to talk Ukrainian regimental tattoos with him, but the call went to voicemail.

I blew air out between my lips. There were too many pieces on the chessboard; it was hard to keep track of everything going on. The pieces needed thinning out somehow.

The sour taste of the whisky remained as I cut back through the RLD, heading east to the station for my gun. I walked down narrow, neon-lit Molensteeg – Little Hungary – thinking about what had happened here with Jan Tőzsér, and the eerie vacuum he'd left behind.

I considered calling Stefan.

A few of the cabins on Molensteeg were empty. The city

was trying to reclaim the sites for businesses, putting them to alternative use. Many of the windows were still occupied by girls, and I couldn't help but think about what became of the 'models' who weren't able to repay Malek his photo-shoot fee – did they end up in these sleazy cabins?

'Boss?' Stefan finally picked up. I could hear him panting.

'Am I interrupting something?' I asked.

'Only five-a-side football.' He caught his breath. 'Welcome break, actually.'

'When you get into work tomorrow, could you do some digging around for a planning application that a company called East–West Trading Services might have submitted to the city?'

'Sure. What sort of plans?

'Retail, or cafés.'

'What's the applicant's name?'

'Why?'

'Er… it might help trace it. If the application was put in through another company, the name of the person behind it shouldn't change.'

I thought about giving him Malek's full name but, fearing that Stefan would check that out too, decided against it.

'Try East–West Trading Services first.'

'Will do. Are you away again tomorrow?'

'I have to see someone early, but I'll be in later.'

'About Holendrecht?'

'It's a separate issue.'

But related, I neglected to say. Not knowing was for Stefan's own good.

145

20

THE DEBATE

BY THE TIME I got back to the houseboat it was dark. Orange street lamps reflected on the rippling water of Entrepotdok. I inspected the lock that Jan Tőzsér had tried to pick before I'd given chase to him the night he'd drowned in the harbour.

Petra was in her usual spot on the sofa, watching TV. I bent down to kiss her.

'You look tired,' she said.

'I feel it.'

I unholstered my gun and locked it away in the cabinet.

'Can I get you a drink?' I offered.

'I just made a cup of tea.'

I paused in the galley, deliberating whether to have the same. Then I reached for the clay bottle of jenever and a small glass, pouring myself a healthy measure.

Petra was lost in the TV screen, the light of it putting her face into sharp relief. I joined her on the sofa. Those cheekbones and that finely proportioned nose – after all these years, I could still appreciate them like I was seeing her for the first time. Nadia shared those features.

'I don't even know what those words mean,' she was saying, perplexed.

'Which words?' I asked, patting her on the knee.

'Sustainable energy security.'

On the screen were five talking heads around a table. One of

146

them was Muriel Crutzen, the energy minister. Her stylish grey hair matched her eyes, and she wore a silk scarf that was casual yet elegant. Crutzen often looked slightly startled, like a fine creature who'd suddenly found herself in the wrong habitat. But her body language was open, conciliatory. Most Dutch voters liked her and looked up to her. Rem Lottman worked for her at the Council of Europe.

'It's an electoral debate,' Petra said.

'Already?'

The elections were months away. They only ever brought the same outcome: some reformulation of the never-ending coalition government.

'Does it refer to the sustaining of energy security,' Petra persisted, ever the journalist, 'or the security of sustainable energy?'

I considered making a joke about how she shouldn't bring her work home with her, but then I remembered Nadia's acerbic comment about me disappearing to Brussels over the weekend.

Instead, I rolled the words over in my head.

Sustainable energy security.

It *was* cleverly ambiguous. The kind of clever ambiguity Rem Lottman might have come up with, maybe?

I looked at my watch. It was too late to call his office again.

'Politicians,' I said ruefully. 'Always hedging their bets.'

'But this is a key issue,' Petra protested.

I sipped my drink. The politicians' voices floated in and out.

'... even Scandinavian countries with abundant oil reserves are moving away from fossil fuels... what I think we can all agree on is the need *not* to rely on Russia for our energy requirements...'

Always what *not* to do. What *should* we be doing?

Don't vote, my dad once told me. *It only encourages them.*

'I saw Nadia this afternoon.'

'Oh?' Petra looked at me.

147

'She wanted me to help expedite her passport renewal.'

'Why? Where's she going?'

'Dubrovnik for the weekend, apparently.'

Petra sniffed. She was hurt that Nadia hadn't ended up meeting us in Rotterdam, I could tell. But she wouldn't admit it.

'It sounded like you at least spoke to her...' I ventured.

'Briefly.'

I pulled my shoes off, grimacing with the effort, and let them fall to the wooden floor with a thud. 'I'm not sure about this boyfriend of hers.'

'Sergei?'

The name was all we had to go on. That, and one other salient point.

Petra was looking at the TV again, clutching a pillow to her chest.

'She was wearing a decent-sized diamond, which he'd given her.'

'Which finger?'

'Not her ring finger. The middle one.'

'Then let her find it all out for herself,' she snapped. 'If the jewellery was given to her with love, she'll be happy. If not, she'll be wiser.'

I knew that my wife's words were directed at Nadia, not me. Still, why couldn't we just have a calm discussion about it?

My phone vibrated. I eased it out of my jeans pocket, checked the display and then answered.

'Johan,' I said, as much to reassure my wife that it wasn't work-related as to greet my old friend.

'You were trying to reach me earlier?'

'Yes, but it's OK. It can wait till tomorrow.'

He waited a beat. 'Actually, are you free for a drink?'

'Now?'

'Yes.'

'Er... Why? What's up?'

'I could use a chat.'

If it had been anyone else, refusing would have been easy. But after what Johan had done for me...

I looked at Petra. She was lost in the political debate again.

'What about a quick one at De Druif?' Johan said.

The bar was practically at the end of my street.

'OK,' I agreed. 'I'll be there in a few.'

*

Gert, the shaven-headed bartender, served us two Dubbel Boks at our table and then gave us our space, which wasn't easy to achieve in a bar as small as De Druif – although there was only one other customer, at the bar, surrounded by empty glasses; the guy was practically falling off his stool.

'I keep waiting for the call,' Johan said. His eyes had a cloudy, preoccupied look.

'Which call? What are you talking about?'

He lowered his voice. 'Some other section of the police force, Henk. Telling me they're going to investigate the Tőzsér shooting.'

'That won't happen,' I said, attacking my beer. But it was easy for me to say – I hadn't been the one to pull the trigger.

'How do you know that?' Johan asked.

How did I? Joost had threatened me over it that very day, at least suspecting my involvement in the shooting.

'We've talked about this often enough, Johan. There are too many skeletons in the departmental closet. Any investigation risks exposing the full informant racket they had going on at IJ Tunnel 3.'

'But what if someone new comes in – decides to clean house?'

I shook my head. 'They already have cleaned house, in their minds. There's a new commissioner. But it's the same old team: Joost, Bergveld... they're all implicated. They don't want the full truth coming out about the Tőzsér brothers any more than you or I do.'

There was the crux of it: Joost, Bergveld, even Lottman and I – we all needed one another to some extent. I took another gulp of the strong Dubbel Bok.

Johan required more convincing.

'We did the right thing,' I went on in a low voice. 'Once Zsolt found out that I'd let his younger brother die in the harbour, revenge was coming, as sure as night follows day. And his "eye for eye" approach would have been to take out one of my family members. You know this.'

Johan looked lost in thought. 'How *did* he find out?' he asked finally.

'Who?'

'Zsolt. About the way his brother died?'

'Who knows?' I'd often considered the question. 'There were enough witnesses down at the harbour that night. Only takes one camera phone.'

I couldn't erase the memory of Bergveld approaching with Liesbeth, right after Jan Tőzsér's head had slipped under the icy water.

Johan's expression clouded over again, as if he were remembering something else. 'So what did you call me about earlier?'

'Oh, yes. I wanted to ask you about a tattoo. I think it's a regimental one – Ukrainian – but you'll know.'

'What does it look like?'

'A star within a star.'

'Hmm.' Johan's eyes narrowed. 'Could you draw it?'

I reached for a beer mat, but I didn't have a pen. 'Hold on.' I walked over to the bar, on which the other customer's face was now resting.

'You think it might be time to send him home?' I asked Gert.

'He's a boat captain. I'm thinking it's better for him to sleep it off here, in case he gets any ideas about taking to the water…'

I chuckled. 'You got a pen handy?'

'Sure.' Gert pulled one from his top pocket. 'Here.'

Back at our table, I drew the star within a star. Johan looked up at me sharply. 'Where did you see this?'

'The arm of a guy I know.'

'You might want to keep your distance.'

'Why?'

'It's Ukrainian all right, but not regimental. It looks very much like the insignia of a motorcycle gang there.'

'What… like the Hells Angels?'

'Worse. It looks like the Ten Guns Motorcycle Club from Donetsk. They're notorious.'

21

FRANK'S BOAT

I GOT BACK TO my boat quickly and checked its hatches, locks and latches. Further down the waterway, the lonely 'iron sentinel' – a disused goods crane – loomed eerily.

In the army, we used to talk about threats as capability mixed with intent. There was no question that this biker gang was capable. What about their intent, now that I'd suspended relations with Malek?

I entered the warmth of the boat. Petra had gone to bed.

My hands shook as I started to fix a drink. I changed my mind and set the bottle back down. My head flooded with questions and foreboding as I clambered into the hammock slung amidships.

How might my young rival Bergveld have handled a snitch like Malek more successfully? How much of a threat would Frank Hals become if I went after *him*?

I fell into a fitful, restless sleep. Through the mists of my dreams sailed a broad ship with masts and ghostly rigging. A ship of death...

I awoke with a start, blinking at the pale dawn, seized with a sailor's premonition that people were about to die. Would I – or those close to me – be among them?

Grabbing my jacket, holster and gun, I let myself out. The dawn moisture was cool on my face. I headed towards the Ibis hotel for coffee and a fresh roll. From there, I'd go on to the harbour.

*

Cautiously, I approached Frank Hals's boat. It resembled a floating fortress, holding its own – in terms of scale – with the cranes, gantries and old grain silos found at the eastern reaches of the harbour. Graffiti ran around the harbour wall, stopping a respectful few metres from either end of Hals's vessel. There was a musty smell of sea salt and warming tar. The dawn mists had burned away; the light was astringent.

Hals was hosing the deck down. He was dressed in a pair of nylon shorts, a short-sleeved shirt and flip-flops. On one of his pale legs he wore a long white sock for varicose veins. As I arrived beside his boat he looked up at me. He appeared to be alone, but no doubt his henchmen were close by.

'Spring cleaning, Frank?' I called across to him.

He stayed silent.

'May I?' I gestured towards the long gangplank.

Hals didn't refuse but watched me, fox-like, all the while.

The wooden planks bowed beneath my weight. Down in the black hull of his boat was a cannabis crop worth tens of millions of euros.

'What brings you here?' he asked.

'Oh, you know. Work… casework. One case in particular.' I looked around. 'Is there somewhere we can talk?'

'Here.'

'OK,' I said, deciding how to begin. 'We thought we had a taxi driver who'd give witness testimony regarding that shooting in Holendrecht. We don't. Yet the case just won't go away.'

He went on cleaning the deck. I looked beyond the harbour wall to the bright sea channel, the route by which contraband has always entered and left this city. Seagulls wheeled around the prow of a huge petroleum barge. It ploughed along remorselessly, churning up the birds' catch.

'All the fingers are pointing to you, Frank. You know that?'

'Let them point,' he said, head bowed, continuing with his hosing – but with no particular aim now.

I changed tack. 'You remember that place we all stayed in over on Brouwersgracht? The squat? D'you know what it's finally turned into?'

He looked up.

'Mondriaan's – Amsterdam's first three-Michelin starred restaurant. Can you imagine, after some of the food we ate in that squat? If you could even call it food.' I shook my head and chuckled.

'All I remember is that place being firebombed by the developers,' he said, the hosepipe in his hand still gushing. Sunlight reflected blindingly off the little rope of water. 'Things evolve.'

That's my line, I thought.

I squatted down on my haunches. 'The boss has got the bit between the teeth with this one, Frank. They want a result.'

'Let them want.'

'Why not give me an alibi? Something I can take back to them.'

'Why should I?'

'Is it not worth anything to you, me sharing this?'

'Not really,' he said, finally turning the water off. 'You're the one who may be needing the alibi, from what I hear.'

I stood up again. 'Oh?'

Now he was facing me. His shoulders were hunched but his energy was electric, battle-ready – I recognised it from days of old.

He looked me straight in the eye. 'I know about your Hungarian friends.'

I stiffened.

'You've got no issues with me,' he added.

If he knew, who else did?

I caught sight of a head, cut off and immobile as if mounted on a spike; it was one of his henchmen peering up from below deck, keeping an eye on us.

'Here,' Hals said, reaching into the top pocket of his shirt for a reefer. 'Relax, old Henk. Take this home with you. Give my regards to Mrs van der Pol.'

I stared at it for a second, then decided against refusing him and took it.

'There's a place in every man's life, beyond which the idealism and naivety of yesterday has to give way. *Has* to,' he said.

Had Bergveld put the word out about my involvement in Zsolt Tőzsér's death? Or had Joost?

I thought too of Johan, protectively.

'Welcome to that place,' Frank added, turning away.

I needed a chance to think, to regroup.

I noted the smaller boats at this end of the harbour, often semi-submerged; the Perspex windows of a couple of them were duck-shit green and almost totally obscured. My gaze swept around and I clocked the old cannon at the edge of Hals's clipper. Its dull, pitted surface was in sharp relief against the strong sunlight.

'Quite a deck adornment you have there.'

He didn't need look to know what I was talking about. 'It's from the *Vrede*.'

The *Vrede* ('Peace') had played a starring role in the Second Anglo-Dutch War.

'Still fires,' he said.

I wondered if City Hall let him do that, too.

'You have an eye for these things.' I chose my next words carefully. 'Would you also happen to know about a stolen Verspronck?'

He turned to face me. 'What?'

There are rumours about you too, I thought. 'The painting of the little girl.'

'What are you suggesting?' he hissed.

The henchman was suddenly on deck beside us.

'Only that you have good taste in antiques, Frank. And that you move in informed circles.'

He backed off a fraction. 'That painting was stolen to begin with.'

I recalled Wester mentioning that there was a question about its provenance – whether it had changed hands during the war.

'It wasn't theirs to give.' He spat out his words.

'What do you mean? Who gave the painting to the Norwegian diplomat then?'

Frank laughed. 'Why would I tell you, when you've given me *nothing*?' He paused. 'But that's where you need to go looking. Not here.' He turned on the hosepipe's tap again, dismissing me.

At that very moment, a text arrived from Stefan. It was lengthy. I read it quickly yet carefully, then considered its import, my downcast eyes shifting from the phone's display to the deck and the precious herbaceous cargo beneath our feet.

'OK then, Frank, here's something for you. Competition's coming your way.'

He stopped.

'A Ukrainian called Malek,' I went on. 'D'you know him?'

Frank betrayed no recognition.

I kept going. 'He's a pimp. He's built up a network of high-class escorts that masquerades as a modelling agency.'

Frank snorted. 'What kind of competition is that?'

'He's branching out into coffee shops, we believe. He's got plans for several sites.'

'Where?'

'The Red Light District, station-side.'

Hals's eyes darkened. With the number of visitors it attracted, the RLD was lucrative for many things, but none more so than the coffee shops. There was a steady ant trail of curious human beings wandering over from Centraal station to the coffee shops at its western fringes. Most of the shops belonged to Frank – for now.

'What's his form?' Frank said.

He was asking me about Malek's police record.

I looked at him with an even expression. 'He's a businessman, you know? Seen to be doing everything above board.'

'What else?'

'That's all I have for now.' I omitted mention of Malek's involvement in the Ten Guns motorbike gang.

Frank ran his tongue over his front teeth, pushing his cheeks up. 'Come back and see me this time tomorrow. We'll talk about the painting.'

'Now's not a good time?'

The henchman shifted his weight from one foot to another.

'Now's certainly not a good time,' Hals said. A sharp, steely timbre had entered his voice.

'Okey-dokey.' I retreated back along the gangplank.

Halfway across, I paused, thinking over what I'd just told Hals. Stefan's text had mentioned plans for cafés, not coffee shops... as any plans destined for the city's official planning department would, I reasoned. But there was little doubt in my mind that Malek was moving into the cannabis trade.

'See you tomorrow then,' I said.

As I looked over my shoulder at him, Frank Hals's face appeared like a portrait of undiluted bitterness.

22

BERGVELD'S BEAT

WALKING AWAY FROM THE shadow of Hals's boat, I called Stefan.

'Boss.'

'So the application classified those plans as cafés?'

'There's a bit of further description, but that's basically it.'

'Did you note down that further description?'

'Course.'

I could hear him flicking through the pages of his notebook.

'Provision to offer coffee, other beverages, cakes and patisserie –'

'They *must* be coffee shops,' I interrupted. 'Especially when you consider the locations, right there in the RLD...'

'Could I ask what this is in connection with?'

'You could ask, but I'm not sure I know the answer myself yet. I'll see you back at the station.' I ended the call and kept walking in the direction of IJ Tunnel 3.

Something was nagging at me.

Something about the Lars Pelt case smelled very bad.

And twenty-four hours was too long to wait for my next audience with Hals and what he might choose to share, or not.

As soon as I got to the station, I borrowed an unmarked police car and drove over to Willemspark, the scene of Pelt's death. It was still early in the day and I was betting that Bergveld wouldn't be there.

*

Bergveld wasn't outside the house, I observed, as I drove past it on leafy Koningslaan – but neither was anyone else. I turned, making a second slow pass, then parked the car on Willemsparkweg and called Wester, who had been guarding the property the previous day.

No reply.

At the prompt, I left a message asking him to call me as soon as possible.

I returned to Koningslaan on foot and walked up to the house.

Something was wrong.

As I entered through the gate and approached the front door, I registered an unnatural sense of calm. The door was sealed with yellow tape – not the white, Amsterdam police variety familiar to me.

I couldn't see any signs of activity through the grand bay windows.

There were buildings on the opposite side of the street, but no one was around. Many of the homes in the area were second or third residences, kept empty. Reckoning that no one could see me, I walked down the side of the Pelt house, feeling a sudden coolness in the shadows there. A rose bush tore at the sleeve of my bomber jacket. I was expecting to reappear in a sunlit back garden full of blooms, but instead I found my feet crunching sharply raked, grey gravel in between manicured bonsai trees. Had Lars Pelt been a Buddhist? I felt like I was intruding on a very personal space. Following a narrow stone path, I approached the back door.

The door had a large glass panel with a clear view of a hallway. The house's interior, with its bare wooden floors, looked glum and deserted. But there was an imposing, fair-haired man standing there, facing away from me. He wore polished black shoes, a green military sweater with epaulettes, and a gun on his hip, the model of which I couldn't distinguish through the glass. I shielded my eyes against the glare and a face appeared not ten centimetres from my own, giving me a start.

Bergveld flung the door open. I stepped back just in time to avoid being smacked in the face.

'Enough!' He launched himself at me. I felt his weight and momentum; I staggered back onto the gravel. Barely had I the chance to regain my balance before I saw his fist nearing my face. I bobbed my head back but his knuckles still thumped into my right temple, sending shock waves through my skull.

'What the fuck are you doing?' I shouted. 'I'm a fellow police officer!'

He'd collected himself together to attack again; I shoved him, hard, in the chest. I'd always seen him as an overgrown boy but there was a solidity to him I hadn't registered before. He hardly even stumbled back as he prepared to come at me once more.

The military man was shouting in the hallway.

I tried to catch my breath as we grappled – our feet crunching gravel, each trying to get the other off balance. Bergveld's strength surprised me. Had he been working out? Or was I, the older man, losing my own strength?

'Bergveld, what the f –' I gasped. Still the military man was yelling, and in my peripheral vision I caught sight of a dull black object: his gun, unholstered…

I moved one foot to the side and swept Bergveld's right leg out from under him. He went down hard amid a haze of grey dust, baring his teeth and clasping his knee.

'I'm a policeman, too,' I said to the other man, who was pointing his handgun at my chest. My palms were up. The gun was a Heckler & Koch P30 semi-automatic. The fair-haired man held it in a two-handed grip, his stare boring into me.

Bergveld was coughing as he scrambled to his feet.

'You're fucking finished, van der Pol!'

'Maybe,' I conceded. 'But not by you. You couldn't finish a school milk carton, Bergveld.'

'You know him?' the military man said, lowering his gun. His accent was Scandinavian.

Bergveld nodded.

I turned and walked away.

'Stop right there!' Bergveld yelled. But I was already in the shadows to the side of the house, pushing aside the rose bush. I could hear his feet on the gravel behind me as he hobbled.

I picked up the pace on Koningslåan, drawing deep breaths. Neither man was following.

As I waited on the corner of Koningslaan and Willemsparkweg, hands on knees, breathing hard, I was unsure whether to go back and try to straighten things out. But something told me that wouldn't go well.

So I went back to the car. There was a parking ticket under the windscreen wiper. I balled it up, looking the length of Willemsparkweg for the traffic warden.

Fuck.

How much longer before Bergveld spoke to Joost, and I got the inevitable call? Hours… if that.

My phone was already ringing.

'Wester.'

'You asked me to call you back?'

'Yeah,' I said, getting into the car. My hand was torn and bleeding from that damn rose bush; my head was throbbing. I started the engine and drove.

'Hello?' Wester said.

'Yes, I'm still here. I just dropped by to see you at the Pelt house. What's going on there?'

'What were you doing over there again? That's Bergveld's beat!'

'I got that.' In the rear-view mirror I could see a dark bruise on my temple.

'It's being turned over to the *Militaerpolitikompaniet*,' Wester said.

161

'The Norwegian military police?'

'Yes. The diplomatic section.'

A dead diplomat.

'But it's not an embassy,' I said. 'It's Dutch soil.'

'That's a point of debate. Jesus, what were you doing there? Why didn't you call me first?'

'Er… I think I did. You didn't pick up. So, how are you guys handling the case now?'

'We're not. The Norwegians are.'

'What happened to the English woman? The one from yesterday – the art insurer? Lucy…' But I couldn't remember her last name.

'Channing-West? I don't know. She was leaving for London, last I heard. Why?'

'You wouldn't happen to have her phone number, would you?'

'I wonder how many men have asked that over the years.' He chuckled. 'The answer's no.'

'Usually is. Where's she staying?'

'I couldn't tell you.'

'Can't or won't?'

I noticed a flash of a familiar colour down Cornelis Schuytstraat, one of the streets of expensive houses leading off Willemsparkweg.

'Henk, what's going on?'

'That's the right question.'

I slowed and made a quick U-turn, the steering wheel spinning in my hand, a horn blaring behind.

'Henk,' Wester repeated, 'what's going on?'

My eyes hadn't deceived me.

'I've got to go, Wester.'

The sculpted end of a maroon Bentley.

*

Another substantial Willemspark residence, all corbels and balconies and gables. The engine of the Bentley was purring in the driveway. Sammy got out, not noticing me cross the street. He walked around to the back door of the car, opening it for Lesoto.

The Ghanaian giant was ending a phone call. 'Yes, that is most satisfactory.' His head sheened with sweat.

'Ah!' he cried joyfully, his eyes widening, 'our friend of Mista Lottman's!'

Then he caught the side of my face. 'What has happened?' He was looking at the bruise. 'Did somebody beat you?'

'No, it's nothing. You should see the other guy.'

'I would very much *like* to see the other guy,' he said with fierce intensity. 'I would like to give him a taste of Ghanaian justice!'

'No, I was just using a figure of speech... never mind. Is everything OK?'

Sammy was unloading bags from the boot: Armani, Bulgari, Chanel, Dior...

'Everything is most satisfactory. Your country has been *most* gracious and welcoming.'

'How much longer are you here for?'

'A little while,' he replied, .surveying the sun-dappled street. 'I like it very much. *So* many nice things,' he said with soft insistence. 'I should like to settle here, find a nice young European bride.'

It gave me an odd feeling, made me think again about the girl in the Verspronck painting.

'Well, good luck with that.'

'I have to make another phone call now,' he said, 'but you must come by and see us again soon. It is pleasant to have friends in the neighbourhood.'

'I'm sure it is.'

I watched Sammy struggle with the shopping bags. Lesoto sauntered off to the side of the house with his phone pressed to his ear, and I thought of the man in Brussels who'd introduced us both.

*

'Rem Lottman's office,' the assistant said in a French accent.

'Can I speak with him?'

'Who is calling?'

'Henk van der Pol, Amsterdam Police Department.'

'What can I say it's in connection with?'

'Mr Lesoto.'

'Did you say "risotto"?'

'No!' Did they ever put the fork down in Brussels? 'There's an "L", not an "R", at the start of his name. Lottman asked me to keep him updated on the matter.'

'I'll be sure to let him know.'

'The sooner the better.'

'Noted.'

'*Merci beaucoup.*'

'*De rien.*'

I drove back up Willemsparkweg, getting out my phone so I could google Lucy Channing-West. I could feel a migraine coming on; the dazzling sunlight streaming in through the windscreen was making my eyes water. Wester had said that the English art insurer was leaving. How soon?

There was too much going on; it felt like a maze, one barrier after another. Finally, I gave up trying to work my phone and drive at the same time; I pulled over as I approached the intersection with busy Van Baerlestraat, my brakes squealing, and switched on the hazard lights.

The browser on my phone showed a *Loss Adjuster with Lloyds of London, 196 Syndicate: Lucinda Channing-West*. It had to be her, but I couldn't find a direct line to call.

If she'd been staying in a hotel it must have been one of the better ones, judging by her wardrobe and preference for executive taxis. There were only so many top-of-the-range hotels to choose from here in central Amsterdam, and directly in front me was the most exclusive of all: the Conservatorium, conveniently close to Pelt's house. I got out of the car, putting a *Police Business* sign in the window so as to avoid a parking ticket this time, and made my way over to the imposing building.

There had to be a better way of going about all this.

My phone was ringing.

Liesbeth.

'I've found her,' she announced.

'Who? The maid from the Royal?'

'Better,' she said. 'Through the maid, the beaten woman herself. Elena Luscovich.'

'Is she OK?'

'From what I could tell over the phone, just about. I'm wondering if I should bring her in to the station.'

'Please do. Right away.'

'She's not saying much,' Liesbeth cautioned.

'Let's see if we can change that. See you back at the station ASAP.'

23

BRIDGES

A CAR HORN BLARED as I stood in the middle of busy Van Baerlestraat. A Mercedes taxi.

I stopped dead. Lucy Channing-West had hailed an Amsterdam Executive Cars cab the previous day when she'd left the Pelt house.

I pulled out my phone and dialled their number.

'This is Officer Henk van der Pol of the IJ Tunnel 3 police station,' I told the person who picked up. 'I need some information about a fare yesterday.'

'Wait on the line,' the woman said nonchalantly.

'Yes?' a male voice barked after a few moments.

I repeated my introduction.

'We've sixty-two cars,' the man said. 'These police requests are becoming too taxing. Far too taxing!'

Police requests... plural?

At least it made my own sound routine. 'The woman concerned is leaving town,' I said. 'It's important that we catch up with her before she does so. She's around one-seventy tall, Caucasian, blonde, English. Smartly dressed. She was picked up on Koningslaan yesterday at around two p.m.'

'All right,' he relented. 'Let me see what I can do.'

I gave him my number.

'Tell me your name and rank again.'

I did. 'And yours?' I asked.

'I'm Max. I'm the owner.'

I considered asking him about the other police enquiries, but then realised the line had gone dead.

From Van Baerlestraat, I drove straight back to the station. I was approaching it when a familiar caller ID flashed up on my phone.

PRIVATE NUMBER.

'Henk.' It was Rem Lottman's voice, thank God. 'You have news about our Ghanaian friend?'

'I do, but I'd like to speak in person.' About Joost. 'I can come back to Brussels. Later today?'

'What's happened?'

'Lesoto is staying in Willemspark, near Lars Pelt's house.'

He was silent for a second. 'What do you make of that?'

'There are a few things becoming apparent, but I'd rather discuss them in person.'

'Today is very difficult. There's a big energy function in Brussels this evening. The minister is hosting.'

'I don't need much of your time.' It reminded me of asking for my father's help and attention, years before.

'Can't you just tell me over the phone?'

'Better in person. I only need a few minutes.'

'All right, old Henk. I'll put you back on with my assistant and you can arrange something. But first... did you get any sense for how long Lesoto might be staying there?'

'A while. He looked to be getting pretty settled in.' I gave him the address of where the Ghanaian was making himself at home.

Then Miss Risotto was back on. 'There is a recess of the Energy Ministers' Summit at around six p.m.,' she said. 'Can you be here by then?'

I thought about what else I had to do. Liesbeth was bringing in the woman from the Royal Hotel, and I needed to find Lucy Channing-West – assuming she was still in town. It was already noon.

'Hopefully,' I replied.

'Should we send a car?'

'Nope, I can find my way.'

Something else I needed to do was dress my wounds.

What is the pattern here? I asked myself as I ended the call and approached the police station. Were the Norwegian military police now involved in the Pelt case because of the man himself, or that priceless painting? Both, presumably. But then there was the Ghanaian giant, too…

My phone rang again as I squealed to a stop. Bloody brakes.

'Henk –'

'Liesbeth. Do you have her? Elena Luscovich?'

'Henk, no. I can't.'

'Can't?' I slammed the car door shut behind me. I walked quickly, away from a loud rumble nearby. 'What do you mean, *can't*?'

'I don't have approval,' Liesbeth said.

'Huh?' I stopped, stunned. 'I asked you to do this!'

'Joost isn't supportive, Henk.'

I was about to say something, but she pre-empted me. 'You didn't tell me that the station was about to close down.'

'What the hell?' The rumbling was getting louder. 'Let's talk about this.' I looked around as I crossed the street, trying to identify the source of the noise. 'Let's meet at the Ibis.'

There it was: the hotel. But moving around in front of it were three large shapes – dark, smoky streaks against the bright light.

'… not sure that's such a good idea –' Liesbeth was saying.

I cut in. 'Be at the Ibis in five minutes.'

One of the bikers was riding a Honda Hardtail chopper; another, a vintage Indian. The third sat astride a Russian-looking machine I didn't recognise. Their bearded faces were impassive beneath their matte-black crash helmets. They wheeled around, liberally using up two lanes of the road, manoeuvring to form a semi-circle in front of me, all the while giving throaty blasts of their engines. As their front wheels edged close to my knees, I could just make out the double-star emblems on their forearms. The chrome of their front forks dazzled.

Please God, don't let Joost see this.

A diplomatic Bentley one day; these guys the next...

'Malek asked us to stop by and say hello,' Hardtail growled over his burbling engine. He had a curled moustache and was missing a bottom tooth.

'Nice of you gentlemen to do so,' I managed.

The smell of hot engine oil mixed with the odour of stale sweat.

'He's not in any trouble now, is he?' Indian weighed in. His expression was hidden behind his jet-black sunglasses.

'Why don't you ask him?' I suggested.

'I'm asking you,' Indian said.

'He's got nothing to fear from me.'

Hardtail narrowed his gaze, trying to make sense of my words. 'What about them?' He jerked his head towards the brick police station and its security cameras.

'None of us.'

Hardtail nodded, apparently having heard what he wanted to. All three began backing their bikes away.

'S'long as it stays that way,' Indian said.

'Well thank you, gentlemen, for stopping by.'

The third man, masked by red facial hair, responded to my remark with a quizzical look. My heart thumped as they roared off down the IJ towards the water; Liesbeth stepped out from the station at that very moment.

*

She was eyeing the bruise on my face like she already knew how I'd come by it. We were at a table in the restaurant where Joost and I had sat the day before.

'All right, Liesbeth,' I said. 'What's going on?'

'You tell me,' she responded. 'I mentioned to Stefan that I

was bringing in Elena Luscovich. He said maybe I should check with Joost first.'

'Stefan said that?'

'He said the station might be shut down.'

I reached for my phone to call him, then restrained myself.

'We just need to think about our careers here, Henk. If we don't have a future at IJT3, we need to consider our options.'

Bergveld's new beat?

'Of course there's a future here. This is the harbour beat. It's Amsterdam. There will always be a need for good policemen and women here. Always.' I smacked the table with an open palm, causing the coffee cups to rattle and heads to turn. I leaned forward. 'It comes down to results. You know that. Whatever political bullshit is going on around us, we have to keep our focus on our cases, especially ones involving violent assault. Where did you leave things with Elena Luscovich?'

'I'm not sure how much we'll be able to get out of her in any event. She wouldn't share anything about the hotel guest on the phone.'

'About the man who beat her into unconsciousness?'

'Yes, him. I even said we may have to open a full investigation, look at the path of the financial proceeds. She still didn't open up.'

'Is she afraid? What exactly did she say?' There was potentially a five-figure sum involved, by way of payment for her night in the sack with her attacker.

'Only that it wasn't the client who paid.'

'Run that by me again. She's saying someone else paid her to spend the night with this thug?'

'Correct.'

'Who paid?'

'I don't know yet.'

I sipped my coffee hastily.

'Why don't you just talk it through with Joost?' she said.

I didn't doubt that I'd be doing so soon enough. I'd be receiving a call from the man at any moment.

'Did you share this piece of information with him?'

'What information?'

'About someone else paying for Elena to spend the night at the Royal?'

'Yes,' she said. 'I had to. He wanted an update, to understand what we were all working on instead of the Frank Hals case.'

'What was his reaction?'

'Henk.' She leaned in too. 'Are you not missing the bigger picture here? *The station is closing.* We're all out of a job unless we find transfers to other stations. Isn't it time to start building bridges rather than second-guessing the cause of everything?'

Liesbeth had to be able to tell me more about Joost.

I tried rewinding the conversation. 'How did he react when you said I'd told you to bring in Elena Luscovich?'

She rolled her eyes in exasperation. 'He was angry – *very* angry. He said you should have been focusing on getting a result with Hals.'

I chewed over that.

'Listen,' Liesbeth said, leaning closer still. 'You didn't hear this from me, but Joost's got some pretty high-stake objectives of his own that he needs to meet. You think he doesn't feel the pressure, too?'

I held Liesbeth's brown-eyed gaze. 'Is this what you and that prosecutor husband of yours talk about at night?'

'No!' she snapped. 'If you must know, I overheard Joost speaking on his mobile in a conference room yesterday afternoon, when he came in to the station. The door was open. He didn't realise.'

I weighed every one of Liesbeth's words, feeling the world tilt slightly. 'What exactly was he saying on his phone?'

'Jesus! I tried not to listen.' She suddenly sounded exhausted. 'But his conversation gave me the distinct impression that he would go to some lengths to do what he needs to.'

'You make it sound like he's got some kind of shadow organisation going on.'

'Henk… Christ. Less of the paranoia, please! We just need to get in line. You were in the army once, weren't you?'

Once.

She took my hands. Surprised, I looked down at her slender fingers wrapped around my battered digits. Blood had clotted on the back of one hand, where the rose bush at Pelt's house had torn it.

'Forget Elena Luscovich and focus on getting a result with Frank Hals.' She spoke softly yet insistently; it reminded me of Lesoto. 'Don't burn bridges Henk, please. Build them instead.'

24

TEAM VAN DER POL

I DROVE BACK TO the houseboat to pack for an overnight stay in Brussels, if it came to that. As I walked across the gangplank my phone rang; it was Max, from Amsterdam Executive Cars.

'Right,' he said. 'Good-looking English woman, around one-seventy tall, picked up on the corner of Koningslaan and Willemsparkweg yesterday at two-sixteen p.m....'

'That's her.'

'The driver took her to a residential address.'

'Where?'

'Amstel 81, beside the Magere Brug.'

The Skinny Bridge. Three minutes' walk from the Royal.

'OK?' Max prompted. 'That give you what you want?'

'It gives me what I need,' I qualified. 'Who did the other police requests come from?'

'Huh?'

'You mentioned other police requests, which were becoming "taxing". Your term.'

'And it's true. Do you people not work together?'

'To a point.'

The door to the cabin of our houseboat was unlocked.

'I didn't catch his name. He sounded like a younger cop.'

'As opposed to the older type?' I asked.

'Well...'

Was it Bergveld? Or Wester?

'What did he ask you for?'

Petra was sitting at the table in the galley, a sweater tied around her neck. She looked surprised to see me back during the day, and more surprised still by the bruise on my temple. I kissed her on the forehead.

'Why are you asking me this?' Max said.

'I want to identify this person, make sure he's really a cop and not someone trying to pass himself off as one.'

'You think I can't tell?'

'Let's see if you can.'

Max harrumphed. 'He asked me the exact same question you did, actually.'

'About the woman picked up at Koningslaan and Willemsparkweg?'

'Yes.'

I doubted it was Bergveld. He hadn't witnessed Lucinda Channing-West getting into that executive cab.

But Wester had witnessed it.

So too had Stefan.

Stefan.

Enquiring at whose request? Not mine.

'Will I get some peace now?' Max asked.

'That depends on your conscience.'

'Oh dear,' Max said, hanging up.

The boat rocked softly as I went through to our cramped bedroom.

Petra appeared in the doorway, leaning against the frame. 'What happened?'

'The bruise? Oh, it was just a scuffle with a suspect,' I said vaguely. I found my battered overnight bag.

'So where's the harbour master sailing off to this time?'

'Brussels,' I replied, easing past her into our yet-smaller bathroom.

She followed me. 'Again?'

'Yes.'

I threw a toothbrush and some other toiletries in; I needed to get to Amstel 81 as soon as possible to catch Lucy Channing-West.

'You'll have people talking,' Petra said.

'How so?' I looked up at her.

'A girl in every port...'

Though she'd become prickly since quitting her job at the paper, she was joking. Wasn't she?

'I'm not sure how well the attaché for the Dutch energy minister in the Council of Europe would take to being called a girl.'

'Rem Lottman?'

'Yep.'

'Is that who you went to see on Saturday?'

'Yes.'

In the mirror, my wounded temple looked even worse, the bruise now green-edged. I thought about changing my clothes but there wasn't time. I did remember to remove the reefer that Frank Hals had given me. That might require some explanation in Brussels, at the European Parliament building.

'Why are you going to see him again? Why didn't you tell me this?'

'I'm doing so now, aren't I?'

I went back through to the bedroom.

'What's wrong?'

'My team is abandoning me for my rivals, the station is going to be closed down because I'm unable to bring charges against a cannabis-growing former acquaintance, and a gang of Ukrainian bikers is personally threatening me. Apart from that, it's a pretty good day.'

I sat down heavily on the edge of the bed, suddenly exhausted by everything going on and the prospect of a three-hour drive to Brussels in traffic.

'Sometimes it just feels like the sky's falling in,' I said.

Petra sat down too, and took my cut hand, much like Liesbeth had.

We sat in silence for a few seconds, then I asked, 'What's going on with Nadia?'

'She's gone to Paris.'

Of course – she'd reckon on not needing a passport for that. 'With Sergei?'

My wife nodded. 'Shopping.'

'Just like my team… finding brighter opportunities elsewhere.'

Petra spoke slowly and deliberately. 'Sometimes in life *you* have to create the sense of certainty about those around you, Henk. Create your own sense of order. What is this trip to see Rem Lottman about?'

I explained the situation with Lesoto briefly, concluding: 'Whatever's going on, there's an element of corruption involved. That much I'm sure of.'

'So be it. But I married a man who didn't just react to his circumstances. I saw someone who had the ability to shape them.'

'Had?'

'Had, has. You should do whatever you need to with Lottman to gain influence over the station and your team.'

I looked at her. 'You mean be complicit in corruption?'

'Just don't become a victim of it, is all I'm saying. The rest is up to you.'

I eyed my watch. 'There's something else. There's a Ukrainian woman who was badly beaten up at the Royal Hotel on Sunday night. We can't find out the name of the guest – her attacker. Joost shut down the case.'

'You want me to find out?'

'Can you?'

'I'm an investigative journalist, Henk. How do you think a lot of these celebrity gossip stories emerge? Even the most exclusive hotels have an army of random insiders – bellhops, maintenance crews and suppliers. There are invariably ways and means.'

'Legal ones?'

'Would I reveal my sources?'

'The victim's name is Elena Luscovich.'

'Then leave it to me.' She squeezed my hand again. 'Leave it to Team van der Pol.'

My phone was ringing again. It was Max once more.

'I have some information for you,' he said.

'I thought we police had taxed you enough?'

'*You* amuse me.'

'I'm flattered. Go ahead.'

'Your woman just ordered a car for Schiphol Airport.'

'The English woman?'

'Correct. We can delay it, but not by much.'

'I'll be right there.'

*

I parked the car on Nieuwe Kerkstraat. Petra had come with me.

'Perhaps one day you'll take me to Brussels,' she said wistfully.

'You really want to go?'

'I've never been.'

'You're not missing much, but let's plan on it for another time.'

We walked around the corner onto Amstel and kissed goodbye. She carried on to the hotel; I stopped beside the Magere Brug.

Two sisters living on opposite sides of the river had built the famous wooden bridge to visit each other. I couldn't help but wonder why they hadn't just lived on the same side. Why did we Dutch have to make things so difficult for ourselves? And yet, the result was something wondrous, particularly at night: a thousand little light bulbs gently illuminating the old drawbridge, reflecting in the rippling currents beneath…

But it was mid-afternoon now. The clatter and rumble of a roller bag's wheels brought me back. Lucy Channing-West had emerged from number 81. Was it a short-let apartment? A friend's place? Dressed in another immaculately tailored suit, she looked up and down the street for her cab, then at her slim watch.

'Hi,' I said, approaching her. 'Henk van der Pol, Amsterdam police. We met at the Pelt house yesterday.'

'A miracle…' I could detect the sarcasm immediately. 'A policeman around here actually showing some interest,' she continued caustically. Her blue eyes held me, took in my bruise. 'I'm afraid I have a flight to catch.'

I made a show of looking around. 'I don't see any means of transport. Tell you what – I'm driving to Brussels; I could give you a lift.'

She looked at her watch again, unsure. 'Is the airport even on the way?'

'More or less. They're both south of here.'

'Most things are. Apart from the North Sea.'

'You've an excellent sense of geography. I can get you there in twenty minutes. Here, allow me.' I picked up her bag, leading her to my car.

I put her luggage in the small boot, then we got into the vehicle. 'It doesn't sound like you've had the best stay here,' I said, glad that I'd cleared out the passenger seat for Petra. Lucy Channing-West's expensive-smelling scent filled the car's interior.

'I've never known any constabulary take such little interest in a priceless artwork.'

'Art crime is a difficult one to assign resources to,' I said. 'People tend to see murders as more important.'

'Yet everyone acknowledges that Pelt's death and the burglary are linked. Do you know how much that Verspronck was insured for?'

I shrugged, heading towards the ring road. 'I thought priceless meant just that: you couldn't put a price on it.'

'It was actually over-insured.'

'What do you mean?'

Her phone rang. She ignored it. 'We had an argument over what we'd insure it for... compared to the amount the Norwegians wanted. Ever since that Munch went missing from their National Gallery in 1994, they've been cautious. But we didn't feel the Verspronck was worth that much today.'

Only a foreigner would say that about a Verspronck.

'It's a nine-figure sum,' she added.

Jesus. Over one hundred million euros?

'Not content with their sovereign wealth fund and all that bloody oil money sloshing around... a nine-figure sum!' She was incredulous. 'Do you have any idea what this will do to us? We're a small syndicate!'

Sometimes when you give people a chance to share their problems, the floodgates really open.

'And why the hell aren't you investigating it?' she demanded.

'How d'you know we're not?' I countered. 'Officer Bergveld –'

'Pah!' She cut me off. 'Don't even mention that man's name. He's done nothing.' She snorted, beside herself now. 'Nothing other than provide the paperwork for the Norwegians' insurance claim, that is.'

I just kept driving, and listening intently.

'Of course, the Norwegians have taken it all over. Their military police.'

I recalled the Scandinavian man at the Pelt house.

'What have they found out?' I asked.

'Nothing that I'm aware of! Their only concern is with substantiating the insurance claim, too.'

I couldn't believe that. The Norwegians would be intensely interested in finding the killer of one of their diplomats, I was sure. Only, they wouldn't have any means of leading an investigation here in Holland on their own. Why didn't they want to work with Bergveld and the Dutch police?

'Aren't they taking *any* investigative steps?'

'You tell me.' She looked at me.

I kept driving.

'It would appear not,' she said. 'Which is very unusual for the police in these circumstances, whoever's jurisdiction it is. Do you not agree?'

I couldn't disagree.

'I offered them everything: help using the Art Loss Register – not that the ALR's in any way difficult to use – but also access to our three-factor model.'

'What three-factor model?'

Her phone rang again. It was the taxi company; she let them know she no longer needed the cab. Then she answered my question. 'There are three types who steal valuable paintings, we've determined. As classified by motive.'

We were already on the E19, nearing the airport. It was too fast. I needed to slow down; I needed to hear this.

'The most common type is the "Delusionals",' she said. 'That is, the people who think they can actually sell the paintings, or hoard them for later sale. But tracking capabilities and auction-house regulations are only going in one direction.'

I thought of the big diamond heist at Brussels airport the prior year, and the gang getting caught as they tried to sell on the stolen diamonds: how do you even begin to sell a famous painting illicitly?

Then I remembered something. 'I thought the painting had already *been* stolen, during the war?'

'The title was legally clear. Your country grants dispossessed owners just three years to challenge a title change. Which brings us to the second type: the "Opportunists". Now these are the tricky ones. Valuable art has turned out to be surprisingly versatile collateral, in different kinds of exchanges.'

'What exchanges?'

'Don't you know?' She eyed me doubtfully. 'It can be anything from favours to large drug deals these days. Artworks are highly portable and can be moved easily across borders. Surely you know all this? Their financial value doesn't even need to be realised for them to allow other important deals to go through...'

A plane screeched low overhead.

'You mentioned three types of fine-art thieves.'

'Yes.' She unbuckled her seatbelt as I approached the front of the main airport terminal.

'The "Nutters". There are some people who just really like staring at a particular painting in the privacy of their own home.'

'Does appreciation of art necessarily make someone a nutter?'

'You haven't met some of these people.'

'Don't be so sure.'

She smiled primly and presented me with her business card. 'Should anything new come to light, please do let me know. And thank you for the ride, officer.'

'It was my pleasure.'

Or it would have been, had I not been thinking of Frank Hals.

25

BELGIUM AGAIN

I CONTINUED ON TO Brussels for my appointment with Rem Lottman, trying to work out the pattern between these events. Had Joost been right all along – at least in part – about the need to focus on Frank Hals?

I passed the turn-off to Rotterdam, and there the traffic slowed. It was past 4 p.m., and I'd agreed to meet Lottman at six. Gripping the steering wheel, I sat up, trying to see past the cars in front to where the hold-up was.

On the other side of the motorway, a car came into view – it was flipped over onto its roof, the tarmac slick-black around it, rainbow colours shimmering over the scene. There must have been a petrol spill. The screams and blares of a fire engine were coming from the opposite direction. Drivers on my side of the motorway had slowed to look. Traffic sped up once it got past the scene, the drivers just nosy about the fate of others.

Petra was calling me.

'*Hoi oi.*'

'I have some information for you,' she said.

'From the Royal? Already?' My wife had accomplished in two hours what we'd taken days to fail to do. 'How?'

'You know I can't reveal my sources,' she said. 'But the woman's client was a sheikh. From Abu Dhabi or Dubai, my source reckons. One of the Emirate countries, anyway.'

'To be clear, we're talking about the guest who booked the suite she stayed in?'

'To be clear, my source isn't sure whether the guy booked the suite himself or not. But this sheikh was in the bedroom the night the woman was attacked.'

'How does your source know that? Was he bringing them room service or something?' He could have been an eyewitness, I thought hopefully.

'Henk, I'm not joking when I say I can't reveal my sources. I may no longer be a journalist, but the journalistic ethic is still part of me.'

'And long may it remain there.'

'Oh look,' she said, distracted. 'There's a fire.'

'Huh?'

She said, 'I'm walking away from the Royal and there's black smoke on the horizon, the other side of the river.'

It seemed symbolic somehow. Was everything about to go up in flames, here *and* there?

'Do you want me to go on and get the sheikh's name?' she asked.

'Yes.'

But I could guarantee that this guy had already left the country, and I could see the connection now anyway.

'Will you take care of yourself in Brussels?' she asked. 'No more nasty bruises, please.'

'I'll try. And thank you. You've earned yourself a trip there, too, once I'm through with all this.'

'Aren't I the lucky girl? Can we stay on the Grand Place?'

'We can stay in the Palace of Brussels if it'd make you happy.'

*

I was still trying to piece together the different peoples' parts in the puzzle when I saw the turn-off to Antwerp Airport.

It was five minutes off the E19 and I was able to park

alongside the terminal building with ease, the structure tiny in comparison to Schiphol's.

I jogged in through the sliding doors, thinking back over the events that had taken place there yesterday morning. Would the same immigration guards be waiting beside arrivals?

No – when I got there, I found two different men.

'*Hoi*,' I said, pulling out my warrant card as I approached them. 'Henk van der Pol of the Amsterdam police force. I was here yesterday morning when a Ghanaian diplomat arrived.'

They conferred for a moment. 'You want Thierry and Loïc, but what's this about?'

'Your guys were suspicious of this diplomat – what he was bringing into the country. I'd like to ask them about it.'

'We're suspicious of everyone, you know that. Who is this diplomat?'

'His name's Lesoto.'

'Hold on.'

One of them disappeared through a grey door.

I eyed my watch. Lottman was one person I couldn't be late for.

The guard reappeared. 'We need some higher-level clearance for this,' he said.

'How about the attaché for the Dutch energy minister in the Council of Europe? Here's his assistant's number.' I waved my phone at him.

'All right, all right. Leave it with us overnight.'

'No, there's not enough time. I'm meeting with the attaché at six – I need to brief him. This whole bloody thing came out of nowhere.'

All law enforcement officials can relate to being hijacked by a last-minute briefing request from a superior.

The guard hesitated, then said in a low voice, 'With that guy, it wasn't so much what he was bringing in.'

'What was it then?'

'What he was taking *out* – without export clearance.'

I thought back to the exchange between Lesoto and myself in the back of the Bentley, when he'd shown me the Ghanaian Star. 'And this is a gift?' I'd asked him.

'Yes,' he'd replied.

'You're going to make someone very happy.'

'*Yes. I am*' – those were his exact words.

Lesoto himself was the happy someone…

And a sheikh had been treated to a night at the Royal with a high-end escort.

The picture was less clear when it came to the Norwegians, but I had no doubt now that a pattern was at play.

*

It was five minutes to six when I arrived at the address that Lottman's assistant had given me: a vast, glass complex just off the Square de Meeûs, a few hundred metres from the European Parliament building. Of all the property makeovers in Europe, this one is the most spectacular: a former industrial slum turned cash volcano.

I stubbed out my cigarette and entered the silvery-blue atrium. Two ornate easels were set up beside the escalators that connected to the atrium's upper level. One easel announced the *XXXII Symposium on Benefitting from the EU*. The text below referred to a twenty-eight-point checklist for securing funds from the Commission.

The neighbouring easel said simply: *ES – Grande Salle*.

The Energy Summit.

I took the escalator up, glancing above me at an enormous glass ceiling. The dimming sky was fractured by what looked to be cracks in the glass.

'We call it the Milky Way building,' a familiar voice said.

Rem Lottman was leaning over the railings, the dark material of his suit jacket bunching around his bulky shoulders. 'That ceiling allows you to see the stars at night.'

Lottman shook my hand. 'The ceiling alone cost one hundred

and fifty million euros and occasioned a memorable opening ceremony. It cracked three days later.' He shrugged and led me into an anteroom, away from the *grande salle*.

I was suddenly confused by where we were. 'What is this place? Part of the Parliament?'

'It's a "public-private", as we call them… it adapts to function. Please.'

We entered the anteroom and motion-sensor lights flickered on.

'I wanted to catch you before the delegates break for drinks,' he said. 'I'm glad I did – you look like you've been in a fist fight.'

I didn't respond to his comment about my bruise.

Down the side of the anteroom was a table on which glasses of champagne and canapés had been set out; at head height ran a band of windows, tinted silver-blue, which gave a panoramic view of the neighbouring room. Through the glass I watched a familiar figure enter – Muriel Crutzen, the Dutch energy minister, hounded by a group of hangers-on.

'Who are all those people?'

The necks and ears of the women sparkled, the wristwatches of the men, too. Their dark suits had a lustrous sheen that was obvious even through the tinted glass.

'Publicists, advisers, consultants…' Lottman replied. 'Advisers to consultants… consultants to advisers to consultants. All sucking on the EU's udders. Of course, they're all lobbyists, really. We all are, in the end.'

Maybe he was right. Had I, after all, not come to Brussels to lobby Lottman for influence over my boss?

White-jacketed waiters sailed around the room with trays of canapés and champagne.

'Those gentlemen in the far corner, glowing faintly orange: they're the nuclear lobby,' Lottman confided.

I narrowed my gaze.

'I'm kidding,' he said. 'Though nuclear is looking increasingly competitive – if you ignore the decommissioning costs. But then, this place is all about building, not dismantling. As in life, you either grow or you die.'

He helped himself to a glass of champagne. 'Want one?'

I shook my head, wishing for a beer. A Heineken would have done. There was none.

'Let me tell you a quick story,' Lottman began. 'It may seem odd that I'm sharing this, but from the time I first met you, I felt I could trust you, Henk. Rely on you even. Anyway, when I arrived here in Brussels, I proposed to the Commission a plan to save the EU half a billion euros of energy costs across their budgets – travel and facilities, mainly. That struck me as quite a win for them and the contributing countries. Can you imagine how the senior Commission member I approached responded?'

I shook my head.

'He told me that half a billion euros was less than two per cent of the Common Agricultural Policy's budget, and that no one would be interested. *No one here is rewarded for saving money. There's never been – and never will be – any glory in cutting budgets.*'

Lottman went on: 'But look at it this way. There hasn't been a war in Western Europe since the start of the European Project. And, judging by how the Second World War went, wars cost us infinitely more than any amount spent here.'

He drained his champagne. 'Enough chit-chat. Our Ghanaian friend – what do you have for me?'

'Something's up, Rem. Something smells bad.'

'Oh?' He stabbed a lobster tail with a cocktail stick.

'I went back to Antwerp Airport, quizzed the security staff there.'

'Why?' he asked, between mouthfuls.

'Because it was on the way here, and I was curious to know why they were suspicious when Lesoto arrived yesterday morning.'

'And why were they?'

'Don't you know?'

'No.' He swallowed, and stared at me.

'Well, it wasn't about what Lesoto was bringing into the country – it was about the things he was taking *out* without export clearance.'

'Are you implying that I misled you? I simply told you that he'd been having trouble with diplomatic pouches at the airports.'

Lottman was correct about that, at least.

'Lesoto is receiving gifts. Very valuable ones. The diamond he showed me is worth many millions of euros. But who's it from, and why does Lesoto have it? And there's more… there's Joost.'

Lottman's eyes narrowed.

'Joost wants me to focus on a drugs case that's not even in our precinct, which should be handled by the National Police Agency. Yet he doesn't want me to investigate a violent assault at an exclusive hotel, or the theft of a priceless painting.'

'Perhaps he believes drug-related crime is more important in Amsterdam than prostitution or stolen art,' Lottman said. 'Perhaps he believes that you're up to handling a prominent drugs case.'

Inwardly I recoiled: how did Rem Lottman know that the assault at the Royal involved a prostitute? Why had that news got through to him, when it wasn't even an approved police investigation?

'Perhaps Joost is right on both fronts,' Lottman added.

'There's a shadow organisation at play, just as there was with the informant-handling racket before – isn't there?'

'Please. Do you not think you're getting a little paranoid, Henk?'

He wiped his mouth with a napkin. For a second, I thought he was going to mop his brow.

'No, I don't.'

'Has Joost mentioned Lesoto to you?' he asked.

'Why would he?'

'He wouldn't,' Lottman said emphatically. 'Which is precisely my point. Why are we even talking about this? What I want is an update on Lesoto, which you promised.'

'But it's all related.'

He hesitated. 'How?'

'You know very well how.'

A svelte woman approached – his assistant, Miss Risotto? *Oil*, I mouthed.

Norway, the Emirates, Ghana: they were all big oil-producing countries.

Lottman had frozen.

As his assistant mumbled something about resuming, Stefan's text arrived: *CALL ME, IMPORTANT.* Lottman was locked in discussion with his assistant, so I stepped away and called Stefan; he answered immediately.

'You're damn right it's important,' I said low and urgent, before he had a chance to speak. 'Why were you calling a cab firm about a police matter without my authorisation? *I'm* your manager.'

'I can explain…'

'You'd better.'

'In two words: continued employment? The station's being closed down –'

'No it's not. Who asked you to track down that art insurer?'

'Bergveld,' he said in a small voice.

'Why?'

'I don't know; he just wanted to know her whereabouts, what was going on with her…'

I was about to read him the riot act but he continued: 'There's been a fire at East–West Trading Services.'

'What?'

'That company you asked me to investigate, the one making the planning application for coffee shops. It's been burned out.'

Malek's place.

'Find him.'

'Who?'

But before I could give Stefan directions, I felt a hand grip my arm.

26

GUILE AND INGENUITY

MISS RISOTTO HAD VANISHED.

So, too, had the bonhomie.

'What matters is sustainably secure energy sources,' Lottman was saying, steely eyed.

It was different to the phrase used by Muriel Crutzen in the TV debate that I'd watched with Petra. There, the energy minister had talked about 'sustainable energy security'.

Words matter, and never more so than when the ambiguity is stripped away.

'Where's it coming through? Rotterdam?'

'Where's *what* coming through?' He took a step towards me, the ends of his polished shoes centimetres from my scuffed boots.

'The oil, petroleum – whatever it is that you're receiving, on favourable terms, in exchange for these gifts.'

He glared ferociously at me.

And then a tiredness and despondency washed over his face. 'When the average Dutch voter gets in from work – with babies crying, baths to run and meals to cook – do you think he or she really cares how the heat and power arrives, so long as it *does* arrive?'

'That's an assumption.'

'That's realpolitik, Henk. And here's some more of it: What natural resources do we have in Holland? Forget about what we once had, elsewhere in the world. What do we have now? Today? Some flat earth and water… some tulips, for God's sake… and then the guile and ingenuity of our people.'

State-sponsored bribery… theft… something worse?

'Don't look so surprised. Governments have always traded treasures for valuable services. You know that.'

I shook my head.

'Look through that window.'

In the silvery-blue panorama, the jewellery and glassware glistened.

'Everyone here in Brussels is biddable,' he said.

I watched them smile, and laugh, and mouth assurances to one another.

'And what are we giving away here, in exchange for national energy security? Tiny little objects dug out of the ground, cut and polished. Dried oil paint on old canvases. Who cares about them, relative to the ability for broader society to enjoy fire, warmth and hot food? The social fabric is at stake here!'

Some part of Lottman had persuaded himself of the virtue of his crusade. Why didn't I just walk away from it all now?

There's a point in every man's life when his earlier hopes and aspirations must make peace with the realities of his circumstances. That is, if he is to become whole. Not good, nor bad – just whole.

'Why did *I* get the call?' I demanded.

'Which call?'

'That day I was in Rotterdam, you brought me here to Brussels to have me chaperone Lesoto. Why me?'

'The Norwegians had changed political course, gone all carbon-lite on us, now they'd made their sovereign fortune. The Russians were never an option, for obvious reasons. The Emirates and the Middle East remain about as predictable as Ajax in an off-season and that left Africa – or more specifically, Ghana.'

'But why didn't you just ask Joost's team to handle Lesoto?'

'Because I trust you. And things haven't been going so well elsewhere, in case you hadn't noticed.'

The beaten Ukrainian escort, the dead Norwegian diplomat… Christ.

'You need to clean house,' I said.

'Why do you think I'm sharing all this? We need new leadership on the ground, Henk. Someone who can see things from all angles.'

'What about the Norwegians?'

He stabbed glumly at another lobster tail. 'It's a mess.'

'Life's a mess,' I said. 'So what happened?'

'When the Norwegians reneged on us, we needed the Verspronck back.'

'You stole the bloody painting back?' I asked, stunned.

'National budgets are not limitless, Henk! Especially not after all this has been paid for,' and he waved a hand around us.

'A man died!'

'I merely told Joost to get the painting back,' he exclaimed, 'by legal means!'

'So what the hell went wrong?'

'There needs to be a full internal enquiry,' he conceded. 'Will you help with it? You're the one standing apart from all this.'

Another call was incoming, this time Petra's.

'I need to take this.' I turned away from Lottman. '*Hoi.*'

'You… you sound on edge,' my wife stammered.

'So do you.'

'When are you back?'

'Later tonight. Why? What's up?'

'I don't know…' There was a rumbling in the background.

'Tell me,' I pressed.

All the while, Lottman was looking on.

'There's a group of guys hanging around the boat.'

'What guys?'

'Making a hell of a racket.' She tried to make light of it. 'They're on motorbikes…'

'What's wrong?' Lottman asked. He was alongside me now.

'Lock the doors and hatches now, Petra. I'm going to call Johan. Where's Nadia?'

'In Paris still,' she said. 'Henk, I'm scared.'

'Hang on. Stay on the line.' I turned to Lottman. 'I need your phone.'

'Why? What's going on?'

'My wife's in danger!'

'Then let me help you. Where is she?'

'Help me by giving me your phone!'

He did.

I knew Johan's number by heart. No reply. He wouldn't recognise the number of course. We were losing time.

'Just hold on, Petra, I'm going to try to call Johan from my phone. I'll call you right back.'

'Don't leave me!' she said. But I had to.

Lottman took his phone back and began dialling a number.

'Henk,' Johan's voice came on the line.

'Johan, where are you? Petra's in trouble.'

'What's going on? Where is she?'

'At the boat.'

'I can be there in ten.'

'Please hurry.'

'What's the threat?'

'The Ten Guns. One of their guy's offices was firebombed. They apparently think I may've had a hand in it, or at least know who has.'

'Jesus.'

Capability, intent.

'Please do what you can,' I said.

'I will.'

As I hung up, I was already walking out of the anteroom,

Lottman following.

'I've asked our security people to send a car around to your houseboat on Entrepotdok. They'll be there in less than five minutes.'

I turned to look at him.

'Let me help you, Henk.'

I let him.

'Just one question,' he said. 'Who's this Johan?'

I realised I'd handed Lottman the phone number of the man who'd shot Zsolt Tőzsér.

*

I was soon back on the E19, charging back to Amsterdam, my speed not dropping below 140 kilometres per hour. I tried Lottman's phone to find out how his security people had fared at the boat, but his line was busy. *Damn it.*

Would he be as good as his word?

For a few minutes everything was quiet – just the lights and signs on the motorway sweeping past – then my ringtone broke through: Johan.

'Are you there?' I asked him.

'At the boat, yes. But it's empty. There's no one here.'

Fuck.

'Stay there, Johan. I'll call you in a moment.'

I tried Lottman again.

'Henk.'

'Rem, thank God. Do you have my wife?'

'Yes, our team picked her up. They've taken her to a safe location.'

'Where? Can I speak with her?'

'At any moment, I'm sure. They'll call you once they've found a secure place.' He paused. 'Just think over our conversation earlier. I need your help clearing up this mess.'

'Please can you arrange for Petra to call me?'

He said he would, and hung up.

While waiting for Petra to get in touch, I called Johan back. 'She's safe,' I told him.

'A lucky escape,' he said. 'But that motorbike gang won't give up easily.'

'I know.' I was thinking fast. 'Johan, is the boat open?'

'It is. Looks like she left in a hurry.'

'There's a spare key under the plant pot beside the door to the cabin. Could you lock it up, but before you do, go down into the bathroom. In the cabinet above the sink you'll find a reefer.'

A reefer containing highly distinctive, local weed...

'Henk, I'm not looking for a hit right now –'

'That's good, given what I'm about to ask: take it back to yours and put it in your gun case with your P225.'

The weapon he'd used to dispose of Zsolt Tőzsér.

'Huh?' he said, confused.

'Wipe everything for fingerprints. Take the gun case and the reefer to the scene of the firebomb and leave it somewhere obvious.'

I gave him Malek's address.

'I don't understand,' he said. 'Leaving a gun at the scene like that: it's a sign among those Eastern European bike gangs that this was a grudge attack. You know that, right?'

I did.

'And it's my army weapon,' he added mournfully.

'It's time to say goodbye to the evidence of Tőzsér's shooting.'

'You're trying to lay the blame on someone else? Is that the point of including the reefer?'

'I'm just directing blame for the firebombing where it belongs. Look, we're wasting time. Please just get over there as soon as possible.'

'There may still be fire crews at the scene.'

'I hope so. That way they'll find the case quickly. They'll be scouring for clues. Be careful how you go about it but I know you can make this work. God's speed, Johan.' I ended the call before he had a chance to quiz me further.

The motorway lights hypnotised me for a few minutes, calming me a little. My speed had hit 150 kilometres per hour. That was OK. But why hadn't Petra called? I tried her number to no avail, then Stefan's.

'Boss.'

'Where are you?'

'Outside the offices of East–West Trading – or what's left of it. I didn't know who you wanted me to find, so thought I'd just come here to await further instruction.'

'You did the right thing. What can you see?'

'The fire's out but smouldering. There are a couple of fire crew members… and a couple of guys on bikes –'

'OK Stefan, stand down. I need you to go somewhere else, down at the docks.'

'What address?'

I gave it to him.

'But that's Frank Hals's boat, right?'

*

I no longer doubted Lottman's word, but waiting for Petra's call was agony. Somewhere past Rotterdam I caught sight of a two-car convoy approaching on the other side of the central reservation: big vehicles, the red and blue lights of the lead car flashing past. I dropped my speed.

Johan called again.

'OK, it's goodbye to the Sig Sauer P225. And a very good reefer, by the smell of it.'

'Good riddance,' I said. 'To the gun at least.'

'What now?' he asked.

'Meet me down at the harbour, would you?' I gave him the address of Hals's boat. 'You'll find one of my guys there: Stefan. I'll join you both soon.' I was still thirty minutes from Amsterdam.

'What's going on?'

'Fireworks, if the plan holds.'

'Count me in.'

Finally, my phone rang again and it was the number I'd been waiting for.

'Petra?'

Pause.

'Petra, are you there?'

'Henk.'

She sounded normal, thank God.

'Where are you? I've been beside myself with worry.'

'These gentlemen wouldn't let me use the phone till now. How on earth did you find them? I must say, they are quite fine specimens of manhood. Which was a damn good thing, given the look of those bikers back there! No shortage of news for the neighbours to gossip about, anyway.'

'Where are you?'

'On my way to Brussels. Where are you?'

'Heading back to Amsterdam.'

Had I just passed her in the convoy?

'Henk! You promised me a trip to Brussels. Will you turn around again?'

'Small matter to attend to down at the docks.'

'As always.'

I said nothing.

'I'll be waiting,' she said, ending the call.

I hung up and began navigating my way onto the Amsterdam ring road – heading towards the harbour.

27

THE BATTLE

'WHAT ARE WE LOOKING at?'

I'd scrambled quietly alongside Johan and Stefan, in the dark shadows behind a couple of dinghies. There was a slight mist in the sky, obscuring the stars. The air was still, the water too.

'Hals has unmoored his boat,' Stefan said.

I'd noticed that. The gangplank was gone. The vessel sat four or five metres away from the harbour wall. He must have done it some time before, given the stillness of the water.

'He's prepared for trouble,' Johan said in a low voice.

The boat was almost totally dark. Just the occasional shadow moving across a porthole. The hoarse bark of a large dog – a guard dog – came across the water.

'The bikers got here five minutes ago,' Stefan whispered, pointing down the harbour wall.

There, a row of motorcycles glinted.

I was still seeing the sodium lamps of the motorway sweep past but, as my eyes adjusted, I caught sight of one of the bikers who'd ridden up to the police station that afternoon. He was still wearing his dark glasses. Another biker emerged from the shadows.

'Looks like they got the message at the scene of the fire,' Johan said.

'Indeed.' I patted him on the shoulder, congratulating him on his work. 'You did well too, Stefan,' I added. 'I don't imagine the fire crews stood a chance of taking that gun case away for examination, once these boys caught sight of it.'

The distinctive marijuana in the reefer had led them straight to the black hull in front of us, but how would they gain access, now that it was floating free? Doubtless that's what they were conferring about, the murmur of their conversation indecipherable. Their air of calm suggested they had a plan.

At that moment, the low trundle of an engine rounded the corner of the dock. A boat came into view, cutting a wide 'V' in the dark water. I recognised the metal shape and dim livery immediately: it was an old police boat, decommissioned. Through the reinforced windows of the bridge, I could just make out Malek's determined expression, bathed pale-green in the light of the boat's instrumentation.

'Where the hell did he get that from?' Stefan wondered aloud.

The boat had an open deck at the back. As Malek pulled up to the harbour wall, the bikers began clambering in, passing down y-shaped objects: Kalashnikov rifles, with their distinctive curved clips.

'Shouldn't we call someone?' Stefan asked.

'Who?' Johan said.

'The station? Tactical firearms? The KLPD?'

'Keep your voice down,' I whispered.

Johan was frowning at his mobile. 'Reception's not good in these farther reaches of the harbour.'

Stefan held up his smartphone. 'Mine's fine –'

'No it isn't.' Johan took the phone and tossed it. It landed beside one of the fibreglass dinghies in front of us with a soft plop. I was only glad it hadn't hit the small, metal outboard motor.

Stefan was too startled to speak.

'That's a new iPhone,' he finally managed.

'Was,' I corrected him. I was glad his call history and location records had disappeared with it.

'You're better off without it,' I assured him. 'We'll get you a new one, don't worry.'

All were now aboard the ex-police boat, and it was puttering over to the larger vessel. I noticed a figure crouching above deck on Hals's boat.

The bikers didn't get within twenty metres of the figure before he stood.

At first, I thought he was carrying a musical instrument – some kind of strange horn. Then I recognised it to be a rocket-propelled grenade launcher, held over his arm. The RPG was pointing directly at the ex-police boat.

The man taking aim must have faced harder shots than this.

Malek's boat engine thrummed, the water around it churning white as it manoeuvred itself side-on. The bristling barrels of the Kalashnikovs pointed up protectively, like cactus spikes.

Frank Hals appeared on deck beside the man with the RPG launcher. Clutching his side, he looked a little like Napoleon, only in shorts.

'You've interrupted my supper,' he called out, his voice clear over the water. 'You should leave now, before I really become upset.'

'You burned down my office,' Malek countered.

'Of course I did. I don't know who the hell you are or where you're from, but there are ways and means of going about business here.'

Malek was silent. I could almost sense his anger pulsing through the night air.

'There are protocols to be observed,' Hals continued.

Still Malek was silent – contemplating a negotiated solution? Heaven forbid…

'Do you have your Zippo?' I hissed at Johan.

He looked confused.

'Stefan,' I said, 'you don't need that scarf around your neck.'

'Huh?'

'It's about to get a lot warmer around here. Hand me your scarf.'
They did as I asked.

'What are you doing?' Johan said.

'Back in the Anglo-Dutch wars,' I replied, unscrewing the cap of the fuel tank on the dinghy in front of us, 'do you know how we really gained advantage over the English?'

I stuffed most of Stefan's cotton scarf into the opening. Both men awaited my answer.

'Hell-burners,' I said, draping an end of the scarf behind the stern. 'Fire ships, that is. Here, untie that rope.'

As Johan set the dinghy adrift, I flicked the Zippo and held the flame beside the straggling end of the scarf, checking the disposition of the bigger boats one last time. The scarf was already damp with petrol and it lit with a little *whoosh*, the orange flame dancing in the darkness but thankfully hidden from view behind the dinghy's stern.

'Help me with this.' The interior of the dinghy held a few centimetres of water, providing crucial ballast. 'Let's get this party started,' I said with a grimace; we gave the stern a good shove, careful not to topple after it into the stagnant water.

Across the water, Malek was saying in broken English: 'So maybe we talk.'

Hals was quiet, apparently considering Malek's suggestion. Perhaps he was impressed by Malek's show of force. At any rate, he wasn't focusing on the dinghy gliding towards the two boats...

'Maybe,' Hals said. 'But at a time and place I choose. Not now.'

It reminded me of the way he'd left things with me, saying he couldn't tell me more about that stolen painting till the following morning. Always *mañana* with Frank. Malek's head was turned towards him, trained on him, or perhaps trained on the RPG launcher beside him – as were the barrels of the Kalashnikovs.

For a second, I thought the fuse I'd lit had gone out. I could only see a speck of orange. It was very quiet, none of the men were speaking. Surely they'd caught sight of the drifting boat by now. The human eye is too good at picking up peripheral movement, especially in times of peril.

The dinghy didn't make it as far as the larger vessels. The whole scene brightened as it exploded, a ball of orange leaping high into the air; I caught the startled faces of the armed bikers, even the one wearing sunglasses.

Burning pieces of fuel tank rained down as the Kalashnikovs crackled into life. There was a hiss as the RPG's white vapour trail snaked across from Hals's boat to Malek's; the windows of the old police boat blew out and fire engulfed the frame, smoke hurrying blackly skywards. There was yelling, and more shooting, and general confusion, and then the whole scene shone a dazzling yellow-white.

I could feel the oxygen rushing past my ears. The police boat's much bigger fuel tank had exploded.

I remembered my dad telling me once about the Allies bombing Dresden, and how the bomber crews would become mesmerised by the colours of the fires burning below.

'Well, you certainly pushed the boat out this time,' Johan said. Greens and rich mauves rippled across his face.

There was laughter from Hals's boat as a loud crack split the air again. Something whistled low and very fast over the water, missing the molten metal of the ex-police boat but smacking into the harbour wall. We felt the impact from our hiding place.

He'd fired his old cannon.

But Hals's fun didn't last long. The force of the police boat exploding had pushed the burning dinghy towards his hull. I swore I could see Hals, reaching for his hosepipe once more, through the flames now licking up the side of his wooden vessel; the fire caught hold in several places as more men emerged on deck. The old clipper was soon listing, and one of the men leapt into the burning water. His shrieking dissuaded the others from joining him.

'Maybe this is the end of Frank Hals, too,' Stefan said, perhaps thinking about the Holendrecht case we could never crack…

'From your lips to God's ears,' I said.

Blue lights flickered in the distance. The drone and dull thudding of a helicopter approached low over the skyline: a police chopper, its spotter light slicing through the thick smoke. The pungent smell was unmistakable – Hals's prized cannabis crop, thirty years in the making, was crackling away, the sparks jumping high into the air.

'Let's take off,' I said.

Stefan had already done so.

Perhaps it was disappointment more than the fire itself that got to Hals in the end. Evidently he didn't abandon his vessel. I never found out what he'd planned to share with me the following day about the stolen Verspronck.

But I got a pretty good idea from elsewhere.

*

Joost's call came in as expected. 'Jesus Christ, Henk, what just happened down in the eastern docks?'

The same old Joost. It appeared he knew nothing of my discussions with Rem Lottman that evening.

'You wanted a result with Hals,' I said.

'I didn't authorise you to bring the bloody Battle of Medway to Amsterdam!'

I couldn't help but be impressed by his knowledge of naval history. The seventeenth-century battle had seen the Dutch fleet trounce England's Royal Navy in the River Medway, near London.

'Multiple suspects dead,' Joost went on. 'Two firefighters passed out, the fumes were so potent!'

'Come now,' I said. 'There are worse ways for a firefighter to wind up on paid leave.'

'There was also a very valuable painting aboard Hals's boat!'

'That's a problem,' I said, suddenly seeing the bigger picture. 'You got Hals's crew to steal the Verspronck back and harbour it for you? Only... he wouldn't then give it up?'

'These are absurd allegations!' Joost yelled down the phone.

So that's why Joost had been so intent on me getting the goods on Hals.

The cornered animal is the most dangerous they say, and I wasn't about to give any intimation of the enquiry coming Joost's way. That news needed to arrive from Rem Lottman.

I wondered how much blame Joost would try to push down onto Bergveld.

I thought too of Lucy Channing-West: it looked like her Lloyds syndicate would have to get used to their loss. But I didn't feel any regret. That *Girl Dressed in Blue* had come from nowhere and gone nowhere; there was always the one in Rijksmuseum for everyone to appreciate.

Lars Pelt, the Norwegian diplomat killed in the re-theft of the painting, was another matter.

For that, and for the woman beaten into unconsciousness at the Royal Hotel, Joost would have to hang.

But first, I wanted to see my family.

28

GRAND PLACE

PETRA AND I STROLLED in the evening sun towards the old main square of Brussels, past the food and drink shops that led to it – the *chocolatiers*, the *biscuitiers* and *sucrecuitiers*. The locals had devised a fine way of trying to kill themselves, with their diet of rich chocolate, strong beer and giant waffles.

'Oh Henk,' Petra said as we entered the Grand Place itself. It was like something out of a Brothers Grimm fairy tale: all intricate stonework and glinting gold, the ornate rooflines in sharp, warm relief thanks to the sun's low rays.

'We *should* have stayed at the Amigo,' she said.

The five-star Amigo was situated just off the Grand Place. But the prices there hadn't been so friendly. Lottman had offered to pay but it didn't feel right. Besides, I liked the Metropole – five minutes' walk away – with its Belle Époque heft.

I was less appreciative of Lottman going radio silent on me. It had been two days since the Energy Summit and the events at the harbour; my three calls in the meantime had gone unreturned.

We entered the square and joined the other tourists in pointing, photographing, sauntering. 'When are we meeting Nadia again?' I asked.

'Nadia and Sergei,' she corrected me. 'In five minutes. Here, at the Brasserie de L'Ommegang.'

It was a stone-fronted building with window boxes and a

large carved goose over the front door.

Had I somehow killed the golden one – my relationship with Rem? The enquiry into the Amsterdam police that I'd pushed for... had it somehow engulfed Lottman too? What was going on? Why wasn't he in contact?

'There they are!' Petra said. I could make out our daughter, sat holding hands with a well-built, fair-haired man who looked several years older than her.

My phone was ringing.

PRIVATE NUMBER.

'This could be Lottman,' I said.

'Hallo?' the voice on the phone said.

'Who's this?'

'Thierry. Immigration, Antwerp Airport.'

'Oh,' I said, disappointed. 'Now's not a good time.'

'Then I'll be brief: Lesoto left for London yesterday. One-way ticket.'

'Add him to the list,' I said. The list of foreign diplomats and dignitaries to be detained for questioning upon arrival at any Benelux or Dutch airport. Already on it was a certain sheikh.

'Look, I can tell you're busy,' Thierry said. 'Is there someone from your team I should coordinate with?'

'Actually, there is.'

I gave him Stefan's name. I'd moved Stefan out of front-line policing, back into station operations and surveillance. It was better for him and the team. This was management: deciding which pieces fitted where on the chessboard.

I hung up as I approached my daughter and her boyfriend. Petra was already chatting away animatedly.

Sergei was smartly dressed and mature, and Nadia appeared to be truly at ease with him. He insisted on buying a bottle of champagne and Petra quickly gave in, laughing. He asked me a series of polite, deferential questions: about my career as a policeman, mostly. Just the one question about the drama at the harbour, which had been all over the news. I asked a couple of questions in return – about his films, his investments – and all the while his pale eyes scrutinised me. Instead of me assessing his appropriateness for my daughter, he was searching me, weighing me up. Perhaps this was just how Russian businessmen had been taught to survive in the motherland.

All the while, the old doubts and bogeymen were crowding around me. What had I managed to accomplish by first dismantling a highly productive police-informant network in Amsterdam and now ending a system that provided cheaper energy to the whole of Holland?

Was I getting my just deserts in Rem Lottman abandoning me?

'What do you think, Mr van der Pol?'

'Please call me Henk,' I told Sergei. 'Say again?'

'Bear hunting? Would you like to try it some time?'

'We're talking about St Petersburg, Dad.' Nadia rolled her eyes.

'Ooh,' Petra said, 'we could go to the Hermitage! Nadia, have we not always wanted to go?'

I was about to ask what was wrong with the branch of the Hermitage in Amsterdam when my phone rang again. It was Johan. I almost rejected the call, then realised how much I wanted to hear my oldest friend's voice.

'Henk, where are you?'

'Brussels, with the family. You?'

'At home. I just got back from visiting the harbour again. There are quite a few onlookers still down there.'

I excused myself from the table. 'That end of the harbour has never seen so much attention.'

'No,' Johan agreed. 'Is there any news?'

'About what?'

'Er… the enquiry, Henk. Whether it extends back to the informants?'

I sighed. 'It's too early to tell. These things take time. There's a big mess with the Norwegians to sort out. But Joost's team is on the way out – that much is clear. And they were the main threat.'

'They can still accuse us,' he said. 'They may have all the more reason to do so, and far less to lose now.'

I couldn't refute that, other than to say: 'As long as Rem Lottman's in our corner, we should be all right.'

As long as…

'All right.' Johan sounded unsure. 'Let me know.'

'Okey-dokey.' I hung up.

I walked back to the table, where Petra was sitting alone. 'Where did Nadia and the bear hunter go?' I asked, surprised.

'He has a name, Henk,' my wife said, finishing her champagne and taking my hand. 'They went to see a show. Told me to tell you goodbye. Let's take a stroll.'

'What show?' I said, stung. 'There *are* no shows in Brussels!'

'Perhaps they just wanted some time alone together. Perhaps they're heading back to their hotel room early, who knows?'

I grimaced. 'I thought you didn't like the sound of him?'

'Whatever gave you that idea?'

'You told me so. In Rotterdam.'

'That's before I met him! I've actually grown quite fond of him. He clearly cares a great deal for her.'

The Grand Place was cast in twilight shadow. On the opposite side of the square was a higher frontage, catching the last of the light. It was dated in gilt – *1697*.

'I guess they have their own lives to lead,' I said.

Petra squeezed my hand.

'As do we. I wonder whether we might do better elsewhere.'

She looked at me. 'What are you talking about?'

'All this history. All this looking back to the golden age – so far in the past. It would be nice to live in a place that was looking forward. That believed its best years were still ahead of it.'

'Oh no,' she said wearily, 'not this again.'

At regular intervals during our marriage – roughly measured in half-decades – I'd floated the idea of moving to the US. Specifically New York City – the part of the country instantly familiar to us Dutch, with our shared history...

'Why would you want to do that, when your career has just got a second wind?'

I didn't mention anything about Lottman's silence.

'Besides...' she said. 'We just agreed to go to St Petersburg in August.'

'Did we?'

'We did,' she said, contentedly. 'Sergei is taking you bear hunting.'

My phone was ringing. I grabbed for it, but again it wasn't the private number I'd been hoping for.

It was Liesbeth.

Which was strange.

'What's up?' I said.

'I just wondered if you needed any help.'

'Help with what?' I asked, confused.

'You haven't heard?'

'Heard what? What's happened?'

'Henk, it's just appeared on TV, as breaking news...'

'What has? Tell me, Liesbeth!'

'Rem Lottman... it appears he's been kidnapped.'

Part III:

Ransom

29

AN UNFORGIVING MISTRESS

THINGS WERE NOT GOING to plan. The woman on the phone was having trouble breathing.

'Where was Lottman going?' I demanded.

The woman was Francine, Rem Lottman's assistant.

I caught my wife glaring at me from across the hotel room. The room was hot, airless; the front of my shirt was damp and I could feel the sweat trickling down my back. What was meant to be a fun trip to the Belgian capital was turning into a nightmare.

'I'm not sure that I can tell you.'

'*Why?*'

'I don't know if I can even talk to you.'

I shifted uncomfortably. Most people would be terrified, I conceded, if they were the assistant to an attaché in the Council of Europe and that man had just been kidnapped; she could easily have been abducted with him.

But what were the facts here? Did we even know for sure he'd been kidnapped? Could he have collapsed, been attacked?

For the media, the inference was clear. And, more than ever, the media shaped police priorities.

'What do you mean by that?' I asked her.

'Mean by what?'

'Not knowing if you can talk to me?'

'I've… I've been given a list of people I can speak to.'

'Which people?'

213

I caught the sharp edge to my question. It was possible the call was being recorded.

'You're not...' she stammered. 'You're not on the list.'

'Who gave you the list?'

The same security personnel who'd failed to protect Rem Lottman in the first place? The ones who'd intervened to save my wife from a Ukrainian biker gang in Amsterdam, when they should have been focused on their man?

Francine was silent, save for her gulps of breath.

'You know that I'm a Dutch policeman, and that I'm well acquainted with Rem. You know we met in the days leading up to his disappearance. Like everyone, I'm just trying to find out what happened to him. Don't you want that too?'

A little cry escaped her.

'Give me *something* to go on!' I yelled.

'Henk!' my wife reproved me.

'I've...' Francine began.

'What?' I prompted.

Did she blame herself? I suddenly saw that this might be a more interesting path to travel down.

'Don't make yourself feel the guilt of not doing all you could have done. Guilt can be a very unforgiving mistress. I should know.'

'I shared pretty much everything with the investigators!' she cried.

'*Pretty much?*'

Petra eyed me once more. She'd stopped flicking through the Hotel Metropole's in-house magazine.

'He went to see his *amie*,' Francine said.

A lover? I assumed there was an 'e' on the end of *amie* – that his lover was female – but when it came down to it, all I knew about Lottman's personal life was that he was a bachelor. Being a senior politician and yet unmarried wasn't so odd these days. Politics could be almost as unforgiving as the police force in

214

the way it treated married life. I gave my wife a glance that was supposed to be reassuring. I'm not sure it worked.

'Please give me more details,' I said to Francine.

'Who's this?' A male voice had come on the line.

'Henk van der Pol, Amsterdam police. I was with Lottman at the Energy Summit –'

'Don't interfere with an official enquiry.'

There was a click and then a continuous, dull tone.

*

Petra set her magazine down beside the full fruit bowl on a low table.

'Lottman was visiting a lover the night he disappeared – according to his assistant,' I told her.

'Really,' my wife said, raising one eyebrow and crossing her arms, a combination that spelled trouble.

I suddenly craved outside air, and a cigarette.

'Henk, we came here to be with our daughter. To get away from all this.'

'All what?' I asked. 'Rem Lottman's security team saving you from a gang of psychotic bikers?'

'And what – *who* – put me in that situation in the first place?' She stood up forcefully.

She was right.

I let my head fall into my hands. My brow was hot and damp.

Petra put her hand on my shoulder. 'This is not your responsibility.'

I looked up at her. 'That's debatable. What's not debatable is that, without Rem Lottman, I'm finished. He was backing me against Joost.'

The Amsterdam police commissioner had wanted to get rid of me for longer than I could remember.

My wife sat back down opposite me. 'I thought you said *Joost* was finished.'

'I thought he was, until now.'

215

She picked an overripe plum from the fruit bowl but let it fall back in again. 'Could there be something else going on here?'

'Huh?' I said, massaging my temples.

'When we first met, what case were you working on?'

How could I forget? The kidnapping of Freddy Heineken in 1983: one of a spate of abductions of high-profile business people – the Van der Valk hotel family, Albert Heijn's grandson... For a brief period in the 1980s, Holland overtook Colombia as the kidnap centre of the world.

Even in that context, the Heineken case stood out, for the ease with which the kidnappers had extracted a ransom of thirty-five million guilders (fifteen million euros) and achieved notoriety. My role in the investigation had been peripheral, but the wounds had barely healed – throughout the police force. If we couldn't keep a man like Freddy Heineken safe, who *could* we protect?

Had those wounds just been reopened?

'It's not about that,' I said.

'Then what is it about? I'm sure the Belgian police will have their best people on this. Let them do their job.'

I didn't want to get into my feelings towards Rem. I didn't understand them fully myself. Feelings of friendship?

No, it was a deeper reliance than that.

'I'm assisting an enquiry into the Amsterdam police force at Lottman's behest. Without Lottman backing it, I'm exposed.'

'You haven't mentioned this.' Having been a features writer for *Het Parool*, Petra was trained to seek the scoop.

'I couldn't. It's highly confidential.' I had to tell her now because I needed her to do something for me. 'The government was running a covert operation via senior personnel in the Amsterdam police force and various foreign diplomats, exchanging gifts for energy-supply contracts with favourable terms. The diplomats were all from oil-producing countries.'

She narrowed her eyes. 'What kind of gifts?'

'Fifty-carat diamonds. A Verspronck painting no one knew existed.' I paused. 'Nights with high-end Ukrainian escorts.'

'That escort at the Royal Hotel who was beaten up?' Her mouth fell open. 'What was Rem Lottman's role in this?'

'It's not clear. I'm realising there's much I don't know about the man. But by the time I confronted him over it – at the Energy Summit – he wanted everything to be cleaned up, and he wanted my help doing that.'

'This enquiry you just mentioned?'

'Yes.'

I wiped the sweat from my forehead. 'The fallout's bad. A dead Norwegian diplomat, a painting taken back from them… a powerful Ghanaian diplomat put on "do not enter" lists at Benelux airports. That sheikh, too… there are a lot of powerful people suddenly upset with us.'

'Willing to kidnap?'

'Who knows? Kidnapping is how powerful figures seek redress in the criminal world and the people involved in this haven't exactly been law-abiding, have they?'

'Have you told the investigating team?'

'I haven't had the chance. They've already shut me out.'

She gave me a sceptical look. 'You'll talk with them in the morning though, won't you?'

'*Cherchez la femme*,' I said. 'Rem's assistant said that his last known move was going off to see his lover…'

Petra was shaking her head when something seemed to occur to her. 'What's his assistant like?'

I recalled seeing Francine the night of the Energy Summit.

'Young, well turned out… now scared. Everything you'd expect of an assistant to a power player who's been abducted –'

'Sexy?'

'You could say.'

Was *Francine* his mistress?

'You always ask the right questions –'

She'd already seen where I was going, and waved her hands in front of her now. 'No Henk, not again…'

'Someone needs to locate and quiz the lover, fast.'

'You're starting to sound like a tabloid editor!'

'Rem would have confided in that person.'

'The police team investigating will find out. Anyway, what about the rest of the family?'

It was a good point. His parents… did he have siblings? 'I'll ask Liesbeth to look into it.'

'Not *that* family,' Petra cried. 'Ours! Don't even bother to ask for my help until you've made time for Nadia *and* Sergei.'

'When?'

'Now, in Brussels! And, the trip to St Petersburg we talked about.'

I had no choice. 'Deal.'

My phone rang before Petra had a chance to say more. It was Stefan.

'Boss – you seen the latest news?'

Picking up the hotel room's remote control, I flicked on the TV.

'The kidnappers just released an image,' Stefan said. 'You should take a look.'

30

THE PHOTOGRAPH

MY HEART ALMOST STOPPED when I saw it: an unkempt Lottman against a dull background, holding up a folded copy of *De Telegraaf*.

I stepped closer to the TV screen. It was yesterday's edition of the paper in his hands. Though he was physically bigger, Lottman looked just like Freddy Heineken in the photo; it was the exact same arrangement as in the photograph taken of the captive beer tycoon in 1983.

What was the wide-eyed expression on his face – surprise? Submission… humiliation… resignation? Was this a man who'd undergone a psychological earthquake, whose every assumption in life had been shaken? Or was there still some political calculation behind those dark pupils, trying to send a message over the heads of his captors?

Three decades ago, I'd stared at an eerily similar image for hours, trying to observe, rather than assume, the dominant emotion. The more I'd looked, the harder it had become, the photo acting like a mirror of sorts, trapping my own feelings – fatal for any objective, facts-based investigation… and yet there had been as much going on in those dark eyes as in one of Rembrandt's self-portraits (the later ones, when the old master had gone broke).

Lottman wasn't in pyjamas like Freddy Heineken. He wore his suit and tie as though everything were normal, although

– like his black hair and thick eyebrows – his clothes were dishevelled; the knot of his tie was severely askew. Evidently he'd been manhandled. His fleshy cheeks had reddened. From anger – or exertion, perhaps?

Or was it the heat in the room where the photo had been taken?

I kicked the bed's baseboard, vexed by my lack of access to the investigation.

Then I looked again at the newspaper Rem was holding up. Dutch was of course spoken in Belgium and *De Telegraaf* was widely available here. Still, the choice of paper was significant. The headline looked innocuous in comparison to the 'original', the title of which was burned into the memories of anyone who'd worked the case: *POSSIBLE TO TRACE HEINEKEN KIDNAPPERS*.

This time it read: *STALEMATE IN BRUSSELS...*

The rest of the headline was hidden by the fold of the newspaper.

I studied the rest of the photo.

The background was different. The original had been just like an Old Masters painting: a mustardy-green in the middle darkening to a blackish-brown at the extremities. This one was dull grey and yet there was a slight shimmer. I took a picture of the digital TV screen with the camera on my phone just before the image vanished, replaced by a perfectly coiffed newscaster in her studio. She was speaking French and describing Rem as a *haut fonctionnaire*, a label that would guarantee him a certain type of police attention here in Brussels.

'Boss, you still there?' Stefan said over the phone.

'Yes, I just saw it.' I eyed my watch. 'We need to get a closer look at that photo.'

'Er... sure. But how?'

It was a good question, to which I had no answer – yet.

*

220

The Federal Judicial Police building on Koningsstraat was where the local investigation would be led from, I knew. I called the main number as I walked over there early the next morning. It rang without being answered or going to voicemail.

Frank van Tongerloo, the *chef d'enquête*, hadn't invited me over – although he hadn't told me not to come either. A Flemish name for the man leading the case in French: nothing about this situation was straightforward anymore. The Flemish disliked the Dutch, I reminded myself – particularly 'haughty Amsterdammers'.

The Brussels air was soft yet already warm; the day promised to be another scorcher. I approached 202 Koningsstraat, a large new building that the Belgian Federal Police were still in the midst of moving into, by the look of it.

It had a bare, high atrium. The only sign of life was the security staff behind a glass wall. I announced myself and was surprised to learn that Commissioner van Tongerloo was available to see me.

He came down five minutes later: a heavyset man with pale, alert eyes that revealed professional mistrust – so often the way with policemen. He wore plain clothes of course, the only item identifying his status the plastic badge clipped to his waist.

I introduced myself, showing him my Dutch warrant card. 'New digs?' I asked, looking around.

'Yes,' he said. 'I can't take you through to Operations, I hope you understand. Come through here.'

He led me across the atrium. I tried to imagine what 'Operations' might look like. Van Tongerloo would likely have a dozen or so specialists – perhaps more, given the status of the victim. There would be a technical team assigned to analysing phone data – and analysing that photo. Other aspects wouldn't have changed so much since 1983: finding fingerprints and witnesses at the kidnapping scene, for instance…

But which scene? Where had Lottman been abducted?

It was one piece of information that I was determined to find out.

He led me into a large conference room that faced back onto Koningsstraat, the tables forming three sides of a square. It looked like we were the first ones to use it.

'Forgive me if this is brief,' he said.

The usual courtesy would have included the offer of a drink, or at least a chair; courtesy wasn't van Tongerloo's priority, clearly. I got the sense that he was taking me in, getting the measure of me.

'That's OK.' I filled the conversational void. 'I was with Rem Lottman at the Energy Summit the night he disappeared. I'm in town for personal reasons; my family's with me. If there's anything I can do to help you...'

He acknowledged the offer with a curt nod. There were many questions he could have asked me at that moment – about Lottman's personal security team on the night of the disappearance, about the state of mind of the man himself – but he didn't. It may have been that he'd found out all he needed to know from Lottman's assistant. Perhaps he was the one who'd cut off my call the previous night, warning me away from the investigation. Certainly his voice sounded familiar as he said, 'The best thing would be for you to enjoy your personal time here in Brussels. If I need you, I'm sure I'll be able to reach you.'

'OK,' I ventured, 'but have you made progress at the scene?'

He shrugged.

There would be offensive as well as reactive moves that his team would be making, but there was no point asking about those now.

It was equally pointless to mention my involvement in the Heineken case all those years ago, or to ask about the photograph, though I was yearning to do so. How had they received it? Electronically, or in an envelope? Directly, or via an intermediary – a family member perhaps? The kidnapping may have happened here, but Lottman's family would surely be in Holland, and hopefully in Amsterdam. I glanced at my watch and van Tongerloo mirrored me; it was as synchronised as we'd ever be.

'Just tell me one thing,' I said as we walked back towards the atrium. Having sized me up, he was now seeing me out.

'Where was he seized?' I asked. 'How was it called in?'

He looked at me, holding me with his investigator's stare. Extending his hand, he said, 'Goodbye, officer.'

*

Outside, I got a Marlboro Red going and started walking over to Place du Grand Sablon – an old square with a busy antiques market where my wife had arranged to meet Nadia and Sergei. Pulling out my phone, I called Liesbeth in Amsterdam.

'Good morning,' she answered brightly. 'How's Brussels?'

'A little too hot for my liking. Are you free to work on the Lottman case?'

'Er... sure,' she said. 'But has it been assigned to us?'

I felt the hair on the back of my neck prickle. 'Let me worry about issues like that, Liesbeth. Could you check out his family?'

'I can try...'

'Start with his immediate family – parents and siblings. Don't approach anyone till you've talked to me first.'

'Right,' she said, hesitating.

'Questions?'

'Not yet.'

'Then get to it.'

I hung up and opened my phone's web browser. The sunlight was so strong that I could barely see the screen, even with the brightness turned up to maximum, but I managed to find out the name of the local police's media spokesperson. In the absence of new case information, the press wouldn't stop printing – and they needed handling by *someone*.

That someone turned out to be Christophe Delors, who also happened to be a crime novelist, Google informed me. The images of him – as far as I could tell while shading the phone screen with my hand – showed a fleshy face that somehow managed to smile suavely.

Hearing the hiss of sprinklers, I found myself looking up at Brussels Park – the large square beside the Royal Palace. There was an octagonal pond among the trees. A couple were stood beside it, leaning into one another. Their dark forms stayed very still, making them look like cut-outs in the bright sunshine. Surrounding them was a sparkling haze of water and wavering heat.

I kept on walking and searching the web on my phone, checking to see if a press conference had been scheduled. There was no sign of one. Then my phone started ringing and I answered.

'Where are you?' my wife asked.

'Almost there. What's the name of this waffle place again?'

'Wittamer. Did you tell the local investigators everything?'

'About the favours-for-energy enquiry? The local case leader hardly gave me a chance. But I haven't given up yet. There's a local press spokesperson, Christophe Delors. It might be interesting to meet him.'

'Henk, I really don't want to get involved –'

'You said that if I went to St Petersburg –'

'You should *want* to go to St Petersburg with your family!'

I didn't recall Nadia's boyfriend Sergei becoming a member of our family. There was a pause, in which I seriously considered returning to Amsterdam.

'All right,' Petra relented. 'Let me hunt around a little, see what I can find.'

'It's Lottman's mistress we need to focus on –'

'Don't push it, Henk.'

*

My wife, my daughter and her boyfriend were sitting outside at the waffle restaurant when I arrived. Sergei looked older in his powder-blue, short-sleeved shirt, the bright sun making his grey hair glint. From a few metres away, he could have passed for Nadia's dad.

'Couldn't you have found a spot in the shade?' I said, squinting.

Petra gestured at the full tables. It was tourist season.

'Nice to see you too, Dad,' Nadia said, with more than a hint of sarcasm. She was wearing a vivid blue summer dress and designer sunglasses, which prevented me seeing her eyes. On the ground beside her was a large Dries Van Noten shopping bag.

I kissed my wife on the cheek and sat in the empty chair next to her.

'How are you?' Sergei asked.

'Hunky-dory,' I said. 'You?'

'Good,' he replied, relaxed and confident. 'It has been a productive trip.'

'Really.' I picked up the menu.

'We ordered waffles,' Petra informed me.

Each cost over thirteen euros.

'Indeed,' Sergei continued, 'there are some very good financial schemes for film-makers here in Brussels.'

'I'm sure there are.'

Petra shot me a look.

What? I mouthed back.

I felt the urge to rebel against everything she was orchestrating here. Who was this guy Sergei, anyway? Fortunately, at that moment a waitress approached. She wore black trousers, a black shirt and a loud pink tie. She must have been baking hot.

'I'll take a cold beer,' I said, closing the menu.

Petra was now making a show of looking at her watch; it was early for a beer, granted.

'We're on holiday,' I said, answering her unspoken concern.

'Leffe, Stella, Heineken?' the waitress asked.

'Anything but a Heineken,' I replied.

'I may join you in that,' Sergei said.

A waiter arrived with two enormous waffles, each accompanied by a pot of melted dark chocolate, a swirl of fresh crème anglaise and a scoop of vanilla ice cream. 'I'll bring some extra cutlery for you,' the waitress told me. She was speaking French but sounded English.

'No need.' The sight and smell of the waffles were making me feel sick.

She returned with two beers, beaded with condensation on the outside. 'Cheers,' she said, smiling and pulling her blonde hair away from her reddened neck as she strode back inside.

She reminded me faintly of Lucy Channing-West, the English art insurer.

Sergei raised his glass. '*Proost.*'

He sipped his beer and sighed, then said, 'Strange business about that kidnapping.'

I looked over the top of my glass at him.

'It's unusual here, isn't it?' he went on. 'A kidnapping. High risk, uncertain reward.'

'If you say so.'

I was suddenly lost in my futile meeting with van Tongerloo, replaying it in my mind. My thoughts moved on to the list of people with potential grievances against Lottman based on the failed favours-for-energy scheme.

Then I realised Sergei was addressing me: '... wondering what gun you would carry?'

I blinked, sweat weighing down my eyelashes. 'Say again?'

'Hunting at the *dacha* – what weapon should I have made ready for you?'

My ringing phone saved me.

'Stefan,' I answered, stepping away from the table.

'Boss, I just got news of something out at Schiphol.'

I waited for him to continue.

'Well?' I prompted when he didn't.

'The security team there opened up an abandoned storage locker.'

'What storage locker? What are you talking about, Stefan?'

'You know how when you leave luggage in a storage locker there, you pay for seven days, and if you don't pick it up they open up the locker and auction off the contents?'

'So?'

'Well, in this case, the contents included a rolled-up canvas.'

'What canvas? Get to the point, Stefan!'

'It's that Verspronck. The one we thought went up in smoke on Frank Hals's boat...'

The sun was hammering down on the zinc table surfaces and the metal-grey cobblestones. I felt blinded as I tried to make sense of the news. One of Hals's henchmen must have spirited the canvas away, before spiriting himself away even faster after the battle at the harbour between Hals, Malek and their hoodlums.

'How d'you know this?' I asked.

'A friend from my training programme was one of the first responders.'

'Who's handling it? Don't say Officer Bergveld.'

'Isn't he leaving the force?'

He had to have been blamed for Joost's transgressions already.

I tried to think. The Verspronck belonged to the Norwegians. It had been gifted to them in exchange for favourable energy terms that had never materialised, then 'recovered' by Joost's team. Only, the recovery had gone wrong. Both the Norwegians and the Dutch had lost out, until now...

'Anyway the police commissioner's office is handling it directly,' Stefan said. 'Perhaps Joost wants the canvas authenticated.'

Appropriated, more like.

Did some Norwegian actor, perhaps one associated with the state, have motive to kidnap Lottman in retaliation? It sounded extraordinary to my ears.

I noticed that Petra and Sergei were watching me.

'When did this happen?' I asked Stefan.

Would van Tongerloo and his team have got hold of the news, and be pointing the investigation towards Norway? If so, I needed to get there first. It was the only lead I had.

'First thing this morning,' Stefan replied.

Or was I clutching at straws? Instinct told me to find out.

'I need to leave.'

31

NORTHERN LIGHT

THE LAST-MINUTE FLIGHT TO Oslo connected through Stockholm, where I called Lucy Channing-West, who represented the painting's insurers.

No reply.

I decided not to leave a message.

Stockholm Airport was loaded with revellers arriving for the midsummer celebrations. No wonder the flight had been so expensive: up here it was New Year's Eve, Christmas and the summer holidays rolled into one. Passengers were laughing – giddy, probably already drunk. One woman my age wore a disintegrating garland of wildflowers around her head. A family was setting out a picnic of open sandwiches, summer fruits and schnapps – all available in the airport shops.

I dialled the other number I had to hand: Captain Magnusson of the Oslo Police District – an old contact from my army days when I'd been training in Norway. We hadn't spoken in years and I wondered if he'd even remember me. No matter – if Magnusson didn't respond, I'd find someone else. One way or another, I had to understand this Norwegian angle…

'*Hallo?*'

'Magnusson? It's Henk van der Pol.'

There was a short pause. 'Henk,' he said. 'God, it's been years.'

'It has – we've got a lot of catching up to do. Listen, I'm in

Oslo on the spur of the moment. I don't suppose you're available for an aquavit?'

'I'm always available for an aquavit. And a chat. With you.'

I recalled his staccato way of speaking; I'd missed the old bruiser.

'But,' he went on, 'I'm leaving. For the holiday. Why didn't you call ahead?'

'Like I said, it's a spur-of-the-moment trip.'

'What brings you up here? Work?'

'Yes. Do you have a moment to talk?'

'I have three, actually. Then I must go.'

'OK.' I chuckled; he'd lost none of his candour. It chimed with my Dutch directness. 'There was a case in Amsterdam recently, a Norwegian diplomat who disturbed the burglary of an artwork at his house and died –'

'Lars Pelt?' Magnusson cut in.

'Yes. You know of it?

'Bad business. We're a small department. We hear of these things. Handled by the *Militaerpolitikompaniet* here, yes?'

'To a point.' Beside the airport gate, someone was warming up an accordion. 'A Dutch diplomat has just been kidnapped.'

'The one in Brussels?'

'Yes.'

'I don't see the connection,' he said.

'I don't either, yet. But I believe there might be one.'

'Why?'

'That's what I'd like to explore. The possibility that some individual, or group, got to know of events in the Pelt case and the stolen painting… and acted upon them.'

'Who? Why?'

'An extreme-right group, perhaps? One taking a particularly nationalistic approach to Norway's affairs? Are there any more Anders Breiviks out there?'

'Oof,' he said, as though he'd been thumped in the stomach.

'No. Thank God. He's a one of a kind.'

'So imagine a milder cousin of his. Similar mindset, similarly upset about things. Blames foreigners.'

'Blames the Dutch?'

I couldn't get into Lottman's moves and motives concerning the energy scheme.

'And able to execute a sophisticated kidnapping?' Magnusson asked sceptically.

'I know this sounds far-fetched, but what Anders Breivik did sounds more so. Blowing up government buildings in the centre of Oslo? Shooting seventy youth workers dead at a camp on Utøya?'

'Sixty-nine,' he corrected me.

'Sometimes these things come out of nowhere.'

'What leads do you have? I can't believe you came all this way without any.'

'I can't say, Olaf.'

A pause. 'I've got to go. But I think you're barking up the wrong tree here.'

'Is there someone I could talk to in your absence?'

'Like I said, the *Militaerpolitikompaniet* are handling the Pelt case. I can't easily get you in there. Let me think about it. I'll send you a text. To this number?'

'Thank you. One other thing – has anyone from Brussels contacted your department?'

'About the Dutch kidnapping? I don't think so. I can't speak for my colleagues. But, like I said, Oslo's a small department. I'd likely have heard. If they had.'

'OK.' I wondered what other questions I should be asking him, but sensed his impatience to go. 'Enjoy the holiday.'

'I will. You too.'

*

By the time I arrived at the Radisson Hotel, beside Oslo Central Station, it was past 9 p.m. and yet so light that the sky made it look like mid-afternoon. After checking in, I tried calling Petra. No answer. I was putting my phone away when I saw Magnusson's text had come through: *Try Freddy Brekhus, Norwegian Sovereign Wealth Fund*. He went on to give me Brekhus's address. *Lykke til*, he signed off – 'Good luck.'

This was a small city, as Magnusson had said – and a very well-resourced one.

I took that thought with me to the bar beside the hotel lobby. Even the airport had been more soulful than this place. The menu reminded me how much drinks cost up here. I tried Petra again – no answer – then decided against the hotel bar, dropping my roller bag off in my room and venturing out into the cool, bright air.

There was a hint of mist as I made my way down to Oslo's waterfront. I reminisced about the time I'd spent here with Johan. It reminded me to give him a call, see how he was doing.

Silvery light glistened off the water. I soon found an old bar: Sjømannen, 'The Sailor'. These kind of places were called 'brown bars' due to their smoke-stained interiors. Smoking had been banned inside, but The Sailor still smelled of tobacco.

The bar was half-full, the conversation among the regular-looking crowd soft and respectful. I ordered an aquavit and took a large sip of the amber-coloured spirit, feeling it warm me inside. We'd lived off the stuff when on leave here.

I shifted around on the bar stool, trying to get comfortable. Norway, the army, taking my oath of allegiance – there was so much I hadn't known at that point of my life, for good and for bad.

'Another one?' the young barman asked.

'Why not?'

I turned the fresh glass in my hands. The first time I'd spoken properly with Rem Lottman, in the back of his stretch Mercedes in Amsterdam, he'd offered me a whisky from the drinks cabinet, telling me that he'd seen something of himself in me – how he'd struggled until he'd found a cause and a mentor. We all need that figure in our lives, he'd told me.

My phone rang. Petra was calling me back.

At least, I assumed she was, but when I pulled out my phone I discovered that it was someone else.

'Johan,' I answered. 'How odd. I was just thinking about you. I'm in Oslo –'

'Henk, I just got a call from the Belgian police. The federal ones, in Brussels.'

'Who?' I said, surprised.

Johan told me the name – not van Tongerloo. Someone from his team, then.

'They wanted to know why Rem Lottman was calling me.'

I paused, stunned. Then the penny dropped: I'd borrowed Lottman's phone to call Johan the night of the Energy Summit, when my wife had been in danger back in Amsterdam…

'It's no big deal,' I lied.

It was the kind of lead that van Tongerloo's technical team would be assiduous in following up on.

'They're not going to ask questions about you-know-who?'

Zsolt Tőzsér, the Hungarian hoodlum shot by Johan.

'I can't see why they would.'

The evidence – the gun Johan had used – had been discarded, but I could feel the transgressions of the past chasing after me, piling up in the present…

'They want me to meet them,' Johan continued.

'Where? Brussels?'

'No, he said one of them would be coming over to Amsterdam.'

'When?'

'To be arranged. What should I do?'

'Go ahead. Cooperate.' I thought for a moment. 'Let me try to find out who this person is.'

'OK.' I heard him exhale loudly. 'That would be good.'

I hung up, looking out of the windows, the light still silvery on the water. Perhaps I was looking at the same sort of scene my dad would have reflected on, some time long ago.

*

A sound cleaved through my sleep – one part of my brain was stuck in a strange dream in which I was being held in a dark cellar; the other was trying to make sense of where I was waking...

I fumbled for my phone, which was vibrating loudly on the wooden bedside table. The caller was Stefan. A switch beside the bed opened the blinds to Oslo's sunlit skyline. It was 6 a.m.

'*Hoi*,' I said hoarsely. I could still taste the aquavit.

'Boss, I just saw on the station transcript that the Lottman investigation's been moved to Holland.'

'Oh?'

'To Tilburg.'

I sat up. '*Tilburg?*'

It was in the south of the country – 'South of the River', as the area was sometimes described. Amsterdammers reckoned it to be backward. Then again, Amsterdammers reckoned everywhere (other than Amsterdam) to be backward.

'What else have you found out?' I asked.

'The KLPD are coordinating the Dutch side.'

No surprise that the National Police Services Agency was involved. I tried to imagine the liaison between the Belgian and Dutch command posts, the joint investigation team, and how that would be working out for van Tongerloo, who would still be leading the investigation... in theory.

It would mean a lot of coordination, and potentially a lot of conflict.

'So they think Lottman's being held in Tilburg?' Immediately something struck me as odd about that, and not just the area's supposed backwardness. 'Have the kidnappers established contact, beyond that photo?' I wanted to look at it again on my phone.

'I don't know.'

'None of this makes sense. Lottman's not even wealthy. At least, he's no Heineken or Van der Valk. And if you've gone to the trouble of kidnapping him in a foreign city, why bring him back to Holland, where the investigative impetus will be greatest?'

Stefan was silent.

The news emboldened me to continue my northern quest. I got up and began pulling on my jeans, unsuccessfully, with one hand. I knew the official investigation was on the wrong path, even if I didn't have the evidence to back that up yet.

'What do you want me to do?' Stefan asked.

Might it be possible to get Stefan closer to the official investigation, as an 'embed' of sorts?

'Keep me updated on any developments you learn of, for now. Like you just did.'

*

Freddy Brekhus worked out of an office beside the National Gallery. The gallery was an austere brick structure on Universitetsgata, a ten-minute walk from the hotel. The small, quaint office building to the side of it was unmarked. I rang the intercom and nothing happened.

I rang again.

'*Hallo*?' a female voice finally said.

'I'm here to see Freddy Brekhus.'

'Do you have an appointment?'

'I'm with the Dutch police. Captain Magnusson of the Oslo Police District recommended that I visit.'

I heard the voice conferring with someone and then the intercom went quiet. Eventually the door buzzed and I pushed it open. The woman sat three metres away on the other side, behind an antique desk.

'We are all leaving for the holiday,' she said. 'Can it not wait?'

'No. Is he here?'

A small rotund man, pin-neat in his suit, appeared in the open doorway to a large office. He wore tortoiseshell glasses and held a little espresso cup and saucer, his pinky finger extended.

'Magnusson sent you?' he said.

'Yes. You're Brekhus?'

Even this went unconfirmed. 'Would you care for a coffee?'

'I would. Thank you.'

He retreated behind his own, much bigger desk. Two computer monitors sat on one side of it. I followed him into the room. The screens were angled so that I couldn't see what was on them. I explained why I was there – the Pelt case, the Verspronck, Lottman's kidnapping. Just the bare bones. Brekhus took small, precise sips from his cup. His assistant brought me mine, which I drained. It was good, strong coffee and it hit the mark.

'Would you mind explaining your role?' I asked.

He stared at me for a second then gave a little shrug. 'I handle the Sovereign Wealth Fund's fine-art portfolio.'

'That must be quite a responsibility.'

'Yes, it's a valuable part of the fund.'

'I imagine you're not eager to share details.'

'The fund likes to keep a low profile, as I'm sure you're aware.'

'The Verspronck – what happened after it went missing?'

He paused. 'The insurers have already confirmed that they will pay.'

'In full?'

'Of course. Do you think that, after the Munch incident, we'd leave such a valuable painting to chance?'

So the Norwegians hadn't suffered any loss after all.

'The Munch incident?' I prompted him to explain.

'Yes, *The Scream*. Stolen in fifty seconds, using a stepladder behind the gallery.' He gestured next door. 'The day before the

236

opening of the Lillehammer Winter Games, with the world watching.' He sniffed. 'Before my time here.'

I sensed that he'd used that line on more than one occasion, perhaps to justify more resources, maybe to ask for more power for himself…

'The world certainly wasn't watching when the Verspronck vanished. Wasn't it overinsured, in fact?'

He arched an eyebrow and finished his coffee stiffly. 'Who suggested that it was overinsured?'

Lucy Channing-West, the insurer, I wanted to say – but it was clear to me now that Magnusson had been right. I was barking up the wrong tree. The Norwegians had no grievances against Lottman. The opposite, in fact: there was a lot to feel grateful for, in Brekhus's office at least. A windfall out of nowhere.

'No matter,' I said. 'I'll see myself out.'

32

BRUSSELS PARK

MY PHONE STARTED RINGING as I returned to the hotel to check out.

'Finally,' my wife said. 'I've been trying to reach you!'

'Sorry, I was in a meeting…'

'So, how's your northern odyssey?'

'I learned something – about how little I know. It was a long way north to come for that insight.'

'Serves you right for deserting us. Anyway, I've done some research for you.'

Petra never ceased to amaze me.

'I met with the Belgian press spokesperson,' she said.

'Christophe Delors? The one writing crime novels?'

It was hard to keep the scepticism out of my voice. Investigative writing, exposing venalities (as my wife had done for a living), I could understand. But spending your days making stuff up?

'He's actually a decent sort,' Petra said. 'Quite helpful, in fact, in the way that people with fragile egos can be, when stroked the right way.'

'How so?'

'I've found the mistress.'

I stopped mid-step. Unfortunately, it was in the middle of a revolving door, which almost hit me on the arse.

'How on earth did you manage to find her? Did you persuade one of the newspapers to review Delors's lousy novels or something?'

'You know I couldn't possibly comment. Except to say that

it was Lottman's mistress who reported the kidnapping to her local police station.'

'Which police station?'

'Brussels Park. You'd better get back here.'

*

My return trip from Oslo consumed the rest of that day and it wasn't until the following morning that I arrived at Rue Ducale, overlooking Brussels Park.

It was pure grandeur – and a strange place to keep a mistress. The buildings here were official – ambassadorial, or even royal. Along the south side of the park stood the Royal Palace and, on the north side, the national parliament. It was as if an ongoing reminder were needed that Belgium, like Holland, was both a kingdom and a parliamentary democracy.

Had Lottman felt at home here? The traffic was constant. Discretion could hardly have been assured. Then again, perhaps this location was a safer option than regular trips to the suburbs. Perhaps Lottman would simply have been perceived as going about his everyday business. Was it not expected in this town that you kept a mistress, anyway?

But Lottman wasn't even married, I had to remind myself. Didn't that make her a girlfriend, in fact?

I went to the address Petra had given me and looked up at the stuccoed face of the building, recognising hints of domesticity through the second-floor windows: a rose tint to the plaster ceiling, a light with myriad gold leaves...

I negotiated the intercom but got no reply from the second floor. Waiting a moment, I turned towards the glint of sprinklers in the park, conscious that I was probably being watched via various security cameras. Van Tongerloo would surely have questioned the girlfriend and asked her to keep him informed. I stepped away from the building, trying to detect any sign of movement in that second-floor apartment.

I rang the intercom one more time and then crossed the

road and entered the park, where I lit a cigarette and strolled further in, the light gravel crunching underfoot. Soon I came to a junction with a wider path that cut across the park at an angle. Squinting down the sun-bleached route, I saw a pond – not the one I'd noticed the couple beside; this one was round, under renovation and ringed with a chain-link fence. My instincts drew me closer, some part of my consciousness becoming alert to an alternative scenario for Lottman's disappearance.

I walked the circumference of the fence. On the ground, among some yew trees, was a yellow-painted lamp that also served as a sign: *POLICE / POLITIE.* I passed through the screen of trees to find a low concrete building: it must have been the best-hidden police station in all of Brussels.

The female desk sergeant greeted me with lassitude – in French – from behind a glass screen. I showed her my warrant card.

'I'm over from Amsterdam working on the case involving the kidnapped Dutch official, Rem Lottman.'

She scrutinised me now.

'Was anything reported here the night he disappeared?'

She blinked uncomprehendingly. 'Are you not working with the federal police?'

So the federals had been here – this was indeed where Lottman's disappearance had been reported. Petra's information was correct.

'They've already contacted you?' I bluffed.

'We contacted them,' she said, now more confused.

'Then everything's fine.'

For a split second I feared that she might fetch someone more senior, but you can never overestimate the power of inertia in these places.

I took that thought outside with me, and wondered again about Lottman's movements during the night of the Energy Summit: had he been due at his girlfriend's? Failed to arrive, and then... what? She'd called her local police station?

I looked though the sun-dappled trees into the shade – the sheltered corners of the park. I thought I could see a men's toilets: had Lottman been up to something else altogether? He wouldn't have been the first politician, married or not, to have courted danger that way.

I dismissed the thought, making a mental note to ask Petra whether she could quiz Christophe Delors further.

Finally, I returned to Lottman's girlfriend's place on Rue Ducale, giving the intercom one last try. To my surprise, a soft voice replied.

'*Oui*?'

*

She was dark-skinned, slim and beautiful, reminding me of the 1980s pop singer Sade.

'Leonie,' she introduced herself.

She wore a white silk dress, the drape of which revealed a lithe physique. Her movements were feline and sinuous as she led me into the apartment, which smelled of spice and expensive leather. My eyes couldn't help but be drawn to her.

We entered a living room with a cream, textured rug and a large fireplace featuring African art. I wanted to ask her what her nationality was – I already had a new theory that I felt sure van Tongerloo would have overlooked, or not known to ask about in the first place.

'I'm assuming you've been interviewed?' I said.

She stood before the floor-to-ceiling windows that looked out onto the park. The lush greenery, breaking as it did for the watering holes of the two ponds, appeared like some urban savannah. It gave the hunt for Lottman a primordial dimension. 'Yes,' she answered at last. 'It was certainly an interview, not a conversation.'

Curiously, there was no guard in the apartment. Was the official team so consumed by developments in Tilburg that they had abandoned her?

'I'm coming at this from the Dutch angle,' I said, 'trying to build up a picture of Rem. Could I just reconfirm the circumstances in which you became aware of his disappearance?'

For a few seconds she said nothing. I looked across at her sculptural features, immobile as the artwork on the fireplace. Time stood still in that chic apartment.

'He came here from that Energy Summit, exhausted. He said he wanted to take some air, so he went for a walk.' She nodded at the view. 'That was the last time I saw him.'

I looked down. Surely there were cameras around, which the official team would be checking... but that would take time. 'Did you see anything?'

'No,' she said. 'It was dark. I suggested he shouldn't go without a security person present. Their attention had been diverted by a situation in Amsterdam, he'd mentioned.'

My wife's.

She continued, 'Rem told me, "It's Brussels Park – how much harm can come to me there?" I was concerned about the homeless people who sleep out there in summer – although most people here in Brussels seem to be homeless, in one sense or another.'

I shifted my weight between my feet, feeling the carpet sinking and springing back beneath me. 'So you called the local police station?' I asked.

'Not straight away. I waited an hour and called his phone, only to hear it ring in the other room – he'd left it here.'

The phone that the Brussels investigation team would have taken away for analysis.

The phone with Johan's number on it.

'Then I waited a few more minutes,' she went on, 'and finally called the police. They came quickly.'

'Can I ask why you assumed he'd been kidnapped?'

She looked lost.

'You reported it as a kidnapping,' I prompted.

'Oh yes,' she said, 'he'd mentioned it just a few days before: his concern that he might be at risk.'

'What exactly did he say?'

'I'm sorry.' She put a palm to her forehead. 'I'm tired. I've already been through all this.'

'I'm the one who should apologise,' I said. 'I can imagine how distressing all of this must be. I knew him too. I feel it as well.'

There was a kindred concern in her voice as she asked, 'Will he be OK? That photo, in the news...'

She shuddered as though an icy blast had hit her. In reality, the room was like a greenhouse, the murmuring air conditioning ineffectual against the beating rays of the sun.

'It's hard to say.'

I digested the new information she'd given me, especially Lottman's voiced concerns. But what had prompted them?

'He was very generous,' Leonie said vaguely.

I doubted she meant as a lover. It was hard imagining the two of them together physically, with Lottman's size and her slenderness. But I didn't sense that she meant it just in a financial sense, either.

A phone rang somewhere in the apartment. I noted her exaggerated, startled reflex. She attempted to ignore it.

'So he'd been afraid of kidnapping,' I said. 'Were there any other signs of him behaving differently of late?'

She paused, adrift in thought. 'He'd lost a little of his confidence. I think he was just a bit paranoid – with good reason, as things turned out.'

'Did he seem depressed? Withdrawn?'

'It's hard to say,' she replied. 'I'm no longer sure how well I knew him.'

'If you don't mind me asking, how long had you two been together?'

'Since he arrived here in Brussels. He took a big interest in my country, in the political changes in Ghana.'

Now we were getting somewhere.

'You've been following what's happening?' she asked me.

I hadn't, but I nodded all the same. 'What's your interpretation?'

'The rebels need funds. But more than that, they need Edouard Tailleur back. You must know of him? He's the one on trial in The Hague…'

Ah yes, Edouard Tailleur. From the media coverage, you couldn't ignore the man: a notorious warlord operating among the Ghanaian rebels in the remote borderland between Ghana and the Ivory Coast, going by the nickname Edouard Scissorhand – or alternatively 'Scissor Man' – owing to his alleged habit of cutting open his victims, alive, with an old pair of sewing scissors.

'Could it be related?' she asked, staring at me.

I met her gaze. 'Did you discuss this with the local investigators?'

'No. I didn't like their tone. I didn't feel comfortable with them.'

'Here's my number.' I pressed my card into her slender hand. 'If anything comes to mind, please call me, at any time.'

I walked towards the front door, then turned around. 'One last question: has anyone from the media tried to contact you?'

Her phone rang again.

'I have a good lawyer, and injunctions ready,' she said. 'One of Rem's gifts to me.'

'Good. Don't talk to any of them, if you can avoid it.'

*

As soon as I left Leonie's apartment, I crossed the street towards the park and called Liesbeth. Waiting for her to answer, I caught sight of the primary colours of the Ghanaian flag – the embassy perhaps?

'Ahoy there,' Liesbeth answered.

'What's new?' I asked.

'I've been researching Lottman's family, as you asked.'

'Found anything?'

'Unmarried, one sibling living in Amsterdam – an older sister.'

It broadly fitted with how I imagined Lottman's family situation to be. 'What about his parents?'

'His father's dead but his mother's still alive.'

'Where does she live?'

'Noordwijk aan Zee.'

Noordwijk: Holland's answer to the Hamptons. Freddy H had owned a villa there. He'd chosen Heineken-green tiles for its sizeable roof. It's funny, the details that stick.

'So, there's Lottman family money after all,' I said.

An old-school kidnapping motivated by the promise of ransom appeared plausible again.

'It would appear so.'

'I'm heading to The Hague,' I said. 'It's a short distance on to Noordwijk.'

'Oh, I already arranged to meet with her. I'm on my way there now... or do you want me to turn around?'

'No,' I said, following a sixth sense. 'Carry on, I'll take the sister.'

'Why The Hague?' Liesbeth asked me.

Another call was incoming.

PRIVATE NUMBER.

'Keep me posted,' I said, switching over to the other caller.

'Van der Pol?' van Tongerloo said. 'I thought I made it clear that your help wasn't needed in Brussels.'

Opposite Leonie's apartment there was a black BMW. I cursed myself for not having noticed it before. Were there listening devices at her place? The secrecy afforded the police's technical teams here meant that I'd likely never know.

'Don't worry,' I told him. 'I'm leaving town now. Just one thing, van Tongerloo.'

'What?'

'You may want to step up your protection of the girlfriend.'

33

'SCISSOR MAN'

I LEFT BRUSSELS FOR Holland by car, calling Liesbeth again as I went.

'On the road?' she asked, apparently hearing the traffic noise.

'How did it go with Lottman's mother?'

'It was brief, but I learned a couple of things.'

'What?'

'The photo of her son – the one in the news – was physically mailed to her.'

'Oh?'

'Yes. The envelope was postmarked *Tilburg*.'

So that's why the investigation had moved there. Though it didn't sound quite right. Wouldn't a sophisticated gang have sent the photo by email, from an anonymous Internet café?

Though, granted, whoever emailed it risked the IP address being discovered. An Internet café could be traced electronically, its cameras checked and staff questioned about who'd sat at which computer – just as a physical mailing location could be investigated… as it apparently was being.

'What's she like?' I asked.

'The mother? If I could use one word to sum her up –'

'First one that comes to mind.'

'Imperious.'

'Hmm.' I let that sink in. 'How did you leave things?'

'She was cordial, but made it clear that she didn't expect to see me again.'

I digested that too. 'What else?'

'What else about what?'

'Mrs Lottman. It feels like you're holding something back.'

'No, not really. Well – I just wasn't sure about my right to question her, that's all. I mean, Noordwijk's hardly in our precinct, is it?'

'Let me worry about that,' I said tersely, feeling the limitations of my reach ever more. It made my next question all the more difficult. 'What's the process for interviewing a suspect at the International Criminal Court in The Hague?'

'Huh?'

Liesbeth's husband was a senior prosecutor. I'd never asked her something like this, and I hated doing it, but there was a first time for everything.

'There's a criminal from Ghana who may be relevant. Or not. I just need to check it out.'

Liesbeth sighed sharply. 'I don't know. Is it even Dutch soil?'

She made a good point. Would I be leaving Holland again so soon? Nothing in Rem Lottman's world was straightforward.

'I could ask Marc if you want, but –'

'No, that's all right,' I said, changing my mind. Trying to interview the Ghanaian defendant in jail would only draw more attention to myself. It was a bad idea, and I had a better one.

'OK then,' she said, confused. 'I'll write up my report about the mother.'

'Please do, and email it to me.'

I hung up and turned the radio on: 3FM, the music channel, playing an annoyingly catchy 1980s track whose name escaped me. 'Let's Hear It For the Boy'? Thankfully, the music faded out for the half-hourly news, which mentioned the Lottman investigation moving to Tilburg, but not much more. The police spokespeople were keeping schtum – apart from to my wife, of course.

*

The International Criminal Court occupied a strange place, and not just because of the countries (primarily America) that still refused to recognise it. Rather, the physical juxtaposition: it was a white, modern structure that visitors like me approached via elegant old residences, pleasant greenery and other signs of civility, yet within its rooms sat some of the most vicious criminals on earth.

Court One was hosting the trial of Edouard Tailleur.

I parked near the visitors' entrance, which was around the corner from the main entrance at 174 Maanweg. The court was a large operation – two tower blocks – its administrators still keen to demonstrate its purpose and workings to the world. Any member of the public could enter and observe court sessions (apart from those involving witnesses who required anonymity). The way in was beyond a cage-like structure, which jutted out into the street that ran down the side of the building. The cage was where defendants entered as they arrived from the nearby Scheveningen Penitentiary – the most heavily fortified prison in The Hague.

I walked through the X-ray machine, which lit up like a Christmas tree. I held up my warrant card and the duty guard took my gun, phone and lighter, and then asked me to try again. He conferred with another guard; eventually the first one showed me to a security locker where I left my possessions.

Court One was a small but high space, with a public viewing gallery behind the glass on the upper level. Arranged around the judges' bench were desks and computer consoles for the prosecution, the defence, security staff, translators and other officials. My attention went immediately to the man behind a glass screen on the lower level.

When you've done this job for three decades, you become aware of a certain energy that emanates from powerful, violent predators – like that of animals in an undisturbed habitat, I imagined. Tailleur was a large man, wearing an expensive-looking navy suit and tie. He sat slouched, with his headphones slightly askew, resembling a beast in repose. The only movement I could detect was his breathing.

The moment I sat down, he looked up at me. *What the hell have you got yourself mixed up in, Rem?* I wondered. *An eye for an eye? One man's captivity for another's?*

In the open dock stood another African man, wearing a beige military uniform.

'Mr NaTonga,' the gowned prosecutor was saying, 'I wish to turn now to how your brigade selected their targets.'

There was a pause as his words were translated.

The prosecutor hadn't yet finished the preamble that would eventually lead to a question before NaTonga replied.

'We have to work from a philosophy... of survival.' A soft, female voice translated his words. 'The Ghanaian regime is – as everyone here knows – very corrupt. There is much bribery, there is much self-enrichment. This is the central history of our land, going back to the British and Dutch years.'

The prosecutor was gesturing helplessly towards the judges, one of whom said: 'Mr NaTonga, if I may intercede. You have been called as a witness in your capacity as a captain of the rebel army, not as a philosopher – though no doubt you have much to recommend yourself in that department. Could the prosecution please rephrase its question more precisely?'

The prosecutor waved his hands in frustration. 'Thank you, Your Honour,' he said, composing himself. 'I would like to explore how Mr NaTonga received orders – in his capacity as rebel-army captain – to attack and abduct villagers in the region to the west of Kumasi. If you look at the document distributed, you will see the map and the coordinates for the area in question.'

Papers rustled through the courtroom microphones. Tailleur's gaze lowered from me to NaTonga.

The captain drew himself up, the gaudy medals of his uniform jingling. 'I receive my orders from God. God understands the centuries-long struggle that my people have been summoned for – first with the invaders, the Dutch and British colonials, and now the puppet government they left in their place, which has led to where we find ourselves today.'

The stenographer duly noted all.

I folded my arms tightly.

The captain continued: 'God gives his blessing and benediction to the struggle to rid ourselves of the men who rape our land of gold and diamonds and oil, and rape our women too, and God must be our judge in the end. This is a struggle that has been going on for many generations of my people, and will continue for many more generations.' The translator placed peculiar emphasis on the first syllable of 'generations', distracting further from the attempts to establish the chain of command between the captain and the man behind the glass screen.

I suddenly saw why the Americans had such a problem with all this – giving a platform to terrorists. For 'terror' was the only word that could describe the coin of their realm.

'Mr NaTonga!' the prosecutor said, exasperated. 'Could you please answer the question as to how, in a military, *tactical* sense, you selected your enemy targets?'

'Our first target must be the corruption and bribery of the current regime,' the translator continued. 'The outsized payments its members and diplomats are receiving from countries such as Holland, for oil, and for the other fruits of our land –'

I sat bolt upright. The man was referencing Lottman's favours-for-energy scheme, surely? Tailleur was staring straight at me.

There was a muted *clack* as one of the judges brought down his gavel. He was saying something about adjourning early for the day.

I got up – feeling Tailleur's gaze track me – and left the gallery. I strode through the atrium to the security entrance and the locker containing my phone and my gun.

The guard helped me retrieve my possessions and I walked out into the fierce light, dialling Stefan as I went.

'That Ghanaian diplomat who was gifted the big diamond...' I said when Stefan answered.

'Lesoto?'

'Yes. Could you try to track him down? I'd like to ask him some questions.'

'Didn't he leave the country?'

'You're right.' I recalled that now. 'See if he tried to re-enter Holland or Belgium, would you?'

'I can try...'

'There were two guards at Antwerp Airport who were very helpful and should be able to assist, if you run into any difficulties getting the information. Check on Lesoto's driver, too. What was his name again?' I rubbed the side of my head. 'Sammy, it was. See if you can find out anything about the movements of either of them. Dig around.'

'OK,' Stefan said. 'Leave it with me.'

I'd intended to go back into the courtroom but decided against the rigmarole of handing in my gun and phone again, opting for a cigarette instead. The judge had said that they'd be adjourning early for the day anyway.

I'd only just finished my cigarette when Stefan called back.

'I thought you'd want to know, sooner rather than later –'

'What?'

'The guards at Antwerp Airport said that one of the other names on that list tried to re-enter the country.'

'Which one?' I was distracted by a sense of activity in the cage of the prisoners' entrance ahead, doubtless the prison transport arriving. 'What are you talking about, Stefan?'

'The list of foreign diplomats and dignitaries to be detained

251

for questioning upon arrival at any Benelux or Dutch airport, remember?'

'Which name?'

'Sheikh Yasan.'

The one who'd been staying at the Royal Hotel in Amsterdam, where the Ukrainian escort was beaten up.

A van swerved past me, at speed.

'What happened?'

'He was denied entry. He turned his private jet around and flew on to Switzerland.'

'Huh. Stefan, see if you can –'

A dazzling white flash blinded me. My hearing went tinny, as though I were underwater.

I groped for my dropped phone among pieces of hot tarmac.

An alarm horn sounded in staccato blasts.

The scene in front of me was one of smoke and twisted metal – where the cage had stood. Next to it, the knotted chassis of a van sat in a shallow crater.

In the midst of all the warped, blackened metal was another vehicle – or rather the remnants of one. The smell was ghastly: scorched plastic; human flesh. I staggered towards the wreckage as uniformed men streamed in from different directions, vivid blue light flickering across their torsos.

Someone held me back and helped me, coughing, to sit down by the side of the road.

Two thoughts entered my head. One was that people had surely died, and I was lucky not to have been one of them.

The other thought: whoever was attempting to free Edouard Tailleur hadn't needed Rem Lottman kidnapped to try and do so.

34

AMSTERDAM MANEGE

I DIDN'T NEED TO go to hospital. I was fine – just shaken. Twenty minutes and a cigarette later, I was driving myself to Amsterdam, unable to resist listening to the news on the radio. It came in instalments: Tailleur had been taken to hospital under heavily armed guard. He was in intensive care. The attempt to rescue him had killed the driver of the van carrying the bomb, and seriously injured one of the ICC's security guards. Hospital staff needed to amputate one of Scissor Man's legs.

There's some justice left out there, I thought, pulling up and parking in front of the IJ Tunnel 3 police station.

Stefan was sitting in the squad room. A radio was on, competing in volume with the whir of an old electric fan.

'Didn't expect to see you back,' he said, looking surprised.

'Neither did I.'

He looked at me more closely. 'Are you OK?'

The heat of the blast had reddened my face and singed my eyebrows.

'It was hot in Brussels,' I said. 'Any luck finding Lesoto?'

'Not yet. He's not attempted to enter Holland or Belgium again.'

I eased myself into my roller chair. 'What about Sheikh Yasan?'

'Nothing to report there either.'

'Then what about down south? Any developments in Tilburg?'

Stefan flipped through his notes. 'The kidnappers have demanded a ransom in four currencies.'

I turned sharply, wincing as my shirt collar rubbed blistered skin. 'How do you know this?'

'Radio.'

'This came through the media?'

'Yes.'

'It's the Heineken kidnapping, move for move. What's the total ransom amount?'

'Approximately fifteen million euros, at current exchange rates.'

'How did I know you were going to say that amount? Next they'll be calling themselves the "eagle" and us the "hare"; telling us to put a congratulations notice in the personal-ads section of the newspaper...'

Those had been the tactics used by Heineken's kidnappers to control and humiliate us.

'You don't buy it?' Stefan said.

'I'm not sure what I buy,' I replied. 'But there's something off about that photo, for one thing.' I went to *De Telegraaf*'s website and pulled up the image of Lottman. 'Don't you think it's been manipulated?'

He came over to look at it over my shoulder. 'Boss, your hair looks burned.'

'Like I said, it was hot in Brussels. Look – there's a shimmer of light, if I can call it that.' It seemed familiar somehow. 'Yet in every other respect it looks like he's in some kind of dark room.'

Stefan went back to his own desk and started typing.

'It's more like a rippling of light, isn't it?' he said.

I felt a jolt in my chest. 'That's what it is: the rippling effect of light reflecting off water.'

'But why's it there?' Stefan asked.

We sat in silence, staring at our screens.

'There's no water near Tilburg,' I said.

'There must be ponds, fountains, paddling pools,' Stefan

mused. 'Perhaps Lottman was photographed through a window, with some body of water outside. I bet the investigative team is looking closely at that.'

'*Hoi oi*,' a cheery voice said. It was Liesbeth. 'Are you OK?' she asked, after seeing the state of me.

'Remind me to pack some sun cream next time. Who are those for?'

She was carrying a little tray of *tompouce*.

'Dessert.' She shrugged. 'I picked them up on my way back from lunch. Want one?'

'I see how it goes around here when I'm away: *tompouce* in the afternoon, the radio blaring away...'

'How else would we hear what's going on?' Stefan said.

'Aren't you supposed to be on holiday with your wife and daughter?' Liesbeth said, helping herself to a slice coated with pink icing. As she bit into it, a pink smudge appeared on her nose, which she quickly wiped away.

I was tucking into one myself, trying to prevent the custard cream squishing sideways as I bit down on the pastry, when my phone rang. I thought it might be Petra asking after my whereabouts – I'd neglected to call her – but the number on the screen was Belgian.

'Officer van der Pol? It's Leonie in Brussels.'

I forced myself to swallow.

'Have you heard the news from The Hague?' she asked.

'I have. I was there when it happened.'

I got up and walked into the corridor, Stefan and Liesbeth munching slowly as they watched me go.

'Tailleur just died in hospital,' she said.

'That's one less violent criminal to worry about.'

'The International Criminal Court will repatriate his body.'

'Good for them. Are you OK?'

'I think so. It looks like Tailleur and his men were not the reason Rem disappeared, then.'

'That's a reasonable assumption.'

Her voice became quieter. 'So what's the real reason he went missing?'

'Ransom is the official theory.' I shook my head; it just didn't feel right. 'It's what we're all trying to find out.'

Leonie was silent.

I looked out of a small window at the road leading into the IJ tunnel; traffic trundled obliviously in each direction.

'Before – when I asked you if he seemed depressed – you said that you didn't feel you knew him that well. Was there anything you left out?'

'Such as?' she asked.

'I don't know, I'm just wondering whether he had any weaknesses we weren't aware of.'

'Weaknesses?'

'Gambling, maybe. Or drugs.'

'He was a senior politician!'

I was silent, allowing a vacuum to form in the conversation.

'I have to go,' she said, flustered.

'Wait, Leonie –'

But she'd gone.

I almost threw the phone to the floor, but I controlled myself and re-entered the squad room.

'How was The Hague?' Liesbeth asked.

'A dead end.'

I sat down.

'You weren't affected by that bombing, were you?'

'Not unduly. Look, do you have that report?'

'On my interview with Lottman's mother?'

'Yes.'

'It's in your inbox.'

'Good.'

I sighed as I opened up my email – the tens of unread messages. One, from Joost, jumped out immediately:

Henk, I'd like to meet to discuss one or two things. Apparently you're in Brussels? Let me know as soon as you're back in Amsterdam. That's not an invitation.

'Weren't you supposed to meet the sister?' Liesbeth was asking.

I was still staring at the email, deciding what to do.

'Henk?' Liesbeth prompted.

'Yes?'

'Weren't you going to meet Lottman's sister?' she said. 'Or d'you want me to?'

'No, I've got it,' I replied, finding the report she'd just emailed and printing it off.

I collected the printout and gathered up my phone and keys from my desk.

'Where do I find her?'

*

The Hollandsche Manege is an indoor equestrian centre inspired by Vienna's famous riding school. Built in the 1880s, it was conceived at a time when Holland's confidence in the world was riding high. It's an improbable venue to find in the heart of Amsterdam today.

I drove up the busy thoroughfare of Overtoom, negotiating bikes, trams and everything in-between, deliberating how I would present myself differently from the official investigators, who would surely have questioned Carla Lottman by now.

The weather in Amsterdam was warm – not as hot as in Brussels, but it made the smell of hay and horse excrement less incongruous to me, as I recalled a much earlier impression: of Africa, and the heat there...

Odd, the power of sudden memories.

I approached the entrance to the riding school on leafy Vondelstraat. The other buildings were mostly residential: substantial and finely detailed, just like on the other side of the

Vondelpark, where diplomats Lars Pelt and Lesoto had been living until recently. An old man in overalls was scraping the pavement outside the entrance with a spade, making my teeth hurt. There was a little front desk, at which a woman sat glumly. A sign announced that it cost eight euros to enter. 'I'm here to see one of the pupils,' I explained, showing my warrant card. The woman didn't react and I barely had to break stride.

The iron and stone neoclassical structure was far more impressive on the inside, with its finely carved balconies and upper-level seating. The sand in the arena was carefully raked. Over it trotted four white horses in a figure-of-eight. A haze hung in the air that aggravated my sinuses.

Carla Lottman was instantly recognisable from the family resemblance. She didn't have Rem's physical bulk but she was ungainly on her Spanish horse – not quite synchronised with the animal's movements as she rose and sat in the saddle. Her face was gripped with concentration. She shared Lottman's dark features – eyes, eyebrows. Her hair was tied up under her helmet.

I made my way over to the instructor, who was yelling directions from the edge of the arena.

'Howdy,' I said, showing her my warrant card. 'I need to talk to one of your pupils.'

She rolled her eyes. 'Not again. Can you at least wait till the end of this exercise? We've been working on this all afternoon.'

I shrugged and leaned over the railing. The instructor stood just the other side of it. 'Carla, quieten your hands and get your heels *down*!'

Carla's eyes were downcast. Or was she avoiding mine? She didn't seem to have a problem with being yelled at – which surprised me, for the sister of a senior Brussels bureaucrat. The scene had the feel of a school pony club from the way the instructor was addressing her, yet it was hardly like Carla was a girl. Perhaps once she'd been a handsome woman; her face now had a sunken, jowly look.

As well as finding out where Carla spent most afternoons, Liesbeth had learned that she didn't have a job. However, she was involved in a number of charitable causes. For example, she volunteered at the famous Botanical Gardens over on Plantage Middenlaan, which was a stone's throw from the police station. It would have been a much more convenient location to pay a visit to, I thought.

Like Rem, she wasn't married.

The instructor strode into the middle of the arena to speak with Carla. I pulled out Liesbeth's report on the mother, which I'd put in my jacket's inside pocket. I'd only just unfolded it and read the first paragraph when I heard a loud snort and sensed a horse bearing down on me. Carla glowered from on high.

'I suppose it's me you're looking for,' she said.

'I've a couple of questions to ask about your brother, if you don't mind.'

'Actually I do mind. Did you not think to make an appointment?'

'I can wait, if you want to finish up —'

'I've told your people all that I have to say. Do you not talk to one another?'

I paused; the horse pawed the sand. 'I just wanted to quickly go over any contact you had with him in the days leading up to his disappearance —'

'I've explained: I *didn't* have contact. We weren't close.'

I noted the way she used the past tense.

The instructor was making her way over.

'Just one other question —'

But I caught the way that the horse was pinning its ears back. I didn't know a lot about horses, but I was pretty sure that this wasn't a good sign. I backed away from the railing before the instructor had a chance to reprimand me further.

I walked up the dusty stairs to the café on the first floor. It was a long, white-stuccoed room with a certain faded glamour. It smelled like a barn. I ordered a cup of coffee and leaned against the once-opulent bar while I waited for my drink.

Carla Lottman had said all she would to me – precious few words – but I'd somehow learned more about Rem's inner life from those few seconds than in all my enquiries to date, including the occasions I'd spent with Lottman himself. I could suddenly see his childhood, and the world that the Lottman siblings must have inhabited together – no matter how estranged their relationship had become. Unlike when I'd talked to his girlfriend, it felt as though I'd been allowed through the stage door, to the life behind the set of his public existence.

I sat down with my coffee, which tasted weak, and pulled out Liesbeth's report on the mother. I read it fast the first time, to see what jumped out. Pulling out a pen and clasping the cap between my teeth, I started circling anything of interest.

Lottman's father had committed suicide forty years ago. Liesbeth had found this out from background research rather than by talking to Mrs Lottman. It lent the suggestion of a curse over the family. Rem had been at Leiden Law School at the time, an accomplishment that the mother *had* spoken about with pride – as Liesbeth had noted. I'd heard or seen somewhere that Lottman read law; Leiden would have been the logical choice. I was just thinking that it was a short journey from Noordwijk, if I happened to be down that way to visit the mother, when a scream pierced the air. Then a neigh, followed by a general commotion.

I ran through to the gallery that looked down on the arena, almost losing my balance as I leaned over to see what was going on. Lying on the ground – on her back – was Carla Lottman. Through a cloud of dust, her face appeared white. The instructor and a man leaned over her. Carla's horse was ambling back into the middle of the arena. It must have thrown her.

I ran down the stairs.

The instructor's eyes widened in surprise on seeing me.

'There's nothing to see,' she said angrily. 'She's just winded.'

'What happened?'

'The horse spooked,' she snapped.

It wasn't the only one.

35

JOOST, REBOOTED

THAT EVENING MURIEL CRUTZEN, the Dutch energy minister, made an appearance on NPO1, the public TV channel. She looked elegant in her fitted suit, but its dark charcoal colour gave her a funereal presence. She wore no make-up, and her eyes appeared larger and steadier than usual as she addressed her primetime audience.

I was back at the houseboat, a jenever in one hand, the TV remote in the other. My first thought was: election stunt. The polls were close and getting closer.

'Good evening,' she began. 'I want to bring you the troubling news about Rem Lottman, a great public servant of Holland and my attaché in the Council of Europe. I have known him for many years, and can attest to the great value he has brought to both my office in Brussels and the country as a whole.'

The last words felt freighted with hidden meaning. Did Crutzen know about the favours-for-energy scheme? She would have been one of the first people that I'd have tried to speak with, had the enquiry that Rem envisaged gone ahead. How high did knowledge of the scheme go?

'The people purporting to be holding Mr Lottman have given us ninety-six hours, or four days, to pay the ransom.'

I sat forward. This was new. There had been no such deadline in the Heineken case.

I eyed my old army watch, checking the date and the time.

'I'm appealing directly to any of you who may know those implicated. I urge you to come forward now and speak with the special investigation team we've set up.'

Did they have no clue who the kidnappers were, then? Or was she bluffing? In the Heineken case, we'd identified the gang relatively quickly – only we didn't know their whereabouts.

I reached for my phone.

'We are a small country. If we work together, then we can bring about the right outcome. But we must work together. So, please, if you know anything – anything,' she repeated, 'about the people responsible for this unconscionable threat, then call one of the following numbers.'

The screen went blue and white, and up flashed two sets of digits: an Amsterdam number and a toll-free one.

I called van Tongerloo.

Crutzen reappeared on the screen, the phone numbers displayed beneath her. 'Please do this now: it could save lives. Thank you for listening and goodnight.'

'Frank van Tongerloo,' he answered.

'It's Henk van der Pol.'

A second of silence. I could hear squad-room bustle in the background. In Tilburg?

'I'm just going into a meeting.' His voice sounded thinner, reedier. Was the pressure getting to him?

'Listen, van Tongerloo. Like the minister just said on national television, if you saw it, we need to work together now. I knew Lottman, and I'm back in Amsterdam. Matter of fact, I just met with the sis –'

'Sorry,' he cut in, 'we have to focus, to prioritise.' Then, as if remembering something, he added, 'We have the police commissioner from Amsterdam arriving at any moment.'

'What?' It was like an electric shock through me. 'Joost van Erven?'

'That's right.'

'What's he doing?'

'Running the Dutch command post, as of an hour ago. I must go.' The line went dead.

*

I remained sitting there, in silence. Then a key scratched in the lock and turned.

'*Hoi?*'

Petra's voice brought me back, barely.

'What are you doing, sat here in the dark?' she said.

I forced myself to stand. 'Let me help you with that.'

'I can do it.'

She managed the fall of her suitcase down the steep wooden steps of the boat, one *clack* at a time.

'Been enjoying the jenever?' she said from the galley.

I mumbled an answer, my head in my hands. I felt the boat shudder in the wake of a passing vessel.

'What's wrong?' she said.

'The Lottman investigation.'

'What?' She stopped in front of me. 'Is he dead?'

'No, but I am. Dead in the water.'

'Why?'

'Joost has taken over the Dutch side of the investigation.'

'Is that so bad? Would *you* want that kind of pressure?'

'Could hardly be worse. You'll see.'

Petra sat down in the leather armchair opposite and let her head fall back, exposing her pale neck.

Something occurred to me. 'Weren't you supposed to be staying another day in Brussels?'

She flapped her arms resignedly.

'What?' I said.

'You left, then Sergei and Nadia did, too.'

'Where for?'

'Paris,' she mumbled. 'Great holiday.'

'Oh well. Like you said, as long as they're happy.'

'Hmm.'

'Hmm what?'

'Hmm nothing.'

'What?' I pressed.

'It's just... Sergei –'

'I thought you liked him?' I said it a little too fast; I caught the feeling of vindication in my voice.

'I do, it's just that he –'

'What?'

'He seemed to lose interest, once you left.'

I felt an odd sensation, and not just from the rocking caused by another passing vessel.

'He lost interest with Nadia?' I clarified.

'No, it was more with the situation in Brussels. But I'm not sure. Nadia wasn't exactly too talkative by the end either.'

In any other circumstances, it wouldn't have meant anything. But Russia was one country pointedly left off the favours-for-energy list. Was that somehow significant?

'How were things left with them?'

Petra's eyes looked red and tired. 'I confirmed that we would still be going to St Petersburg in August, if that's what you're asking.'

'And?'

Petra shrugged. 'We are. I guess.'

The timing of Sergei and my daughter meeting coincided precisely with the build-up to Rem's abduction. Was it possible that Sergei was part of an operation – an intelligence gatherer of some kind? His question at the waffle house came back to me: *Strange business about that kidnapping. It's unusual here, isn't it?... High risk, uncertain reward...*

Perhaps less so in his motherland.

*

I slept badly that night and retreated to the hammock slung amidships so as not to disturb Petra. A tarpaulin was flapping on a nearby building, sounding uncannily like loose sails at sea. One of the neighbours was remodelling an old brick packing-house just behind us, extending it upwards and sideways and every which way instead of into a sensible arrangement of rooms. *Listen to the buildings*, the chairman of Amsterdam's public housing committee, Jan Schaefer, had advised back in the 1980s.

Fat chance these days.

I got up and went to stand at my usual spot in the cabin – beside the little shelf I'd fixed up for coffee or an evening jenever – looking out over the dark water.

At some point I must have laid down and drifted off, as I dreamed that Joost was pushing his mother along in a wheelchair. Where, why? His face was taut and I surprised myself when I realised, on waking up, that I'd felt empathy for the man. By the time dawn light spilled into the cabin, I was resolved: I would meet him, just as he'd requested in his email. The sooner the better.

*

This time, we wouldn't be getting together in a cramped operations rooms at the IJ Tunnel 3 police station, or the Ibis hotel just over the road. He had about eighty hours left to help find Rem Lottman.

'There's a bar near the Binnenhof called Barlow,' he told me over the phone. The Binnenhof was the seat of the Dutch parliament. Ministers, including Muriel Crutzen, occupied the buildings nearby. It was back in The Hague – forty minutes' drive from Amsterdam at this hour.

I arrived with ten minutes to spare, stubbing out a cigarette as I entered Barlow. The bar was curiously nondescript, its interior decorated in various inoffensive shades of brown, designed not to draw attention... presumably Joost's reason for choosing it. At the counter I ordered a double shot of espresso. There was an unshaven man beside me, jotting down something in a notebook.

A journalist?

Just as I had that thought, a text arrived on my phone from

Joost, directing me to meet him outside. I drained my little ceramic cup and left three euros on the countertop.

He'd grown slightly in stature, somehow – though he remained a head shorter than me. His boots were polished, like a drill sergeant's. 'Let's go to the Holiday Inn Express,' he said.

'You know all the best places.'

Not even a flicker of a smile.

'How are you?' I persisted.

'Busy,' he replied. 'While I remember, we're taking one of your men for the investigation. The one specialising in surveillance.'

'Stefan?

'That's him.'

Good. He might yet become my 'embed' in Tilburg.

I didn't say anything as we entered the Holiday Inn on the other side of the square. Joost led me through to an atrium area – a quiet corner, another study in taupes and neutral browns. What was it with this town? *The world may be going to hell*, it seemed to say, *but we've no comment.*

'Look, Henk, we may as well get straight down to it,' he said, pulling at the knees of his pleated trousers as he sat. His voice was low. 'I know about the enquiry that was planned. I know about the role Lottman was considering you for, before he went missing. I know everything, in fact.'

'How convenient.'

'What did you just say?'

'It's convenient that you know everything.'

I'd actually meant that it was convenient for him that Rem had gone missing.

He glared at me. 'I'm represented in a private capacity by Vincent van Haaften. Do you remember Vincent?'

How could I forget? He'd represented Frank Hals, and the Tőzsér brothers too.

'A *single* word of slander, of innuendo…' Joost warned, leaving the sentence unfinished.

I nodded knowingly, asking myself who might have more motive for taking Lottman off the board than the man sat opposite me. It was a crazy hypothesis, but it was no crazier than anything else unfolding around me.

'So you'll be heading down south, to Tilburg?'

He gave a short shake of his head. 'Oh I'm staying right here, Henricus, where I belong.' He sat back, gesturing through the walls of the hotel to the seats of national power nearby.

It was a long time since anyone had addressed me by 'Henricus'.

'It's a lot of responsibility, handling the Dutch command post,' I said.

'Don't worry about me. Our Belgian friends will still lead.'

'Van Tongerloo?'

He smiled tightly. 'The original crime was committed on their territory. We wouldn't want to steal their thunder down in Tilburg now, would we? Deny van Tongerloo his glory in event of a successful outcome?'

Nor the opprobrium of an unsuccessful one.

He looked at his watch.

'Let me ask you something,' I said. 'Do you not think it odd, the way in which Lottman went missing?'

Joost gave a short laugh. 'Is there anything normal about a high-profile kidnapping?'

'Well actually yes, there may be, in this case. There are parallels with the Heineken case – that photo, the initial ransom demand. But the way the photo was postmarked Tilburg, drawing the investigation down there... does it not strike you as unusual that the kidnappers would allow that to happen – or that they'd bring Lottman onto Dutch soil at all?'

'You're not privy to all the facts.' Joost smiled tightly again. 'You never were.'

'And now this deadline,' I added.

'What are you implying?'

'I'm not implying anything. I'm inferring –'

I stopped as Joost's attention switched to a man who'd just walked into the hotel lobby: the foreign affairs minister – a stocky man full of bonhomie. One of those people who you want to say hello to out of pure recognition – only to realise that you only know them from TV and the rest of the media. Joost's body language was attempting almost telepathically to draw the man's attention, while trying to seem like he wasn't. Trying to be recognised, simply put.

Frustrated, Joost turned back to me and said: 'Why do we have to keep having this conversation, Henk?'

You asked for it, I felt like saying.

'Why can't you work within the lines?' he continued tersely. 'Are you afraid of boring old progress – afraid of success, even? Or worried that you won't have anything left to blame things on if the normal way doesn't work out for you? Is that it?'

Something reminded me of my dream about him: the pity I'd felt, perhaps.

'Would it make sense to see a psychologist?'

'Yes,' I said, not missing a beat, 'I think you should.'

The air changed. 'You're an egomaniac – and a dangerous one, van der Pol,' he hissed. 'And you're not listening. I know everything.'

He leaned in closer, much closer, so I could feel his breath on me. 'I've news for you.' The venom oozed from his voice. 'I know about the call Lottman made to your old army buddy.'

Blood started thumping in my temples.

'I know *everything*.'

36

SEA AIR

I DROVE BACK TOWARDS Amsterdam. Perhaps I'd see Johan, though I needed to compose my thoughts first. There was nothing I could offer him by way of help or reassurance now. Certainly, I didn't want to rattle him.

I did need to know what was happening, for Johan's sake, but my guess was: very little. Joost and I had arrived at a curious point of equilibrium, each apparently knowing just enough about the other to do real damage if one of us chose to. The question was whether that equilibrium would now hold, or what might upset it.

A few kilometres along the E19 I saw the sign: *Noordwijk aan Zee*. Liesbeth's report had mentioned that Rem grew up there – that his mother still lived in the seaside resort.

It was a place I'd visited numerous times, but it was like I was seeing it through new eyes: the hotels, apartment blocks and tourist spots, the gauzy sea.

Turning onto the beachfront, it all changed: large houses, many of them thatched, generously spaced out among the dun-brown heather like a scene out of Middle Earth. There were poppy-like papaver flowers, and the brightness repeated in the dog rose and barberries that dotted my vision.

Each residence was different according to its owner's tastes. I thought I glimpsed the gaudy Heineken roof, its tiles glinting bottle green.

I turned up one of the lanes, Grotiusweg, which led away from the seafront: the houses were large and compound-like, the village-like appearance from afar entirely deceptive.

As I travelled past them, I looked at the signs on the houses (there were no numbers): *Solstice*, read one beside the gates to a residence that resembled a glorified barn. Perhaps the owners had made their money in the flower business; this area was also known as the 'bulb belt'. Although, these days, the house was just as likely to be owned by the manager of the Dutch national football team.

I slowed the car and wound down the window, hearing the blaring horn of a vehicle behind me. A Range Rover roared past. Beside the road blossomed lilac-coloured tarragon and yellow primrose – the colour spectrum was somehow sharper here; all my senses were heightened. The salt air was astringent.

Then I saw it, the next house – *Sand Hedge*.

The Lottman residence truly was a compound, with a high metal gate, intercom system, and a driveway curving out from behind the namesake hedge. I couldn't see any surveillance cameras but didn't doubt their existence.

There were no reporters beside the gates.

Over the puttering diesel engine of my car came the keening cries of gulls, wheeling above. From the corner of my eye I caught sight of one spiralling down towards the sea.

It would have been insane to call on Lottman's mother unannounced, though I was sorely tempted to. I checked my watch – 11 a.m. – then put the car back in gear and drove on, dodging a woman walking determinedly the other way with her black Labrador. I immediately saw the family resemblance, though her eyes were different. Rem and Carla's dark gaze must have come from the father.

Mrs Lottman wore an outdated golfing cap with a turquoise plastic visor. I pulled over, and she turned to me.

'Mrs Lottman?'

'Do I know you?' she asked coldly, fixing her pale eyes on mine.

'Could I have a word?'

'Who are you?'

Liesbeth's summary of her as 'imperious' was spot on. Her face was creased with lines, but her eyes were alert like a young woman's.

'I –'

'Are you a journalist?'

She looked at her dog, checking its reaction to me. It was more interested in a butterfly. 'Whoever you are, please stay away from my property, or you'll be hearing from the police.'

She stalked off towards the house.

There was an intensity of mood about the place, an almost electrical charge. I drove slowly around the bend in the lane, watching her silhouette in the rear-view mirror against the shimmering sea before it disappeared from view.

A few metres further on, I stopped and sat in the car for several minutes, leafing through Liesbeth's report. Circled by my own pen was a reference to Lottman's time at Leiden Law School. What struck me now was how little distance he'd travelled from home.

*

Leiden Law School: just ten kilometres away, and older than Holland itself. Hugo Grotius, referred to as the 'Mozart of International Law', had started his studies at Leiden in 1594, aged eleven. Being made to feel old was not a new phenomenon. I grimaced, putting my smartphone away.

Physically, old Leiden was Amsterdam in miniature, all canals and plum brick buildings. I passed Van der Werfpark, taking a moment to admire its willow trees. The space occupied by the park had been cleared two centuries ago, when a gunpowder ship had exploded. I raised an eyebrow, recalling last week's events in Amsterdam harbour.

It was the main building of the law school that I was making for – the third floor, where I found the office of Professor Jan

Hawinkels. He was as tall as me and was also my age. His attire consisted of the obligatory spectacles (frameless) of the typical professor, and a well-tailored, cream linen suit. He had a full head of grey hair and an erect posture.

His teaching responsibilities for the academic year had ended, he'd explained on the phone, but a law professor's responsibilities never ceased, apparently. He was busy editing a book – something about the convergence of European and Dutch law. He'd confirmed that, as a junior lecturer, he'd taught Rem Lottman back in the day, and had offered me half an hour of his time. 'A legitimate distraction,' he'd allowed.

Something else was working in my favour here: I was pretty sure that those carrying out the official investigation wouldn't have made contact with him. They'd need all the resources they could get for checking leads and for observation operations down in Tilburg. Without a good reason, 'background' interviews such as this one wouldn't have extended beyond Rem's immediate family and the people currently in his life.

'I've seen it all on the news, of course,' he said as I entered his office. The room was more bright and modern than I'd expected. On the walls hung portraits of Hawinkels posing with official-looking figures, including Barack Obama. There was the faint smell of pipe tobacco.

'I know it's a shock to everyone,' he went on, a bemused look in his eyes, 'but when you've really come to *know* someone, their mind, like I did with Rem...' He shook his head. 'I wondered if I should encourage the law school to do something about it – only, what?'

'Leave it to the official enquiry,' I advised. 'Let them do their job.'

'You speak as though you're not one of them.'

'Professional distance – keeps us all sane.' I changed tack. 'So what was Rem like back then?'

He blew air sharply between his lips. 'It didn't surprise me that he went into politics and got as far as he did. He had a very quick, pliant mind. Would you like some coffee?'

'I'm fine, thanks. I don't want to take you away from your work.'

'It won't – I'll have it brought up. Would you like a cup? I'm having one.'

'Thank you.'

He picked up the phone, pressed a button and said, 'Coffee for two please, Elke.'

'What made him exceptional?' I persisted.

'As I said, his intelligence, and he was very adaptable. I remember, one time, I asked the class to prepare a case for the moot courts. When was it?' He pinched the bridge of his nose. 'Four decades ago...' He shook his head. 'Anyway, I'd given each student one side of the case to prepare. As it happened, there were three absences due to flu that day, all students who'd prepared the defendant's side, so I asked if anyone would be willing to swap sides. Of course no one was, because they'd all done their work by then. So I picked Rem, who happened to be sitting at the front of the class. And he argued that side of the case as though he'd prepared it all along.'

'Don't they say that's the hallmark of a great politician? To be able to inhabit each side's perspectives?'

'*I feel your pain*,' Hawinkels said, quoting Bill Clinton. 'But to extemporise like that, in a complicated legal case... to dissolve into someone else's identity...'

A bright, smiling lady with a bob haircut appeared, carrying a tray with two coffees.

'Thank you, Elke.'

Hawinkels emptied a sugar sachet into his cup and began stirring. When the door closed again he said, 'Then the father committed suicide.'

I tried to imagine the impact of that on Rem.

'He ended up taking six months off,' the professor continued. 'That's a long time for a man with Lottman's ambition.'

'Yes and no. Yes, Rem was a young man in a hurry, but the legal training process is a long one anyway.' I had the sense of Hawinkels finding firmer, more familiar ground. 'Three years of law studies here only got them into the Netherlands Bar Association and their local Bar; they then needed to complete another three years in a law firm with supervision before becoming fully qualified, so they were in it for six years, minimum. Seven years now: we require a masters' degree as well these days.'

I sipped my coffee, comparing Lottman's journey to my own in the army and the police force.

'What did he do?'

'The father? Ran sandpaper factories.'

I'd meant what had Rem done with his time off, but this was interesting. 'Where?'

'Across Scandinavia.'

It made me think of Norway; I couldn't help seeking a connection. There was none, of course. Trading routes across the Baltic… historically, it wasn't unusual for the Dutch to have business interests up there.

'There's still a family company?' I asked.

'You haven't investigated this?' Hawinkels looked surprised. 'They sold the company shortly after Rem's father died, but there's family money, absolutely. Trusts and trusts of the stuff. Which perhaps explains what has now happened.'

'Maybe.' I tried to preserve my veneer of knowledge about the case. 'It's discreet money though, isn't it? Hardly well known.'

'That's Noordwijk for you.'

'Do you have a connection to it?' I asked.

'There are several connections, in fact. Donations to the law school, and Mrs Lottman's fundraising abilities shouldn't be underestimated. She sits on the local Bar Association. Mrs Lottman was an advocate herself, as I'm sure you're aware. She's well connected with the local police.'

There was something advisory in that last remark, a warning

in there. We sat in silence for a moment as I digested things.

Hawinkels eyed his watch.

'Do you ever feel there's a curse on wealthy families in this country?'

'Is it specific to our country?' He steepled his fingers and smiled ruefully. 'Look at the Kennedys, the Gettys, the Hearsts. Haven't they had their share of kidnappings?'

Patty Hearst, kidnapped in 1974, was the most often cited example of 'Stockholm syndrome'. We'd had to consider that, too, back in 1983.

'You're right,' I conceded. 'It puts the Heinekens and Van der Valks in context. The Lottmans too, possibly.'

'Maybe they're all trying to expiate something – a guilt of some kind. The murderee cultivating their murder... wasn't that what someone once postulated?'

I preferred a simpler explanation. 'We ditched Catholicism for Calvinism, but we can never quite get rid of our guilt, can we?'

'Guilt for what?'

'If only we knew, maybe we could do something about it.'

He gave a chuckle, then looked again at his watch.

*

As I walked to the car my phone rang.

Stefan.

'*Hoi*,' I answered.

'Can't you get me out of this? It's a circus down here.'

'Is it fair time already?'

Tilburg Fair was the biggest in Europe.

'Very funny,' he said. 'You know I'm talking about the media, now counting down the hours these bloody suspects gave us. Maintaining this information blackout is a nightmare.'

Tell me about it, I felt like saying. Stefan was almost three decades my junior, and was now my primary source of official case information.

'And it's sweltering,' he complained. 'Thirty-three degrees.'

'Well, enjoy it while it lasts. The recognition, that is: your posting there came from on high. What's happening, anyway?'

'They're putting together an arrest team.'

'Who is?'

'Southern Regions. They're fielding the AT and the OT too.'

I was surprised that the arrest team and observation team hadn't come from the National Police Agency, but perhaps the KLPD had its hands full coordinating with the Belgians – who were still theoretically leading all this.

'Sounds like make-or-break time for van Tongerloo,' I said.

'Yep. They're readying the ransom payment.'

'Huh?'

'Or at least some of it. I don't know – access to information is very limited.'

I swallowed, starting to sense a miscalculation on my part. 'Who are the suspects? Where exactly are you all?'

'The Utrecht forest.'

There was a lake in that forest. Water reflecting off glass...

'Right by the Belgian border?' I asked. 'The Reusel crossing there?'

'Yes, a remote hut nearby. Everyone here believes it's the stronghold.'

The proximity to Belgium might make sense after all. Had the kidnappers crossed the border to scramble the investigators' efforts – to *brouiller les pistes*, as van Tongerloo might have put it? There were smart cameras at the Reusel crossing: another inordinate number of images to sift through, even when assisted by computers.

'Stefan, who are the suspects?' I pressed.

'We've been sworn to secrecy,' he said hesitantly.

I bit the inside of my cheek until I almost broke the skin. 'Come on Stefan, it's me. What's going on? What led you there?'

He paused. 'The OT. They tracked the mailing of that photo of Lottman from a postbox in Broekhoven.'

It was an area populated by several well-connected criminal families.

This was starting to hang together.

'How did they ID the suspects? CCTV? Witnesses?'

'It started with CCTV images, but those proved unreliable,' he replied. 'Then they got lucky and found a witness. That was before I arrived.'

There was a pause, in which I could hear official voices and possibly dogs... Stefan's name being called...

'And you?' he asked. 'What are you doing?'

'Talking to you,' I replied, ready to hang up. 'Please keep me informed.'

*

I still wasn't ready to accept that Rem Lottman was in a cabin in the Utrecht forest. The doubt drew me back to Noordwijk, to Mrs Lottman's residence – to warn her not to pay the ransom. It was all so different to the way we'd progressed the Heineken case. I was sure that the 'proof of life' – the photograph of Lottman – had been manipulated.

I drove slowly back up Grotiusweg and parked twenty metres beyond her gates. From the glovebox of my car, I removed a flat cap and pulled it on. A band of sweat formed around my forehead as I stared at the glinting gates.

I put my gun and warrant card away in the glovebox and exited the car, fingers trembling faintly against the closing door. Whatever I did next, it was very important that it wasn't reported to Joost.

I walked along the lane, away from the gates, staying close to the black metal railings that ran around the Lottman compound. There were no breaks in the fence. I was watching out for cameras as well.

Rounding a bend in the lane, I saw that the fence extended a good thirty metres further. It must encircle the property. It struck me that it had done nothing to protect the

Lottman family in the wider sense.

I walked back to the car and got in. I was about to leave when I heard a grating sound and saw the gates slowly open.

A dark, top-of-the-range Mercedes nosed out into the lane, the driver's head turning to look both ways. The windows were slightly tinted, the sun flashing off them; I couldn't make out the driver's features. The car looked official. Governmental? Nothing was visible through the rear window.

The car pulled out, purring away from me towards the seafront and the main road through Noordwijk. Quickly, I locked up my car and jogged over to the gates, which were still closing. Just before they clicked shut, I slid through the gap and stepped onto the driveway.

I pulled the cap down further over my eyes, my heart beating hard. A nightingale emitted its warbling song. I paced up the driveway, which curved around the tall hedge designed to confound prying eyes.

Into view came a vivid green lawn. Pink roses bloomed from islands of moss and lichen that were intended to bind together the earth and sand, to protect it from coastal erosion.

Something felt very wrong.

The house was on the highest point of the rising ground but was relatively modest; it wouldn't have looked out of place in a less salubrious Amsterdam suburb. Built from grey brick, with flat horizontal lines, its picture windows looked out onto the sea from beneath green-and-white striped awnings.

I crouched down. From the west came the insistent, indifferent sound of waves. It was amazing how quickly it happened – I hadn't noted any cameras pointing my way.

'You!'

He came out of nowhere, his bulk appearing before me as I sprang up. I recognised too late the plain-clothes police type.

As I turned on my heels – 'Hey!' – his weight was on top of me. I fell face first into rose thorns and then a soft bed of earth.

37

IN CAPTIVITY

'YOU REALLY ARE MAKING a mistake,' I told the arresting officer. Big guy, heavy jaw.

He led me to the back of Leiden police station, not a kilometre from where Jan Hawinkels worked.

'I'm a policeman.'

'So you said.'

He raised a large hand before I could speak again. 'I know, it's all there in your car – your warrant card, your other ID...'

Did I not even resemble a cop now? My torn, muddy face couldn't have helped. You don't get a second chance to make a first impression, they say.

The officer spoke to the desk clerk. 'Another one found at the Lottman place in Noordwijk.'

She sighed and pulled out a charge sheet. 'Fire away.'

'Trespassing,' the officer said, 'resisting arrest, impersonation of a police officer, failure to produce valid ID...'

As if in some horrible cartoon, the clerk had trouble keeping up.

'Name and address?' she asked eventually.

'Henk van der Pol,' the arresting officer answered for me. He flipped a page of his notebook and read out my home address on Entrepotdok.

'No possessions?' the clerk asked.

The officer turned to me. 'OK, hands up.'

He patted me down. 'These.' He handed her my car keys and lighter. 'And just the clothes he stands in.'

She took my fingerprints and sealed them.

'Come this way,' he said.

'Where's the magistrate?'

'Relax.' He placed a hand behind my shoulders, guiding me. 'All in good time.'

A commotion erupted at the door: another arresting officer pushing in an old, dishevelled man who was jabbering drunkenly about Holland no longer belonging to the Dutch. The desk clerk dutifully flipped to a new sheet.

'Shoplifting,' the arriving officer said over the drunk's babbling. I was steered past him towards the stairs leading down to the cells. 'He's got a bottle of rice wine in his inside pocket...' the policeman was saying. 'Again.'

*

They're just like you imagine them from the movies, the cells. A concrete room – bare but for a bed, small sink and toilet. My arresting officer retreated through the steel door, which creaked on its heavy metal hinges and then slammed shut.

I pounded it once. 'The magistrate is supposed to validate the arrest, damn you!'

'He's coming,' I heard the retreating voice say.

I kicked the foam mattress off the bed. If the grey and lime-green colour scheme was meant to be calming, it wasn't working.

I replaced the mattress and sat on it, elbows on knees. Between my two soiled boots was a line of ants making their way determinedly along a crack in the concrete. The police had means of keeping me for up to thirty days if they could get a magistrate to agree. I stood up again and paced the small cell.

How long I'd been pacing for I don't know, but finally I heard footsteps. The observation hatch opened and a voice said, 'Sit on your bed.'

Away from the door, in other words.

I did so.

The door groaned open. There stood my arresting officer. 'Come with me.'

He led me past another cell, which contained the jabbering drunk, and into a room where the magistrate was sitting. He was my age or a bit older and had a tired, decent air about him.

'You say your name's Henk van der Pol of Entrepotdok, Amsterdam?'

'Yes.'

'You claim you're a police officer?'

'I am.'

'Have you checked that?' the magistrate asked, craning his neck.

The arresting officer looked blank.

'Do it.'

He turned back to me. 'You have the right to a lawyer. If you can't afford one, a public one can be made available to you. You don't have to answer any questions. Do you understand?'

'I understand. Now can I make a call? I'd like to tell my wife what's going on.'

He looked me squarely in the eye, then reached inside his jacket pocket. 'Here,' he said, 'just use mine.' He pushed the phone across the table.

It would be his work phone: a withheld number. My wife didn't answer.

'Petra, it's me,' I said into the voicemail void. 'I've been unavoidably detained in Leiden, I'll call you when I can get back to Amsterdam.'

The magistrate nodded, as if confirming I'd done the right thing. 'If you're who you say you are, this shouldn't take long. Though I have to ask: what in God's name were you doing at the Lottman residence without ID?'

'I was following a lead. Maybe not in the best way.'

'I'll say.'

The door opened and the arresting officer looked at me, expression bovine. 'There's a call for you.'

The magistrate eyed him, then me. 'Take it,' he allowed.

I stood up and followed the officer through to a neighbouring interview room with a desk and a phone.

I picked up the handset warily. 'Hello?'

'How bad do you want things to get, Henricus?'

The room temperature felt like it dropped several degrees.

'I've got options,' Joost said. 'I could even get you into Scheveningen at short notice. How d'you feel about that?'

The heavily fortified prison was ten minutes away, if that. Nothing felt far apart anymore.

I laughed sharply. 'Even *you* couldn't twist the justice system in such a warped way, Joost.' I was thinking of the magistrate on the other side of the wall. He wouldn't be biddable. That wasn't how things worked here in Holland.

'Who needs to twist anything?'

Joost let the question hang there and I felt a chill pass through me again, like a ghostly form entering and then leaving my body.

'You've ignored a parking fine. The new legislation applies to policemen too, as I'm sure you're aware.'

'What the fuck are you talking about?' I said.

The arresting officer eyed me sharply.

'Corner of Koningslaan and Willemsparkweg,' Joost explained. It sounded like he was reading notes. Less so as he continued: 'I'm sure you remember. Norwegian guy named Lars Pelt lived in a house nearby?'

Dimly I recalled getting the ticket. Under new legislation, people could be jailed for unpaid fines if arrested for a separate offence.

'That crime scene belonged to Bas Bergveld,' Joost went on.

Of course: I'd received the ticket while involved in a fracas with Bergveld, one of Joost's boys.

'By extension, that crime scene belonged to me,' Joost continued. 'And you fucked with it, causing me a lot of problems. So now I'm fucking with you. Do you see how this works? Are you getting the idea? It's really not that complicated.'

'No.'

'Scheveningen accepts the full spectrum of prisoners – from minor to the most serious. It's certainly a possibility.'

'Aren't you forgetting something?'

'I don't think so, but please enlighten me if I am.'

'I'm supposed to have received three visits before being liable for arrest for an unpaid fine.'

'Yes. But then you haven't exactly been in your precinct much of late, have you Henk? Gallivanting around the place as usual, interfering when you're not needed or wanted. Should my men attempt to pay your houseboat a visit? Ask after you with your wife?'

'This is bullshit.'

'It is and it isn't.'

'Don't you have work to do in Tilburg?' I said, seeking the high road.

'Not really,' he replied. 'You'll see.'

What did he mean by that?

'Actually, you won't,' he continued. 'Because you'll be in a police cell down in the basement of Leiden police station until after the situation in Tilburg is resolved.'

The phone went dead.

*

I must have scraped my knuckles against the wall; they were bleeding. From down the corridor came music, the volume turned up, perhaps to drown out the verbal assaults of the drunk. He was ranting about Johan Cruijff and the glory days of Dutch football.

Every half an hour the music on the radio stopped for news: Tilburg... the standoff at the stronghold reportedly containing

Rem Lottman... less than two days to go. Something about difficulties within the joint investigation team... had Stefan mentioned this?

It was coming from another world now.

I didn't have the right to make phone calls. This was standard practice, I knew; it prevented accomplices being tipped off, evidence being discarded. I sat on the hard, cold floor with my head in my hands, imagining my phone ringing in the glovebox of my car – Petra and Stefan trying to reach me in vain.

Food trays appeared in the hatch and then vanished. I recalled hearing somewhere that Edouard Tailleur had refused food at Scheveningen, his lawyers complaining that it was impossible for his African palate.

I squeezed my eyes shut until squiggles and stars exploded behind them.

*

Dreams and odd visitations came and went. At one point Sebastiaan Bergveld appeared, entering my cell like a ghost. Hadn't Stefan confirmed that he'd left the force?

'This has nothing to do with you,' I said aloud.

The observation hatch opened, two eyes fixed on me.

Bergveld leaned against the wall, one foot casually crossed in front of the other.

'But I'm invested,' he said. 'Involved.'

It sounded like something I might have said.

'I want to talk about the evening of the Energy Summit. Rem Lottman's security team going to your home on Entrepotdok – why did you arrange for that to happen?'

'I didn't.'

The Ukrainian biker gang had, but I couldn't reveal that or what I'd gone on to do to neutralise the threat. The double bind...

'Didn't you cause Rem Lottman to be kidnapped, van der Pol?' Bergveld said point blank, pushing himself off the wall with the ball of his foot before vanishing into the cool, stale air.

The observation hatch closed, the eyes vanishing into darkness.

Radio reports continued to filter in between the drunk's commentary on the 1974 World Cup final. The hut on De Flaes Lake in the Utrecht forest…

The arrest team ready to storm it…

Perhaps this was *meant* to be: perhaps I was *supposed* to know what it felt like to be held in captivity.

Relief? Was that the dominant emotion I'd seen in the photo of Rem Lottman, holding up his copy of *De Telegraaf*?

If I could just get rid of my sense of guilt, perhaps I could escape once and for all.

The radio announced that the ransom was partly paid. Stupid, stupid woman. The proof of life had been doctored for sure.

Tilburg, the radio announcer continues, *a news helicopter has spotted smoke canisters being fired into the hut…*

'Penalty!' the drunk shrieks.

The hut on fire.

… reports of shooting…

The hut ablaze.

Holland loses; the drunk wails.

My head lolling and straightening sharply.

Van Tongerloo's distinctive Flemish voice crackling through: *plausible intelligence… good reasons for the decisions taken…*

All occupants of the incinerated hut presumed dead.

When I pressed my eyes shut again, flames appeared in the dark behind my eyelids.

*

A key turning woke me, the door's heavy metal hinges groaning as it opened. *'Meneer van der Pol,'* the arresting officer announced. *'Het is voorbij.'*

It's over.

For that, I wanted to lay the bastard out cold.

That was what the arrest team had said to Freddy Heineken in 1983, when they'd found him alive.

38

BRUSSELS PARK, AGAIN

I WALKED OUT INTO the sunlight, squinting – dazed, like some night creature.

My car was back in Noordwijk.

I took a cab, the driver waiting for me while I retrieved his fare from the glovebox. My phone was there, too. As expected, the battery was dead. I plugged it into the car's charging dock and paid the cabbie, who was loitering amongst the crowd outside the Lottmans' gates.

I drove away fast. My phone lit up with six missed calls: two were from Petra, three from Stefan. The last one was from Leonie, Lottman's girlfriend in Brussels.

I was just about to call my wife when Stefan's name flashed up on the phone.

'*Hoi*,' I answered. I needed to clean my teeth.

'I'm glad to hear from you,' he said. 'Where've you been?'

'I needed to take a break.'

'I thought you were already taking time off?'

'So this was time off from time off. Hey, you're answerable to me, not the other way around. What the hell went down in Tilburg?'

'Things happened fast.'

'That much is clear.'

'Forensics are still working on the hut, but it doesn't look promising. Everything inside it was incinerated.'

287

'So now they're searching for Lottman's DNA?'

'Yes, but they're worried about co-mingling. The heat was intense. We're talking about dust there now.'

'Jesus.'

'At least we didn't pay the full ransom,' Stefan said.

'How much was paid?'

'A quarter of the fifteen. Almost four million.'

If my week had been bad, spare a thought for Mrs Lottman. Carla Lottman, too.

Something else occurred to me. 'The kidnappers demanded the ransom in four currencies. Which one was paid?'

'Rubles.'

I pulled over by the side of the road, just ahead of the turn onto the E19.

'The payment was tracked?'

'To a point. It went to a bank in Russia. You can imagine how well that's proceeding. I don't expect there'll be a joint investigation team there –'

'Where in Russia?'

I waited. Cars and lorries thundered past, the larger ones rocking my car.

'A bank in St Petersburg.'

*

By the time Petra called me I was halfway back to Brussels. I'd wanted to hold off speaking with her; I needed to structure my suspicions about Sergei...

'Henk, where in hell have you been?'

'In hell is about the right description for it. On the Lottman trail. You've probably seen it on the news; I'm sorry I couldn't update. Did you get my voicemail?'

'Jesus Christ, Henk, that was three days ago!'

'Yes. Have you heard from Nadia?'

'No!' Pause. 'Why?'

'Listen to me, this is confidential to the investigation: part of the ransom was paid to a bank in Russia.'

'It's not so confidential to my old employer. *Het Parool* are already researching a story about it.'

'What about Sergei?'

'What *about* Sergei?'

'The timing of him meeting Nadia. Him being from St Petersburg, which is where the bank is and where the money went...'

'So, is everyone in Russian a villain now? When did you become so xenophobic?'

It was an absurd allegation.

She said, 'If you must know, that St Petersburg account belonged to a Lottman family trust, as the *Het Parool* journalist has discovered.'

They'd paid the money to themselves.

Perhaps the father had established an outpost there. Mrs Lottman hadn't needed any advice from me after all.

'Where *are* you?' Petra demanded.

'Returning to Brussels. The girlfriend, she's not answering her phone –'

'Christ,' she said, exasperated. The line went dead.

*

There were uniformed police in front of Leonie's apartment.

I flashed my badge. 'What happened?'

'The woman on the second floor,' an evidence technician said. 'Gone.'

'Where?'

He shrugged.

I recalled my last conversation with her after Tailleur's death. While I'd been busy concluding that she was safe from Ghanaian warlords, she was searching for reasons behind Rem's disappearance. I'd asked whether he had any weaknesses – gambling, drugs... *He was a senior politician*, she'd exclaimed before putting the phone down on me.

289

I glanced up at the second floor. 'What's left up there?' I asked the technician.

His face mask was pulled down below his glistening stubble. Brussels was still baking hot. 'What's your interest in this?' he asked.

'I've been working on the Dutch side of it.' I realised that I hadn't shaved in a while either. 'Mind if I take a look inside the apartment?'

'Yes,' one of the uniformed officers said, stepping in front of me.

*

I sought shade near the cooling burble of the fountain in the centre of the park.

There, I called Francine, Lottman's assistant. I wanted to quiz her about any travel arrangements she might have been involved in making for either Rem or Leonie, but her phone number was no longer in service.

I called Petra instead. She answered.

'I'm sorry about going radio silent on you,' I said. 'Sorry too for suspecting Sergei. It was wrong of me –'

'Henk,' she cut in, 'leave the case alone now. You're not in a position to do any more. What is there to do, anyway? Rem Lottman is dead.'

I swapped the phone to my left hand, running my right palm over my damp brow.

'You're right,' I said.

The water from the fountain in the centre of the park sparkled. I looked up the east–west gravel path, towards Lottman's girlfriend's apartment, and for one crazy second I imagined him standing there, staring down at me. My gaze lowered to the police activity at the ground-floor entrance.

'Come back to Amsterdam,' my wife said wearily.

'OK.'

She hung up.

I glanced at my watch. It was 10 a.m. I'd be back in Amsterdam for lunch, traffic allowing.

Only I couldn't return to the car just yet. I stood there with my senses unnaturally alive. I could distinguish the sound of each distinct vehicle that made up the background traffic noise.

There were too many oddities.

How could Rem have been taken here, in Brussels Park?

I glanced through the trees at the different flags flying. *Listen to the buildings,* Jan Schaefer had said.

Practically every building around Brussels Park was high security; almost every one would have camera surveillance. How could Rem have been forcibly taken without the incident being caught *somewhere*?

How could he have been bundled into a car, or a waiting van, without someone raising the alarm – someone other than Leonie? Why would the kidnappers have picked *this*, of all places?

Walking around the perimeter pavements, I saw just how many cameras there were.

'Stefan, where are you?' I left a message. 'Call me.'

I got back in my car and drove.

*

I was making good progress towards Amsterdam and Petra. The news commentary on the radio was comparing Lottman's death to the assassination of Pim Fortuyn.

Fortuyn had been a rising star of Dutch politics when he was shot dead on a Hilversum street just ahead of the 2002 general elections. How had Rem felt about that pivotal event? It was just one of many questions I wanted to ask him now that he'd gone.

'This is different,' a pundit was saying. 'However brilliant he was, Rem Lottman was a bureaucrat, not an elected official.'

Like this was a consolation?

'But it's the same,' another commentator contended. 'The same aftermath, of confusion and unease. How could this happen in Holland, in this day and age?'

291

'What about the funeral?' a third voice asked.

There'd already been a crematorium, I felt like calling in.

'My understanding is that the family will handle it in private.'

'Let's turn to consider the upcoming elections,' the first pundit intervened, steering the conversation away tactfully, 'and how this turn of events might affect the narrowing election polls...'

The temperature fell as I headed north. I checked my phone again and, as I did so, Stefan's name flashed up.

'Where've you been?' I answered, turning the radio down.

'In the final debrief for the joint teams down here –'

'Did anything new come up? How was it?'

'Like a wake. Nothing new.'

I paused out of some sense of respect.

'What happened with the investigation of the kidnapping scene?'

'What do you mean, what happened?'

'Brussels Park – all the camera footage.'

'We couldn't get access to most of it,' Stefan said.

'Why?'

'Those buildings are mostly foreign embassies – overseas missions. Try asking for the US Embassy's security footage. "Good luck", was the comment doing the rounds.'

I shifted position. 'So what's happening now?'

'Enquiries are ongoing, as they say – though CCTV is often flawed in any case, as we saw in Tilburg.'

'Saw what in Tilburg?'

'The mailing of that *Telegraaf* photo there,' he replied.

'What about it?'

'Don't you know?' He paused, surprised. 'The enquiry started with CCTV images of the street where the mailbox was located, but those images proved hopeless. Then they got lucky and found a witness. That was just before I arrived in Tilburg.'

'Who was the witness?'

'A snitch, it turned out.'

Not again.

'Why did the CCTV images prove hopeless?' I pressed.

'The image was only a partial view, and…'

'What?'

'It got recorded over.'

Fuck. Due to incompetence, or a cover-up?

'Did you see the image before it was lost?'

'Briefly.'

'Describe it.'

'You couldn't see her face anyway –'

'Her?'

'Yes, definitely a female.'

'Why not?'

'Why not what – male?'

'No, Stefan! Why couldn't you see her face?'

'She was wearing a cap.'

I almost lost control of the car. 'With a tinted visor, like a golfing cap?'

Could Mrs Lottman have mailed the photo to herself, just like she'd sent the money to one of her own family's accounts?

'No, it was more like a baseball cap…'

Or was it ridiculous to think that Mrs Lottman might be involved?

No, not at all.

Suddenly, things clicked into place.

39

REQUIEM FOR A DUTCHMAN

THERE SHE WAS, with her black Labrador, far down the beach. There were no houses from here to the south of the Lottman residence – just a barely beaten path to Katwijk, the next town along the coast.

'Mrs Lottman,' I yelled.

She was facing out to sea. The wind was blowing a fine sandstorm. The helm grass – planted to hold the dunes together – hissed with resistance.

I jogged over to her. The dog sat beside her, its head mimicking her orientation towards the waves. Flag attachments clanked distantly.

'Mrs Lottman,' I shouted, breathing heavily.

She turned her head to look at me, and must have recognised me from before, in the lane outside her house, because her eyes were like steel.

'Who *are* you?' she said.

'Police,' I replied. 'I knew Rem.'

Her eyes remained on mine for a second longer before she turned back to the water, which was suddenly lit a golden-white.

'That photo of him that appeared in *De Telegraaf*: it was taken right here in Noordwijk, wasn't it? Through one of those picture windows.' I nodded over my shoulder. The green-and-white awnings were only just visible on the rising ground. 'There's a play of light in that image. A very characteristic play, it turns out.'

Those rippling reflections ran deep in my forebears' consciousness. Or perhaps *un*consciousness: maybe that was the reason why it had taken me this long to recognise the distinctive light patterns made by the North Sea.

The Labrador's tail thumped the sand.

'Want one?' I offered her a cigarette.

She didn't move a muscle.

'No one could have kidnapped Rem in Brussels Park,' I went on, cigarette waggling in my mouth. It took me three attempts to get it lit. 'Not without help from some very well-connected people, that is.'

We stood for a second in silence, the gulls wheeling above.

'Where did he go?' I asked, exhaling smoke. 'Has the girlfriend already joined him?'

Her eyes – just visible in profile – were glassy.

'I can see now why he was so obsessed with the Heineken kidnapping. Freddy H came back alive.' The lit end of my cigarette brightened; the smoke vanished upwards from my mouth. 'Whereas Rem's dad – your husband – didn't.'

Her clenched jaw quivered.

'But why?' I persevered.

At some point, I was going to get a telling reaction.

'Why all this trouble? The false trail to Tilburg, all that police time there wasted… why did Rem want to dissolve into –'

'Get away from my boy and I!' she shrieked.

I raised a pacifying hand.

Then I raised the other, in a gesture of surrender, as two darkly clothed men approached quickly across the dunes. The cigarette dropped from my mouth. Both men had semi-automatics drawn in military, two-handed grips.

I stepped away from Mrs Lottman and her dog, just in case one of the men got trigger-happy. The dog had done nothing wrong.

'Don't move!' the man on the left shouted in Dutch. 'Get down on your knees!'

Was this Lottman's security team, diverted by my wife on the night of the Energy Summit?

Only, my wife *hadn't* diverted them. Lottman himself had done that. *I've asked our security people to send a car around to your houseboat*, he'd told me.

'Get down on your knees!' the other man echoed, the bill of his black cap pulled down over his eyes, the gun's muzzle trained on my torso. The dark dot lowered as I did what he said.

No, these weren't private-security individuals. They didn't have the uniforms, the earpieces or the other giveaway gizmos that came with rent-a-cops.

Once certain that I posed no immediate threat, they disarmed me and cuffed my hands roughly behind my back. Then they pulled me back upright and led me across the dunes, one walking behind me, the other leading the way.

I considered the last time I'd been arrested, and the speed with which it had unfolded; I recalled the official-looking Mercedes that had driven away through the gates of the Lottman residence, just moments before. Had Rem been in that car, looking out at me from behind those tinted rear windows? Had he alerted security, while being spirited away once the investigative focus had moved south?

A black van came bouncing over the sand, its white halogen lights dipping and rising; it slowed as the sand deepened and then it stopped, engine idling.

What else had Rem Lottman engineered?

We made our way towards the black vehicle in single file. From behind me came the determined footfall of the gunman following us, as well as the indifferent boom and hiss of the waves…

The side door of the van rattled open.

'Nice of you gentlemen to offer me a ride,' I said, as my head was forced down and I was bundled into the back.

There were grooved metal benches down both sides of the

interior. Two big guys were sitting on one of them. They looked like secret service men.

My hands were re-cuffed in front of me so that the men could see them, and then the door slid shut and someone thumped the side of the van. My eyes adjusted; it wasn't total darkness – there was a smoked Perspex window in the roof, like a dim skylight.

The men looked at one another silently as the wheels spun in the sand – would they need to get out and push?

Finally, the van found purchase and we lurched forward.

At all times, one of the men was looking at me. It impressed me how they knew to alternate, their eyes bright in the purple-grey gloom.

'Where are we going?' I asked vainly.

Not back to Leiden, I grasped, after we'd been travelling for a while at speed. My inbuilt compass told me that we were heading south, though. The traffic sounds suggested a motorway.

I had the sense of other vehicles joining us, forming a cavalcade; red and blue flickered through the crack in the side door panel. I stifled a belch, a nauseous taste rising up my throat. Had the Lottman family delivered me into longer-term captivity?

Lottman would certainly know how to do that, and more besides. How to create investigative chaos between the Dutch and Belgian police... How to make his mother protective, complicit... How to manipulate his girlfriend, who'd temporarily engaged with me merely to ensure that the *pistes* truly were *brouillé*d?

You artful bastard, I thought, as the flickering grew brighter; we were slowing through a short tunnel or an archway. The side door rattled open and in flooded light. We were in The Hague all right, but not at any prison.

Rather, at the heart of government.

Alighting from the Mercedes in front of us was Muriel Crutzen.

*

The energy minister's office, on the top floor of 73 Bezuidenhoutseweg, was a light, modern space – *open for business*, it seemed to announce to visitors.

'Nice digs,' I said. Light reflected warmly off the wooden floors and bookcases. With us were one of the secret service agents and a tall young man in a suit who I took to be an adviser of hers.

Crutzen was harder and more compact in person than on TV – like a tightly coiled spring, barely able to contain her energy and determination. Everything about her connoted ruthless competence.

'I'll get straight to the point,' she said.

'Please do.'

She paused, surprised by my words. 'Rem has gone, for reasons you appear to understand.'

'Could we just test that hypothesis?'

'Please, you know better than anyone about the scheme he was running.'

'He?'

'Yes,' she said sharply. 'Not us. *He.*'

She paused again, letting that distinction sink in.

'You're the one who challenged him about it.'

'Maybe,' I conceded. 'But why did he take off so suddenly? The last time I spoke with him, he was talking about an internal enquiry. Something changed. What?'

Her features altered, turning reflective. 'We're still trying to piece together exactly what happened.'

'You're still saying in public that he was kidnapped?'

'We're still trying to piece together exactly what happened,' she repeated.

Perhaps if the adviser wasn't in the room we'd be having a different conversation; I looked at him pointedly, but he didn't take the hint.

'Maarten,' she said, 'please could you check on that meeting.'

I waited for Maarten to run along. There was only the secret service man, Crutzen and myself left now. Once the heavy doors closed I said, 'What was the sequence of events here, minister? When I saw Rem at the Energy Summit, he asked me to lead an internal enquiry.'

Same night as the battle in the harbour.

I thought too about the painting – the Verspronck that had sent me up to Norway. It had been stolen and apparently lost aboard Hals's burned-out ship, yet it was later discovered in a Schiphol storage locker. The connecting thread, I now saw, was no girl dressed in blue but rather...

'Joost.'

He'd jettisoned Bergveld and appointed a notorious defence attorney.

You're not privy to all the facts, he'd barked at me in the Holiday Inn, just a few hundred metres from where we now stood...

What campaign had Joost been mounting against Lottman?

Crutzen sighed, holding up a printed email. 'The Amsterdam police commissioner has indeed been assiduous in his approaches to the various ministries: foreign affairs, security, justice... even interior and kingdom relations. Attempting to press forward with his own review concerning the unusual scheme set up with our oil-producing partners – a scheme that he claimed was Amsterdam-based.'

I didn't doubt that Joost had his own narrative worked out about the beaten-up Ukrainian escort and the painting and the Norwegian diplomat who'd died during its 'recovery' and... quite possibly many other things that I wasn't even aware of.

Crutzen pressed her lips firmly together before continuing.

'The cabinet is united in its decision to treat this as a matter of national security. The Lottman file has been sealed.'

I needed to think fast. Joost had made his move, and he'd misjudged it here in the big leagues.

'Is Lottman alive?' I sought confirmation.

'We just don't know. But if he is, there's no way back for him.

Rem's prospectively up to his neck in scandal.' She paused. 'Perhaps it's better now that the public *believe* him to be dead from a failed kidnapping.'

I nodded. 'You haven't looked for him?'

'Where would we start? Every country he dealt with could – in theory – have reason to offer him safe harbour.'

It was true, I now saw. Freddy Brekhus's contentedness up in Oslo. If there was one thing my Norway trip had shown me, it was that the Norwegians bore no grievances. The opposite, in fact. And then there was Captain NaTonga's claims at the ICC about the payments to the Ghanaian government; Sheikh Yasan, too, flying off to Switzerland... None of the governments of these countries had reason to bear a grudge against Rem Lottman. Rather, each had been the beneficiary of his lavish generosity. A generosity that one of them was now repaying?

'He could be anywhere,' I acknowledged. A remote island off the Norwegian coast, a gated community in Abu Dhabi or some oil-rich African enclave...

'There have been haphazard sightings from Lapland to Tanzania,' Crutzen said, 'but nothing concrete –'

'Why Tanzania?' I wondered aloud. 'That's the other side of Africa from Ghana.'

She shrugged evasively. 'Just intelligence chatter.'

But nothing frivolous would ever come out of Muriel Crutzen's mouth, I thought.

'The fire down in Tilburg... are the teams there still looking for his DNA?'

'Investigations are ongoing,' she replied. 'These things take time.'

Especially with Dutch elections imminent and the polls narrowing. Lottman's apparent death could only help the status quo. The shock of his passing would privilege the familiar. This was realpolitik all right.

'Before disappearing, Lottman wrote me a classified

memorandum.' She picked up another sheet of paper. 'He said that there was an ideal man to run any enquiry – a man who would understand things from all angles.' She looked up at me.

A warm sensation spread through my chest.

'Rem's judgement was clearly compromised in many respects,' she went on, 'but on this matter, I'm rather inclined to trust his views.'

I shifted my weight from one foot to another. 'Yet Lottman's no longer with us.'

'But Mrs Lottman very much is. And she happens to be persuaded of your investigative abilities as well, based on your rather… *challenging* conversation with her this morning.'

So, Mrs Lottman was what Jan Hawinkels had claimed. *Her fund-raising abilities shouldn't be underestimated,* the law professor had told me. Was she helping her son's former party with their election efforts? I was starting to lose track of all the different arrangements and alliances.

'That's the deal we've worked out, anyway,' Crutzen said.

'What deal?'

'For you to assume a role here in The Hague.'

'What role?'

'To be defined. No matter – we need you inside the tent, van der Pol.'

I shook my head in disbelief. Was this really happening?

'You're central to the enquiry,' she said. 'Possibly you underestimate your power?'

'Hardly, relative to yours.' I laughed. 'Do you use that line often?'

She winked.

The door swished open. Young Maarten stood there looking at her with eyebrows raised and a leather document wallet by his side.

'Yes?'

He walked over to her in his polished shoes and whispered something about the king.

She nodded once.

'Please wait here,' she said, leaving me in the room.

*

With me was the secret service man, one of the two gunmen who'd accosted me on the beach. At least he'd taken his baseball cap off. He was smiling affably now, but stood beside the door, making it clear that I'd be staying put.

I looked past him through the big windows at the treetops of the Haagsche Bos, fully in leaf. It reminded me of Brussels Park – the secrets that the famous square had refused to yield.

Do things evolve?

It's funny: unlike some of my seafaring ancestors, I've never considered myself to be a mystical man, but sometimes I do wonder whether there is a certain karma at play in life, if I can call it that – a lesson that we're intended to learn, at some point along the way. This was the second time a paternal figure had vanished on me.

Dad was driven away in Cape Town, you see – his face hidden behind the smoked glass of a VW prison van. Manslaughter of someone on his boat in the merchant navy, the charges read. The details were never quite made clear to me.

The charges were dropped, I learned, when I finally found the courage to enter the police station – only to be told that Dad had already left. 'You must be young Henricus?' the old custody sergeant had said in his Afrikaans accent. 'Your dad's somewhere else now, son. He's someone else's problem.'

The sergeant had handed me a photo of him, from when Dad had been in his custody: my father holding a little tray of letters and numbers in front of his chest – his prison number. It was the last I ever saw of him. There was the occasional cryptic postcard, and then not even that.

We're all hostage to something.

*

Muriel Crutzen and young Maarten swept back into the room with fresh purpose. 'I need to leave for an appointment with the prime minister, to brief His Majesty about the Lottman dossier. It's one meeting I shouldn't be late for.'

'No,' I agreed.

'May I have your answer?'

'About what?'

'The role.'

'Shouldn't we define it a little?'

'In time. Don't worry, it will be acceptable in terms of rank and pay package.'

'Could I at least run a move to The Hague by my wife?'

Petra would be popping the champagne corks over this one. The Hague was a stone's throw from her favourite cousin in Delft.

'Briefly,' Crutzen allowed.

'I'd also like to take the family somewhere nice for a couple of weeks. Our holiday this week got interrupted...'

Watching me intently, Crutzen nodded. 'Perhaps it might help you to find the requisite' – she sought the *bon mot* – 'perspective.'

'Perhaps,' I said. 'I've always wanted to go to Zanzibar, actually. It's an interesting crossroads, that part of the world.'

She shot me a quizzical look.

Maarten was eying his watch anxiously. 'We really need to go –'

'Stay in touch,' Muriel Crutzen instructed, hastily gathering up her papers.

'Oh, don't worry,' I said. 'I won't disappear on you.'

I hope you enjoyed *The Harbour Master*. I began writing it because, when I started living in Amsterdam, I couldn't find a Harry Bosch, a John Rebus or indeed a Kurt Wallander-type story set there – which struck me as odd, given how Holland neighbours Scandinavia and lends itself just as well to crime fiction.

The kernel of *The Harbour Master* came from writing a newspaper article about the way the Dutch tackle human trafficking. I found myself invited on an undercover operation with the Dutch National Crime Squad into the Amsterdam Red Light District.

Henk's journey started out there, and it continues on. Please try the first two chapters of the next book, overleaf. I'd love to stay in touch as well so please consider signing up at www.DanielPembrey.com to receive my author news every few months.

Finally, if you did enjoy *The Harbour Master*, it is always hugely helpful as an author to receive a short review on Amazon and/or Goodreads. I'd be so grateful.

We (Henk and myself) hope to continue the journey with you,

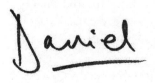

1

IF YOU GAZE INTO THE ABYSS...

'DON'T GO IN THERE.'

I was standing outside a set of double doors on the nineteenth floor of the Ministry for Security and Justice. The brown-carpeted anteroom was dim; much of it was in shadow. I'd been summoned for an after-hours meeting.

'Not yet,' the man added.

He was the assistant to the justice minister.

'What's this about, anyway?' I asked.

'I'm unable to advise,' he replied, his dark features dimly lit by his computer screen. The soft clacking of his keyboard resumed.

I eyed my watch again. My wife was waiting back at our hotel to have dinner. Apparently, global security considerations no longer respected office hours.

I paced over to the tall windows. It was dark outside and The Hague's skyline winked, orange and white. The westward panorama took in the twin white towers of the International Criminal Court and, far ahead, I could make out the inky darkness of the North Sea... landmarks in the case of Rem Lottman, the politician who'd been working for the energy minister, Muriel Crutzen. She'd encouraged me to consider a job here in The Hague. I still didn't know exactly what it involved, but perhaps I was about to find out.

I turned back to the assistant, about to say something, when the double doors to the ministerial office flew open and there he stood.

'Henk,' he said, appraising me. 'Is it OK to call you Henk?'

'Is it OK to call you Willem?'

He smiled and stepped forward, shaking my hand firmly.

Willem van der Steen was of medium height and a stocky build, with wiry grey hair. His white shirt was open at the neck; his sleeves were rolled up. He looked like he'd be a tough bastard in a fight.

He was a vote winner, *'strong on law and order in uncertain times'*. *'We Dutch remain liberal – within limits'* was another of his election slogans. He was known to be a copper's friend. He'd started off in the force and gone on to run Southern Regions. In some ways he'd remained an old-fashioned bruiser – but now he was one with formidable powers.

He released my hand and led me into his office. There was a pattern to the appearance of these ministers' rooms, I was discovering: modern, workmanlike, unpretentious. In van der Steen's case, I glimpsed an oil painting in the shadows: a marine vista, choppy seas. A ship sat in the centre, listing, valiantly holding its course.

There was a circular glass table strewn with papers. A phone sat in the middle.

'A conference call ran long. The Americans like to keep us late.'

It begged questions that I couldn't ask.

'Drink?' he asked, closing the door behind us.

The offer surprised me.

'Still or sparkling?' he added, correcting my misapprehension.

'Still.'

He poured a glass for me, emptying a small bottle of water.

'Please, take a seat.'

I sat on the opposite side of the table.

'You come highly recommended,' he said, emptying another bottle – sparkling – into his own glass.

'Indeed?'

He sat down. 'The energy minister.'

No surprises then… or none yet.

I waited for him to go on, struck by a tightening sensation in my chest – a wariness of what might be coming.

'You're over from Amsterdam?' he asked. It was as if he were softening me up with small talk. He knew where I was from, surely.

'Just for a few days.'

He studied his fingernails, which were slightly dirty. It looked like he might have been doing some gardening, and not quite managed to scrub away the soil.

'What I'm about to tell you, I'm sharing in confidence. Is that understood?'

'Of course.'

I wondered how much was in my file. Did it mention that my wife was a former features writer for *Het Parool*, the Amsterdam daily newspaper?

'We've got a situation over in Driebergen.'

Driebergen, near Utrecht, was the headquarters of the old Korps Landelijke Politiediensten (KLPD) – the National Police Services Agency. The KLPD was now a unit within a single, newly merged Dutch police force. Not everyone had been happy with the unification. Office politics.

'What kind of situation?'

'There's a specialist team over there who are investigating child exploitation. You may be aware of them?'

I stayed silent, but I knew about the team, more or less. They always seemed to be in flux, given changing police priorities and public perceptions.

'It's a six-person team,' van der Steen went on. 'It needs to grow, but before we grow it, we need to clean house.'

'Oh?' I took a sip of water.

'We had a series of busts lined up. Mid-level members of what we'd managed to identify as a major paedophile network.

The busts went bad.'

I noted how the minister used 'we' for what was being described as a tactical operation. The justice ministry oversaw the police of course, but van der Steen's words implied an unusual level of involvement.

'We now believe we've identified a kingpin in the same network,' he went on. 'In your neck of the woods, it turns out, Henk. We can't risk an operational failure this time.'

'You say the bust went bad... How?'

'All the addresses had been hastily abandoned by the time the arrest teams arrived. Cleared of any computer material, cleaned almost forensically. Every single one.'

'Addresses in Holland?'

'Three of them, yes. The other addresses were in Belgium, Luxembourg and southern England.'

I gave a low whistle.

'All recently vacated.' His words reinforced the point.

'A tip-off?'

'Almost certainly, but by who... that's the question.'

'An insider – a plant?'

'That's one theory. A theory that needs proving or disproving, and fast.'

'And you want me to look into it?'

His grey eyes held mine. They shone in the low light, like steel.

'Why me?' I asked, shifting in my seat.

'Four reasons,' he said, holding up the stubby fingers of one hand. 'Evidently you're a man with experience of life.'

I was fifty-six. 'Thanks for reminding me.'

He smiled, briefly. 'You've got an outsider's perspective. At least, that's what I'm told. Don't underestimate the value of being able to sit outside the tribe and see what's going on, in ways that others can't.'

Funny – the energy minister had told me they needed me 'inside the tent' after the discoveries resulting from the Rem

Lottman case. Now they wanted me back outside again – but under their supervision. Things evolve.

'And as I said, you come highly recommended. We wouldn't be having this conversation if you weren't.'

I nodded impatiently. 'That's three reasons. You mentioned four.'

He locked eyes with me. 'There's no one else willing and able to do this, Henk.'

In my thirty-plus years as a policeman in Amsterdam, I'd seen a lot. But child abuse cases were known to be different. The images that the investigating teams had to look at each day, the victims' stories they encountered... you can't leave that stuff at the office, can't go home and forget about it. It gets into your mind, your dreams.

'If you take this assignment, it will change you,' van der Steen warned.

'Does that point to an alternate explanation?' I said, stepping back from the precipice of the decision he'd asked me to make. 'That someone on the team turned? Went native?'

Turned into a paedophile, in other words.

He shrugged. 'That's another possibility. These operatives have to stare at a lot of images. Perhaps, yes, it could... *release* certain things in certain men.'

He was looking at me searchingly.

'I don't pretend to understand what motivates older men to become interested in young children,' he went on. 'And let's be clear about this. We're talking about the sick stuff here, Henk. There's a lot of it going on all of a sudden. As many as one in five of us may have leanings that way, one police psychologist in Leiden is now loudly proclaiming.'

I took a sip of water, wondering what response that hypothesis had got from the psychologist's colleagues on the force.

'There's another point to consider – and I'm sure I don't need to spell this out for you as a seasoned policeman.

Investigating the investigators: it's not for everyone.'

It contradicted the bond of loyalty among police personnel. I'd been in the army, which had the same ethos – though it was for reasons of survival there.

'A plant, looking for a plant,' I said meditatively.

He gave me a tight smile.

'How would that work?' I asked.

'We'd get you a regular job on the team in Driebergen. You'd be one of the guys. But we'd also pair you with someone from the security services.'

'A handler?'

'You could put it that way, yes. We'd work on your cover – give you an alternative identity of sorts.'

'My existing one's not unblemished.'

'I'd be suspicious if it was. You're a human being.'

There was a crushing silence.

Sexual exploitation, trafficking, drugs, corruption, aggravated assault, homicide cases even – I'd worked them all, but the one area of policing I'd stayed away from was child abuse. Every cop felt in their heart the Friedrich Nietzsche quote: '*Battle not with monsters, lest ye become a monster, and if you gaze into the abyss, the abyss gazes also into you…*'

'I also read about your altercation with the Amsterdam police commissioner.'

My old friend Joost. In abeyance since the Lottman case, but still there… still ready to cause problems in all areas of my professional and personal life.

'Take this assignment, and that problem goes away.'

I didn't doubt the justice minister's ability to make it so.

'And if I say no?'

He paused, choosing his next words carefully.

'Then, like the others I've offered this assignment to, you'll walk out of here. You'll forget this conversation ever happened and, as agreed, you won't mention it to anyone. In your case,

Muriel will no doubt send you off to some other ministry. Somewhere easier. Environmental protection, maybe...'

I grimaced. 'Just how important is this to the justice ministry?'.

He leaned forward, pressing his palms onto the table. 'I'd say it was vital... but that would be understating it.' He paused for effect. 'You can judge the decency of a society by how it treats its women and its children. If we're not protecting our children, then what the hell *are* we doing?'

He was good, van der Steen. He knew what drove us. The real coppers that is, not the Joosts of the world.

'It's an unusual case,' he continued. 'Outwardly, it's all supranational networks, technology, and collaboration with counterparts from other countries. In another sense, it's a classic little locked-room mystery.'

'How so?'

'At least one of the six men – yes, they're all men – in Driebergen is rotten. Your job, if you think you're up to it, is to determine which, and to ensure that the rot stops there.'

I tried to visualise the airless environment I'd be entering, the smell of it – but couldn't quite get there.

'How do you know the insider is on that team?'

'If you decide to proceed, you'll see the file.' He paused, and then asked with finality: 'Is the mission clear?'

I found myself nodding slowly, and added a more emphatic nod.

'Think about it,' he concluded, sitting back again but still scrutinising me with those steely eyes. 'Talk to your wife – *in general terms* – about a possible posting in Driebergen. You're married?' he asked, as if he might have misheard or misread something.

'Yes.'

I eyed the painting over his shoulder. The ship, attempting to hold its course in the gathering storm, listing badly.

'With a daughter,' I added.

'Then think it over.' His lips twitched. 'But not for too long.'

2

THE FILE

'*DRIEBERGEN?*' MY WIFE ASKED, mouth agape.

'It's near Utrecht.'

'I know where it is!'

'Keep your voice down.'

'Don't tell me to be quiet, Henk. It's not The Hague, nor Delft – like we agreed!'

'No.'

'What do you mean, *no*?'

'No – you're right.'

We were sitting in the bar of our hotel. The lighting was low; the room was full of flat, grey shapes and figures. I was tired of negotiating everything with everyone. Wasn't life supposed to become easier as you neared retirement and cast off children and responsibilities? My life seemed to be going in the opposite direction.

I signalled to the barman for more drinks.

Petra clamped her hand over her cocktail glass, narrowly avoiding the candle flame as she did so. It guttered.

'OK, *one* more drink.' I corrected my order, raising my empty, sudsy glass.

'But why Driebergen?' Petra demanded.

'Because it's the headquarters of the old KLPD.'

'I know that. I was a features writer once, remember?'

How could I forget? I felt like saying.

'You were talking about a role with one of the ministries here,' she said. 'Why go there?'

'Because the minister asked me to.'

A fresh Dubbel Bok arrived. *Thank God.*

Petra's face was screwed up with incomprehension in the flickering light. As soon as the barman left she said, 'Which minister?'

My voice was low. 'The justice minister. It's a confidential assignment. They've got a problem with one of the teams there, and that's about all I can share.'

My wife had been a journalist for as long as I'd been a policeman. In putting up a 'Do Not Enter' sign, I might as well have confessed everything on the spot. It was just a matter of time.

But I was taking van der Steen's warning seriously.

'Well,' Petra said, crossing her arms, 'I'm not leaving Amsterdam without good reason.'

'Last week you said that you couldn't wait to get off the houseboat and be nearer Cecilia in Delft.' Cecilia was her favourite cousin.

'Oh, I'll be getting off the houseboat all right,' she said. 'And finding dry land. In Amsterdam, close to our daughter.'

Our daughter Nadia wouldn't be leaving the nation's capital any time soon. Her social set could only countenance living in one Dutch population centre, and it certainly wasn't Driebergen.

'Should we get something to eat?' I suggested. 'It's late.'

'*Too* late.' Petra sniffed. 'I'm no longer hungry.'

I sighed exasperatedly, craning my neck. 'Can I see a menu?' I asked the barman.

'We only do snacks. The restaurant, over there, serves food.'

'Of course.'

We sat in silence.

Finally I said, 'OK. I'll tell you the mission I've been asked to undertake, but you mustn't share it with anyone.'

'As though I would!'

'*Anyone*, Petra. Not Nadia... *no one.*'

'Why would I share it with Nadia?'

'You won't.' I paused. 'And you must promise me that.'

'Fine,' she said.

'Van der Steen wants me to look at the team investigating child abuse.'

Her eyes narrowed.

'One of them is suspected of passing on police information to suspected paedophiles.'

Her head dropped.

'They need to plug the leak.'

'Why?' she said, looking up again, her face screwed up in a silent wail. 'Why this, of all the roles you could have taken?'

'Because someone needs to do it.'

'But why you?'

'Would you rather I crossed the road?'

'Oh, don't do your lone-knight thing with me, Henk.' Petra had her head in her hands.

She was right about most things, but not everything.

No one is.

'Child abuse.' She was mumbling. 'There's a reason child offenders live in mortal danger in prison and the rest of society...'

'Well, maybe if there were more women on the team in Driebergen, things would be different.' I was thinking about Liesbeth, a team member of mine who had a knack of winning trust and gaining insight into cases. She was the one who'd helped me break open the Lottman case, with an early interview she'd done...

'So it's women to blame now, is it?'

'That's not what I'm saying. I'm just speculating that it's not healthy to have an all-male team –'

'Therefore, some unfortunate woman – or group of women – must now bear a further cost for these men's depravities?'

Jesus, was this not difficult enough without turning it into a full-on gender war?

'Looking at those images changes the neural pathways,' she cried. 'It rewires the brain!'

'Please keep your voice down.'

She shook her head. 'If it's true of legal porn, it must be doubly so with this.'

I was about to challenge her on the pornography point but her words rang true. I thought again of those six men in the office in Driebergen...

'I don't want you looking at that stuff.'

'All right.'

'I'm serious, Henk. I don't want that stuff in your head, and in our house, and in our bed!'

'All right, dammit! Then I'll make that the condition with van der Steen – I'm there to watch the watchers, but not to watch. Now, can we please get something to eat, before the restaurant shuts down and I shut down, too?'

*

At the justice ministry the following morning, van der Steen's assistant led me into a small meeting room. A beige paper file marked *Confidential* sat on the polished wooden table.

'You can't take it away,' he said.

It felt like an unnecessary piece of theatre – I had my smartphone with me, able to photograph anything inside the file.

'In a few moments, someone from the AIVD will drop by to introduce himself.' The Algemene Inlichtingen en Veiligheidsdienst is the Dutch secret service, charged with 'identifying threats and risks to national security which are not immediately apparent'. It carries out operations at home and abroad, working with more than a hundred different organisations and employing over a thousand people – all of whom are sworn to secrecy about their work.

'My handler?' I clarified.

The assistant didn't answer my question.

'I'll leave you to it,' he said.

The door clicked shut behind him and I opened the file. There appeared to be two parts: a review of the operation van der Steen had mentioned (the bust that had been lined up and failed), and then an overview of the team in Driebergen, SVU X-19.

The nomenclature was familiar. 'SVU' stood for 'Special Victims Unit', the 'X' denoted that it didn't appear as a matter of public record, and the '19' distinguished it from other teams operating in that same capacity.

Conscious that I had little time before my handler arrived, I turned back to the beginning, scanning each page in turn. There are different ways to digest files but I like to avoid reading ahead, instead reliving the experience of the investigation – what was known at which point.

As I discovered, Operation Guardian Angel had grown out of a routine police check in Liège, Belgium. A Belgian police team had paid a house call to Jan Stamms, a convicted sex offender, to ensure that he was abiding by the terms of his early prison parole. They took a cursory look around Stamms's suburban, semi-detached house, including his basement – where they heard a distant cry. The lead officer assumed that the cry had come from the neighbouring property.

Luck (or its absence) can come in many forms in police work, and in this case it was a throwaway remark by the lead officer's partner, Veronique Deschamps, to the neighbour, who happened to be out in her front garden: 'That's quite a pair of lungs someone in your household has,' Deschamps reported commenting.

'But I live alone,' the neighbour replied, perplexed.

Veronique Deschamps then insisted on a more thorough search of Stamms's property. The first team still missed the sealed-up door in the basement, so good had Stamms's handiwork been, but his clear nervousness prompted them to persist and bring in search dogs, who quickly found the location of a passage down to a second basement.

In the concealed chamber were two four-year-old boys, a basic latrine, cameras and lighting equipment… plus a computer with editing software and thousands of hours of video footage. The room also contained a set of workmen's tools.

The twin boys required immediate medical attention. The video footage was too distressing for the local police team to review. However, by interviewing Stamms over a thirty-six-hour period, they elicited a confession to the existence of a video-sharing venue on the Dark Web called 'Night Market'.

I found myself nodding admiringly as I read the report. The Liège team had covered an impressive amount of ground before handing over the case to the Belgian Federal Police, who in turn discovered that Stamms had tried to resolve a payment problem with a receiving bank account in Amsterdam. The Federal Police speculated that the payment to him was in exchange for his supply of video footage. A growing belief that the network was centred in Holland caused overall control of the case to pass to Driebergen.

The door opened and the assistant asked, 'Do you want a drink, by the way?'

I blinked in consternation. 'No. How much longer do I have?'

'A few minutes.'

'Who is my handler, anyway?'

'His name's Rynsburger. You'll meet him soon enough.'

The name didn't mean anything to me. I waited in silence for the assistant to leave again, returning immediately to the file. There was a lengthy section on the build-up to the arrest teams going into the various different locations to apprehend the mid-level suspects already mentioned by van der Steen…

I wanted to take in all the details. But more than that, I needed to get to the section on SVU X-19 itself. Van der Steen had suspected that the leak (resulting in the failure of the arrests) had come from SVU X-19 – only why?

If you decide to proceed, you'll see the file...

I flicked forward, thinking that there must be an elaborate Joint Investigation Team, with investigators from the various countries involved. Any one of them or their immediate colleagues could have had access to information about Operation Guardian Angel, and leaked it...

Aware that Rynsburger might walk in at any moment, I skipped to the final section. Dumbstruck, I took in each of the SVU X-19 team members' short bios and photos in turn.

Manfred Boomkamp was a twenty-year KLPD veteran.

Jacques Rahm was from Luxembourg's Police Grand-Ducale.

Tommy Franks, formerly with the London Metropolitan Police's Flying Squad, was on secondment from the UK's national Child Exploitation and Online Protection agency.

Ivo Vermeulen represented the Belgian Federal Police.

And there was a fifth nationality involved: Gunther Engelhart was from Germany's Bundeskriminalamt.

SVU X-19 *was* the Joint Investigation Team. They'd built a mini states-of-Europe in Driebergen.

I sat back, and exhaled hard. Was it some kind of experiment? Did they believe that it would be more efficient to centralise the joint investigative work? Had the rationale been to avoid precisely the kind of intelligence failure that had then occurred?

And what of my ability to take on these men?

I leaned forward again, reaching into my inside pocket for my phone, when there came a rap at the door. It swung open to reveal a tall, white-haired man in a tailored navy suit. He was rheumy-eyed.

'Henk van der Pol?'

I didn't deny it.

'My name's Vim Rynsburger, I believe the minister has mentioned me. We'll be joined by a psychologist shortly. Please, come this way.'

About Us

In addition to No Exit Press, Oldcastle Books has a number
of other imprints, including Kamera Books, Creative Essentials,
Pulp! The Classics, Pocket Essentials and High Stakes Publishing
> oldcastlebooks.com

For more information about Crime Books go to > crimetime.co.uk

Check out the kamera film salon for independent, arthouse and
world cinema > kamera.co.uk

For more information, media enquiries and review copies please
contact > marketing@oldcastlebooks.com